TITLES BY KAT SIMONS

Tiger Shifters Series

ONCE UPON A TIGER
ALONG CAME A TIGER
HERE THERE BE TIGERS
HER TIGER TO TAKE
TO TEMPT A TIGER
DOWN WILL COME TIGER
TO CATCH A TIGER
WHAT A TIGER WANTS

Praise For Kat Simons' Tiger Shifters

Once Upon a Tiger

Along Came a Tiger

Here There Be Tigers

"The whole book was spellbinding and I was absorbed in the story."

> ~*Night Owl Reviews*, TOP PICK

Her Tiger to Take

"This is a great read for those like me who want strong characters who feel real and are written in a way that you feel an emotional connection and empathy with as they work to be together."

> ~*The Romance Reviews*, TOP PICK

To Tempt a Tiger

"I definitely want to stay involved in this world and visit more of the couples and their friends and family."

> ~*The Romance Reviews*, TOP PICK

Down Will Come Tiger

"The chemistry is a smoldering inferno of heat but this relationship is slow burning because of personal demons and emotional distress and these strong, compelling characters draw readers in and capture their hearts…"

> ~*Night Owl Reviews*

"These are the types of characters you don't see often and they are anything but predictable....Together, they work to get the justice they have sought for so long and find a love they never expected. It is a story of loss and pain but also hope and second chances. "

> ~*The Romance Reviews*

HERE THERE BE TIGERS

Tiger Shifters

KAT SIMONS

T&D
PUBLISHING

For my beloved Eddie. I miss you. You were a super dog.

ACKNOWLEDGEMENTS

This book has been a long time in coming. It was actually the first novel I wrote in the Tiger Shifters world. I was encouraged to expand on the tigers' story by my lovely friend Louise Fury after she read the initial short story Mate Run. I owe her a huge thanks for her encouragement. Without it, I might not have explored the tigers' world more.

I would also like to give a great deal of thanks to the people who helped me bring this book to publication, who continue to encourage my writing and publishing exploits, and who provide excellent shoulders to lean on when things get crazy. There are too many to name. I thank you all! But I would like to add a few specific thanks: Kemberlee Lugo, Peter Shortland, MK Tipton, Stacey Agdern, Leanna Renee Hieber, Mala Bhattacharjee, Elizabeth K. Mahone, Lise Horton, Hope Tarr, Stacey Klemstein, and Linnea Sinclair. A huge thank you to you all, my dear friends.

Thank you to all the readers who've embraced the Tiger Shifter world. Your continued support is priceless, and I am truly grateful to you.

Finally, I would like to thank my beloved family. I couldn't do this without the love and support of my husband and two beautiful boys. Thank you for everything, my loves! I also need to thank my parents and sister. They were the first to get behind me on this writing thing, and after all these years, they're still right there supporting me. Thanks!

HERE THERE BE TIGERS

Tiger Shifters

KAT SIMONS

Chapter One

Nila De Luca dug through her backpack in search of her cellphone as she waited by the luggage carousel for her duffle. Exhaustion weighed heavily on her limbs after the long flight from India to New York. The delayed layovers in Paris and DC hadn't helped, but at least she was already through customs. Now all she could think about was dropping into the spare bed at her grandmother's house and sleeping for the next three days. She'd have to get back to work after that—there was a leopard in a Texas zoo due to give birth in a few weeks, and because of anticipated complications, the resident vet wanted Nila on hand, since big cats were her specialty.

Until then, she was off duty.

She yawned, still pawing through her backpack for her phone as the luggage started coming down the chute.

A slight shiver moved down her back, which she wrote off to the air-conditioning working overtime. Even at ten o'clock at night, August was muggy and hot in New York. She was so worn out that when she felt the jab of a hard, blunt object against her ribcage she didn't react at first.

Then a quiet, deep voice whispered close to her ear, "Stay calm. Do exactly what I say, and I won't shoot you."

Fear and confusion shot a jolt of adrenaline through her. She glanced down. Hidden from the rest of the room by her backpack was the business end of a very ugly looking gun. She swallowed and tried not to panic, but her heartbeat tripled and her breathing sped.

"What do you want?" she murmured, carefully lowering her bag. She didn't want to make any abrupt moves, but someone else in the crowded JFK luggage area had to notice a friggin' gun.

To her dismay, the barrel shifted to her lower back and she felt the man behind her move closer, no doubt covering his weapon.

"If you cooperate," he said against her temple, "you might survive this. If you resist, I'll kill you first then hunt down Leo and Rossa and kill them, too. And I'll make sure their deaths are slow and painful."

"Why?" she hissed as another spike of panic flashed through her. Her father and grandmother were her only close family. Why would anyone want to hurt them?

She tried getting a look at her abductor from the corner of her eye, but he wasn't leaning far enough forward for her to even glimpse a hair color.

"Someone would like to talk to you," he said, putting his free arm around her waist. To strangers, it probably looked like an embrace from a boyfriend.

"Listen, buddy," she said, "I think you've got the wrong person. I'm just a vet. Unless you've got a big cat in need of medical help, I'm of no use to you. And if you do have a big cat that needs a vet, you just have to ask."

His chuckle sent a shiver across her shoulders. The fine hairs on the back of her neck rose.

"We'll have to see what he says, won't we?" the man said. "But he might let you live if you prove useful."

This made no sense. She hated when things didn't make sense. It drove her crazy. The pet peeve sparked irritation that quickly turned to anger. "Buddy, you're messing with the wrong woman. I'm a ball buster."

"Oh, I have no doubt you are. Let's go." He nudged her with the gun, hard enough she was sure to have a bruise.

She sucked in a breath. "What about my luggage?" She spotted her duffle dropping down the ramp.

"Won't need it."

He butted her with the gun again, and she either had to move or risk being shot. To buy herself some thinking time, she walked slowly with a limp.

"What are you doing? Move it."

"I can't, damn it. I hurt my ankle a few days ago. It's still killing me."

"Your ankle will be the least of your worries if you don't move faster."

His response told her two things: he hadn't seen her walk into the luggage area, because she was lying through her teeth about the injury, and he didn't want to get caught. That last part was good for her. She just had to find a way to attract the attention of someone who could help without getting everyone in the area killed.

Even as that thought crossed her mind, she passed a small family, the mother standing beside a stroller discussing something with one child while the boy in the stroller pulled at her skirt.

Fuck. There were too many people in here. That should have worked in her favor. Someone should see the gun. But no one seemed to notice anything beyond their own baggage hunt. If she called attention to her kidnapping, the man might start shooting innocent people.

"Where are we going?" she said, still limping to stall their progress.

"Parking lot. Then a short drive."

She was very certain she wouldn't survive getting into a car with this man. Who the hell was he? Why on earth would he kidnap her? He had to know who she was because he knew her father and grandmother's names. Yet she wasn't rich, and she didn't have the kind of job that inspired kidnappings. What the hell was going on?

As they stepped out of the sliding doors into the muggy night, she caught a brief glimpse of the gunman in the glass door—dark hair with shadowy eyes, pale skin, taller than her 5'3" by almost a foot, and he wore a dark, short sleeved shirt. The doors had opened too fast for her to see more than that, though. She glanced down at the arm still around her waist, covered in dark hair and well-muscled. Those muscles were relaxed but felt coiled and ready to react if she so much as breathed the wrong way.

He nudged her in one direction just as another man hurried up to them.

"Taxi? Taxi, sir? Going into the city?"

She tried catching the man's gaze to let him see her distress, but his full focus was on the man behind her.

"Get out of my face," the kidnapper spat.

"Hey, no need to be rude." The driver raised his hands in surrender. "Just offering."

Then the cab driver glanced at her and winked. She had just enough time to frown. In the next instant, the driver pushed her to one side, the surprise move freeing her from the gunman's hold. She stumbled away as a low growl from behind her raised the hairs on her arms. Before she caught her balance, she heard a painful sounding crunch then the driver had her elbow and was maneuvering her away from the kidnapper. She glanced back long enough to see the other man holding his wrist. He looked up, glaring after her, and his eyes seemed to glow yellow.

She sucked in a sharp breath and turned away when he started toward them.

"He's coming," she said.

"Let's move."

The driver tugged her into a trot. Then into a full run.

She threw her backpack over her free shoulder and did her best to keep up as they wove through the throngs of people on the sidewalk. He rushed her toward the parking lot, ducking around the long line waiting for a taxi.

"Whoa, wait." She tried to nudge his big body back toward the luggage area. "We have to find a security person or airport police." Panic continued shooting adrenaline through her blood stream, mixing badly with her confusion.

"Security can't help with that guy," the driver said without altering his direction.

"And you can? Who are you?" She tugged him to a slower pace, though she didn't dare stop moving.

A quick glance confirmed the gunman was still behind them. Fortunately, he was caught up in a tangled mass of people and luggage, but that wouldn't delay him for long. Her rescuer urged her to a quicker trot, pulling her attention back to where she was going. She looked longingly at the nearest entrance into the airport, wondering where to find an official who could help.

"I'm a friend of your grandmother's," the man said. "Rossa sent me."

Startled, she tripped on an uneven section of concrete. He caught her before she fell, helping her regain her footing with surprising strength and ease.

"Trust me." He held her gaze for a heartbeat.

The brief look stunned her to silence. His expression was hard and serious, his gaze intent. He was also probably the most handsome man she'd ever seen, now that she stopped to actually look. Short, shaggy brown hair, light eyes, classically handsome features.

But it was the hum of her instincts that gave her pause. Those same instincts had served her well her entire life, keeping her safe in her travels around the world and helping her work with injured, angry cats that could outweighed her by hundreds of pounds. Now, her instincts were whispering that the man before her was saving her life.

Trust him.

Her quick, certain insight got brushed to the back of her mind as he pulled her into a run toward the parking lot.

"You know my grandmother?" she asked.

"I'll tell you everything when we're safe. This way." He led her between the rows of cars, down a ramp to a lower level, then up another row of cars.

"That man was trying to get me to the parking lot."

"Probably because he has a car here, too."

"Are you working with him?"

"No."

She tried getting a look at his face, but he was a step ahead of her so she couldn't see his expression. Her instincts continued urging her to trust him.

The skin between her shoulder blades crawled with the knowledge that the gunman was still somewhere behind them. The man beside her didn't give her the willies like the other man did. Hell, this guy had stopped her kidnapping, and he claimed to know her grandmother. He knew her grandmother's name.

Though, so had the kidnapper.

But since she didn't feel the need to get away from this man, and he was making sure she did get away from the gunman, she decided to listen to her instincts.

"You're not a taxi driver are you?"

"No."

This time, she heard a hint of humor in his voice. "That man's still following us."

"I know. We're almost safe."

"Right." Unintended sarcasm slipped into her tone.

He flashed a half smile that nearly made her stumble again. Holy hell. When he smiled, he was stunning, even in the awful, overly bright parking lot lighting. How was that even possible?

She decided adrenaline was warping her sense of reality and shook off the strange effect his smile had on her. She had more important things to do just then. Like survive.

"You know what that other guy wants from me?" She panted, stretching to keep up with his longer strides.

"Yes. We'll discuss it later."

"We need to go to the police."

"He has people inside the NYPD."

"My kidnapper?" That seemed…extreme.

"His boss."

She wanted to ask more, but he shoved her in front of him. She heard a beep beep as car door locks disengaging. He opened the passenger side door of a large, black SUV.

"Get in."

She didn't bother arguing. She could do that later when she no longer felt the other man hunting them. That was the only way to describe it. She couldn't hear him or see him anymore, but she knew her kidnapper was still back there somewhere, almost as if she could feel him. Fear tingled along the back of her neck.

She held her breath while her rescuer climbed in beside her and locked the doors. She started breathing again when he backed out of the parking spot. She still couldn't see the other man.

"Did you break his wrist?" she asked as she scoured the area for any sign of the kidnapper.

"Yes."

"Where's his gun?"

He handed her the weapon, grip first. "Now, duck down. Just in case."

After one last glance around the parking lot, she did as he suggested. She hated guns, so she checked the safety, and then set the weapon on the floor, stepping on it to keep it from sliding under the seat. She couldn't stand having it in her hands. The feel of them disgusted her.

The fact that he'd handed her the gun had gone a long way toward confirming her instinctive reaction to trust him, though. But now she wanted answers. Who was he? How did he know her grandmother? What the hell was going on? Why did she trust him?

"You're going to answer my questions when we're safe, right?" she said from her undignified crouch. She had to concentrate on not throwing up as the adrenaline took its toll.

"Probably." He glanced down and smiled again, the look quick and lethally sexy. Then he returned to focusing on his driving. "My name is Mikhail Chernikov, by the way. Call me Mitch. I hate Mikhail. Only my grandmother calls me that. And it's a pleasure to meet you, Nila."

His last name sounded familiar. Where had she heard it before? When her memory failed her, she gave up and asked, "Where are we going?"

"Somewhere safe."

"Is there a reason I'm trusting you?"

"I just saved your life?"

Nila let out a long, slow sigh. "That's what I thought."

CHAPTER TWO

Nila shifted slightly in the seat to gaze up at Mitch, her lower back protesting her position. She'd remained hunched over for at least ten minutes, and she was pretty sure they were out of the airport now.

"Can I sit up?"

He didn't answer for a moment, then nodded.

She straightened with a groan and stretched her back. "Forty-eight hours of travel, cramped planes, long layovers, crowded airports, followed by a run through the parking lot have not done my body any good at all."

He glanced at her out of the corner of his eye. "I would have to disagree with that."

"Meaning?"

"Your body looks just fine to me."

She narrowed her gaze at him, but he was watching traffic again. "You said you know my grandma? Why don't I know you?"

"Actually, my grandmother and yours are friends. I just met your grandmother for the first time two days ago. She told me

11

to call her Rossa." He smiled slightly.

"What's your grandmother's name?"

"Elizaveta Chernikova."

Ah, that was why his last name sounded familiar. Her grandma had talked about her Russian friend. Apparently, they Skyped and everything.

"So how did you happen to be at the airport?"

"I was coming to collect you. At Rossa and Leo's request."

She blinked at that. "I don't know you. Why would my grandmother and father think I'd go anywhere with you?"

"Because I'm very handsome?"

The answer was so outrageous and unexpected, she laughed. "I don't climb into cars with strangers just because they're handsome. And my father would definitely not send you to pick me up just because you're handsome."

"So you agree I'm very handsome?"

She rolled her eyes. "You're all right."

He grinned, his teeth flashing white in the darkened interior of the SUV. The expression added to his appeal but also gave him a deliciously wicked air.

"Your grandmother was supposed to call you," he said, "tell you to expect me. Sorry I was late. Got caught in traffic."

"Damn. I was hunting for my cell when that man pushed a gun into my back."

She leaned over and dug through her backpack. When she emerged with her phone, she turned it on. Sure enough there was a voicemail from her grandmother. As she listened to the beloved voice telling her a family friend would be collecting her and to check her email for a picture of the man, she detected the strain in her grandma's tone.

"Why was she worried?" she asked Mitch as she checked her email.

"You could tell from a voicemail?"

"I know my grandma."

He shrugged.

When he didn't reply after a few moments, she said, "Are you avoiding my question or do you not know?"

"Why your grandmother was worried? I know. And since someone just tried kidnapping you, I'd say her worry was justified."

"But why? How could she have known I was about to be kidnapped? She's never mentioned being psychic." Nila paused, then admitted, "Though she's a firm believer in giving the Evil Eye." She shuddered.

Mitch smiled, but no humor reached his eyes. "The reason for her worry is a long story."

"Longer than it will take to get to her house?"

"Actually, we're not going to Rossa's. She's on her way to a safer spot with Leo."

"Whoa, whoa. Why do they need a safer spot? Where the hell have they gone?"

He glanced at her, his expression thoughtful. "You're more concerned with their welfare than the fact that a man you don't know is taking you somewhere mysterious?"

"First things first. I'll worry about you in a minute. Besides, my grandma vouched for you in her voicemail and sent your picture so I'd know who you were." She held up her phone to show him the photo. "And I trust her." Her grandma's instincts were almost as good as her own. If Rossa De Luca said this guy was a friend, Nila would give him the benefit of the doubt. For now, anyway. "So where are she and my dad? Why didn't they meet me at the airport? I was stuck in DC for hours. Why didn't my grandmother call me there to say you were collecting me? What the hell is going on?"

Mitch released a long breath. "Your father's got a safe location in mind, but that's as much as I know." He nodded toward the hand she had clenched around her phone. "Leave your cell on. Rossa said they'll call as soon as they can. As for why they didn't come to collect you… That was actually the original plan. We were all going to meet you at the airport so your father could explain everything in person. Then one of Petrov's tigers showed up—"

She stopped him again with a raised hand. "Tiger? There's a tiger on the loose in New York?"

He shook his head. "I'm getting ahead of myself. The guy who tried to kidnap you? He works for someone with a lot of connections, someone extremely dangerous—Petrov Dubrovsky. And Petrov wants you dead."

"What?" Her voice rose and she had to take a deep breath. "Why the hell would someone I've never heard of want me dead?"

"Your past has caught up with you, and your family will be in danger until we can work something out."

"My past? I don't have a past. I lead the most boring life ever."

He gave her a disbelieving look. "You take care of big cats and travel around the world, looking after animals in sanctuaries and reserves, because you're considered the foremost expert in your field. What in that life is boring?"

She snorted. "Okay, so my job is great and I love it. But it's all I do. And I've only been doing it for seven years. And while I'm very very good at it, nothing about it should have attracted the attention of kidnappers. At least not in this country. Now answer my damned question."

"You're not going to like the answers I give you."

She waited. He remained silent. She glared. "Talk, or I'm going to start calling you Mikhail."

That earned her a snort of reluctant laughter. "Fine. I'll tell you what I can, but I'd rather you heard the story from your father. You'll believe him."

"Fine. I'll call him."

"Don't panic if you can't reach him. He said they might be in places where the cell service was bad."

"I'll panic if I damned well want to," she groused and hit the speed dial for her dad's phone. When it went right to voicemail, she tried her grandmother's phone. Voicemail. "Damn it." She stared at the screen as worry ate at her. "You're sure they're okay?"

He didn't answer immediately. She turned as far as the seatbelt would allow and stared at the side of his face. "Are they in trouble, Mitch?"

"You're all in trouble."

"Why? Why the hell would this Dubrovsky guy want to hurt us?"

"He's your birth mother's mate."

She blinked, thinking she'd misheard him. "My birth mother is dead. She died when I was born."

"Actually… She didn't. She returned to her people and mated with one of her kind. Unfortunately, he found out about you. You shouldn't even exist." He refused to look at her despite her stare.

"Telling me I shouldn't exist is rude." She wasn't entirely sure why that was the next thing out of her mouth, but it was all she could think to say as the overwhelming news turned her world upside down. Her mother hadn't died. She'd left her and her father and gone off to marry another man.

She frowned. Mitch hadn't used the word husband. "Why did you call Dubrovsky her mate? That's a weird way of saying her lover, husband, boyfriend, whatever."

"Because that's what they were. A mated pair. He caught her in the Mate Run and she conceived—"

"Wait." She held up a hand to stop him. Again. "Nothing you're saying makes any sense. I detest when things don't make sense. It irritates the hell out of me."

"Yeah, Rossa warned me about that. You really should wait to hear this from your father."

"Well, I can't reach my father right now. You know what's happening. You're going to explain." When he hesitated further, she actually snarled. "Mikhail, I swear to god…"

"Fine." He tossed her a glare of his own. "Just don't call me Mikhail." Then he faced the road again. "And don't say I didn't warn you. You're not going to believe half of what I tell you."

"Tell me anyway. Start with this business of my birth mother still being alive. Did my grandmother and father know?"

"Was alive," Mitch said quietly. "I'm sorry. She died a few weeks ago."

Well that just made it all worse! Now she couldn't even contact this woman who'd abandoned her, even if she wanted to. What the hell? "Did she and my dad have an affair? Is that why her…mate wants me dead?"

Mitch shook his head. "Her relationship with your father was before she married Petrov. She gave birth to you, waited for her cycle to begin again, and then took part in the Mate Run."

"The Mate Run? What the hell is that?"

"That is a much longer part of this already long story."

She rubbed her forehead. "You're giving me a headache."

"I'm not surprised. You've been travelling for days. You must be hungry. We can stop…"

"I'm too worried and nauseated to eat."

"Well, I'm starving, and a hungry…man is always a bad thing." He flashed her an arched look.

She snorted, trying not to laugh. How the hell could she find him charming in the midst of this nightmare? For all she knew, this was an elaborate part of the kidnapping. Her grandmother could have been under duress when she left her voicemail. The email picture could have been sent by anyone using her grandmother's account. She had no real reason to trust this man, despite what her generally good instincts were telling her. Hell, she couldn't even be sure his name was Mikhail, Mitch, whatever.

Staring at the side of his face, she pursed her lips. There was something strange about him, and she couldn't put her finger on exactly what it was. Nothing bad, just…he didn't feel like other men. That didn't make sense. His presence was more pronounced maybe? Like he took up more space and air than his actual body mass would indicate. That sense of otherness reminded her of the cats she worked with. Which was so weird, the thought momentarily made her forget her myriad questions.

She shook off the strange idea, putting it down to jetlag.

He pulled off the road at the next exit and went through a fast food drive thru. He ordered enough burgers to feed an army.

"You're going to have to eat all those yourself. I'm a vegetarian," she commented.

"That was the plan. You said you weren't hungry."

"Get me a coke."

Once they were back on the road again, she motioned with her free hand. "Continue with this explanation."

"Try your father again," he said instead.

She barely held her patience as she rang her dad, then her grandmother again. Both phones went straight to voicemail. "Damn it."

"They're okay," Mitch said, his voice quiet and full of understanding.

She swallowed back her worry. "I don't know what I'll do if anything happens to them. They're all I have." She forced down the threat of tears, not wanting to cry in front of a stranger. "Okay, you're up," she said when she was sure her voice would be steady. "Mate Run? Dubrovsky? Mother alive longer than I was told. I shouldn't exist. Someone wants me dead. Time to explain all that."

He devoured the last of his second burger before saying, "Your mother was a tiger shapeshifter. Humans and tigers can't have children. At least, that's the prevailing wisdom. But you exist so obviously the prevailing wisdom is wrong."

She stared at him, not even blinking, certain now that she was hearing him wrong and wondering if maybe this was all a dream. "Tiger shapeshifter?"

He nodded.

"Like…werewolves?"

"Similar idea. Different species."

"You're talking nonsense, you know?"

He sighed. "I told Leo this would be better coming from him."

"My father thinks my birth mother was a…weretiger?"

"He doesn't think. He knows. She told him. She wanted him to be prepared for… Well, for what might happen with you."

"With me? Because I shouldn't exist?"

"Because a lot of tigers would want you dead if they found out about you, and others might want…other things."

"Other things?"

"It's complicated. Just, let's say your connection to your mother was best kept secret."

"So, she just left, and—" Nila stopped suddenly as something she'd never thought to worry about occurred to her. "What was her name? My mother?"

"Anaya. Anaya Pujari."

Nila closed her eyes briefly. Her dad had told her the truth of that at least. For some reason, knowing hadn't lied about her mother's real name made a difference in all this craziness. "I keep thinking I'm going to hear the fasten seatbelts ding any minute, and I'll wake up from all this as my plane is landing."

"I'm sorry."

She waved away his sympathy. Too much and she might really break down in tears. "Keep going. Why would these… weretigers want me dead if I shouldn't exist?"

"That's probably a story best told once we reach my cabin."

"Your cabin?" She raised her brows. "That's the safe place you're taking me? Isolated is it?"

"I promise, I'm not going to hurt you, Nila. I'm just trying to protect you."

"You'll pardon me if I'm a little suspicious since you just told me werewolves exist."

"Tigers."

"Sorry. Weretigers. So no werewolves?"

"They exist, too. They just don't have anything to do with this."

She rubbed her forehead again.

"I've got some pain relievers in the glove compartment."

She sighed. "This is just a little too much to take in on jetlag."

She shuffled through the contents of the glove compartment as she searched out the little bottle of pills, looking for anything that might give her a clue about the guy she was trusting with her life and the lives of her family. She found the car registration, the bottle of aspirin, and a toy from a fast food kids' meal.

"You have kids?" she asked, waving the little robot thing at him before putting it back. She glanced at Mitch's hand and confirmed he didn't have a wedding ring on.

"No kids. No wife or girlfriend." He shrugged. "Not likely to be either."

"Not likely—why? Are you gay?" That would be very disappointing.

He chuckled. "No. I like women. Just… It's not important." He nodded at the now hidden toy. "That belongs to one of my nephews."

"Ah. Okay. Back to this weretiger nonsense."

He shook his head. "Why bother when you don't believe what I'm telling you?"

"Because someone wants me dead for reasons I don't understand."

"Right." He finished off his third burger. "You sure you don't want to wait and talk to your father? Or at least wait till we get to the cabin and can be more comfortable?"

She growled. "Why are you stalling?"

"I'm not. I just don't want to keep telling you things you aren't going to believe."

"How long before we reach your cabin?"

"Couple more hours. It's in the Adirondacks."

She shuffled the two pain pills in her hand. She hadn't swallowed them yet, hesitating despite the fact that her instincts still told her she was safe with Mitch. She felt so off balance, so outside what she had always believed to be the real world that she didn't trust anything at the moment—even her instincts. Talk about going down a rabbit hole. She felt like Alice discovering Wonderland was full of monsters. She stared at the pills. If she took them would she shrink? The idea was so absurd, she laughed.

"What?" Mitch asked.

"Nothing. I'm just tired." Her head was killing her, but she tucked the aspirins into her pants pocket, deciding taking any drugs right then might not be a great idea.

"Sleep," Mitch said, gently. "We've got time."

Sleep sounded really good right then. Maybe if she went to sleep, she'd wake up on the airplane, this would all be a dream, and she could forget she'd ever heard of weretigers. She blinked. Tigers… "Wait, you said a tiger showed up when you were with my dad and grandmother? What was that about?"

"Ah. Yeah. When we were planning to come get you, one of Petrov's…associates showed up. We got away, but afterward, Leo decided it was safer to split up. He didn't want Petrov using him and your grandmother to get to you."

"And my dad thought I'd be safer with a stranger?"

"With me, yes."

"Why you?"

"I know what we're dealing with and how to protect you from the people after you."

"The weretigers."

"Yes."

She shook her head. "None of this makes sense."

He didn't answer and she didn't press him. She was overwhelmed, exhausted, and not sure she could take on anymore anyway. Instead, she tried her dad and grandmother's cellphones again. Still nothing. It was almost midnight. Where the hell were they?

She confirmed her phone battery was good for the rest of the night, then looked out the window. They were on the highway heading north into the Adirondacks. The combination of sparse highway lights and darkness beyond lulled her, and without her permission her eyes closed. She snapped them open and blinked, but exhaustion still weighed on her.

"Nila." Mitch's voice was quiet, calming. "Sleep. You're safe with me. You can rest."

Hell. She might as well sleep while she had the chance. Could be just the thing to wake her up from this nightmare. "Don't tell me if I drool," she said. "I don't want to know."

She closed her eyes, leaned her head against the window, and let exhaustion take her. If Mitch was going to kill her, she was a dead woman anyway. Might as well be rested when she faced her future.

Or lack of one.

CHAPTER THREE

itch waited until he heard her steady, even breathing before he glanced at her. Nila De Luca wasn't what he'd been expecting from a human-tiger shifter cross.

First, she was smaller than he would have predicted, given the size of her father and the fact that she regularly dealt with large, muscular animals. Mitch had never seen Nila's mother, though. Tiger children did tend to take after the same sex parent. Daughters looked like their mothers and sons like their fathers. So it was possible Nila looked like her mother.

He wasn't sure if he could call her pretty, exactly, either. Striking was a better word. The kind of unique beauty that made a man stop and take notice. He glanced at her again. Yes, striking was a good word for Nila.

Her thick, black hair was pulled back in a messy ponytail revealing sharp, angular features softened in sleep. Her caramel skin had been smooth to the touch, a sensation he still felt on his palms. Those dark eyes of hers were full of fire and intelligence. The delicious mix of cinnamon-sugar sweetness and her natural essence caught around his libido, making him think things he shouldn't given the circumstances.

The urge to touch her made his fingertips tingle.

He flexed his hands around the steering wheel and forced down the impulse. She wasn't just some ordinary human woman he was free to seduce. She was important. More important than she could ever guess.

Nila represented hope for his people at a time when it looked like their species was fading into extinction. There were too many males and not enough females. And the decline in female numbers was getting worse no matter what they did. They wouldn't survive very long this way.

Unfortunately, most of the elders didn't agree with his grandmother's solution to the problem. They'd actively derided her research and all the money she was pouring into alternate options.

They couldn't dismiss her ideas anymore, though. Nila was living proof that Elizaveta's theories were at least partly true.

Humans and tiger shifters could have children.

There were legends of this being possible, but most tigers didn't believe the myth had any basis in reality. Nila proved otherwise, and her existence might just be the key to his people's survival.

It was up to him to keep this hope for their future alive.

He glanced at her again. It was too easy to forget her significance and just see the woman—the sexy, tempting, delicious-smelling woman. A dangerous distraction, that sharp shock of attraction and stirring lust. He couldn't afford to forget what they faced. Petrov Dubrovsky was rich, powerful, and connected in both the tiger and human worlds. Every detail Mitch's grandmother had given him on Petrov had only increased Mitch's concerns. Petrov wouldn't be easy to elude. If Mitch let himself forget the danger, forget Nila's significance, he could get them both killed.

No, any attraction he felt for her would have to wait. In the end, it probably wouldn't matter anyway. He would never be allowed to compete for her if she proved able to have children with tigers. Better for him to keep his emotions under control and his feelings strictly protective.

He glanced at her one last time as her scent filled his head. Then he focused on the road.

Keeping his attraction in check might be easier said than done.

Nila bolted upright with a shocked gasp and blinked at her dark surroundings. Momentary confusion and panic made her heart beat faster.

"You okay?" Mitch asked.

The sound of his voice brought reality, and the untenable situation she was in, crashing back. A different kind of panic tightened her stomach. "Did my dad call?" she asked even as she looked at the phone she clutched. "Damn it. Where are they?"

"I'm sure they're fine."

His tone was calm, assured, and because she wanted desperately to believe him, she nodded and let out some of her tension on a long breath.

Glancing out the window, she tried judging their location. Thick woods lined the road. Highway lights were infrequent, leaving the inside of the SUV darkened and giving a feeling of being insulated from the world outside.

She glanced at her phone again. Almost two a.m.

"How long till we reach your cabin?" she asked.

"Not long now. Maybe another half hour."

"Do you get good cellphone reception?"

"You'll be able to call your father from there. Do you want to try him again now?"

She looked at the bars on her phone. They were coming in and out of reception, but maybe she could get a call through. She rang both phones and got both voicemails again. The tight feeling in her gut twisted hard.

"What if this Dubrovsky has gotten to them? What if they're in trouble and need my help?"

She glanced at Mitch, half hoping and half dreading any reassuring platitudes he might offer. He didn't, though. He just reached out and squeezed her hand still gripping her phone. The contact sent a jolt of sensation and odd emotion through her. His touch was much more comforting than a stranger's should have been.

"Thanks," she muttered as he let her go and carefully wrapped his hand around the steering wheel again. "Did I drool?" she asked in a lame attempt to lighten the heavy mood.

He raised his brows. "I thought you didn't want to know."

"I don't. You're right."

He gave her a side glance and smiled. Damn that smile was deadly. If her situation wasn't so complicated and scary, she'd be very tempted to seduce Mitch Chernikov.

She glanced at his hands. He had beautiful hands, with long fingers and wide palms. Very masculine hands she had no trouble imagining running over her body.

The muscles of his forearms flexed in the dim light, drawing her attention. She loved men's forearms—so much strength and sexy maleness. What would those muscles feel like under her fingertips if she drew her hands up from his wrists to his elbows?

Nila shook off the thoughts, knowing she was trying to distract herself with sex. She couldn't afford that, not now, not when things were so precarious. Hell, she wasn't even entirely sure what her situation was since she couldn't believe half what Mitch had told her. So sex was off the table. A first for her. It wasn't normally something she denied herself when attracted to someone.

They spent the rest of the journey in silence. She kept her attention on the passing woods, checking her phone every few minutes. She was going to drain the battery at this rate, but she couldn't stop herself from fingering it on to make sure she hadn't missed a call, a text, even an email from her family.

By the time they turned up the steep drive to Mitch's cabin she was ready to jump out of her seat. When she unfastened her seatbelt, though, Mitch stilled her with a gesture.

"Stay in the car while I check the area."

She frowned but settled as best she could while he climbed out of the SUV. For long moments he just stood there, staring into the woods, his head up. What the hell was he doing? He turned in a slow circle, his gaze lifted to the cabin behind her.

She turned in her seat to take in the two story home. It was hard to tell in the dark but it looked like a nice, luxurious retreat. With luck it had an indoor toilet and running water because after the long drive she really had to use the bathroom.

When Mitch finally motioned her out of the car she was practically bouncing in her seat.

She followed him up the three porch steps to the front door, waiting with barely contained patience for him to unlock it and let her inside. He stepped in ahead of her, checking the room first before holding the door open.

She took in the first floor at a glance but didn't notice many details. "Bathroom?" she asked.

"Sure. That door by the pool cue rack." He pointed. "I called a neighbor and had him get the water running so the tank should be full."

"Thanks." She hurried to the small, half-bathroom. When she finished she splashed water on her face and made an effort to not look in the mirror. Her nap had taken the edge off her exhaustion, but she didn't really want to confront the circles under her eyes yet.

She stepped out of the bathroom checking the bars on her phone, again. She had a good signal, thank god. "I'm gonna call my dad again," she said without actually looking up at Mitch. She hit speed dial for her dad's phone as she returned to the front porch. She stared into the darkness as she listened to the phone ring.

"Nila, are you all right? Is Mikhail with you?"

The sound of her father's voice made her shoulders slump and her head spin with relieved dizziness. She started breathing again. "Dad. Are you okay? What the hell is going on? Is grandma with you?"

"Your grandmother is right here. We're both fine. You?"

"I'm fine. Yes, I'm with Mikhail." She smiled to herself as she used the name he hated. "This guy is safe, right?"

"Your grandmother swears we can trust him."

"You have your doubts?"

"What has he told you?"

"That Anaya was alive until a few weeks ago." The silence from the other end of the line made Nila's stomach flip and she closed her eyes. "Is he telling me the truth, dad?"

"Yes."

"Dad." She wanted to cry and curse all at once. "Why did you lie to me? How could you do that?" Her chest ached at hearing the reality of his betrayal directly from him.

"What else has Mikhail told you?"

"That he hates being called Mikhail."

"Nila. What has he told you about your mother?"

"Ridiculous stories that I don't believe."

Another telling silence.

"This isn't really happening," she muttered. "I'm still on the plane, sound asleep."

"I'm so sorry, love. I never meant for you to get hurt."

"Then why did you lie?"

"I hoped you'd never have to find out the truth. It was too complicated."

She wanted to laugh at the understatement. "Complicated? That my mother was alive until recently? That she ran off with another man after I was born? Or that I'm the daughter of a mythical shapeshifting creature? How is that complicated, Dad? Seems perfectly straight forward to me." Her voice grew louder with each question. She breathed deeply, forcing herself to calm down.

"Don't," he said. "I know you're hurt. I know you don't understand all this. And I wish more than anything I could be the one there explaining."

"Then why aren't you? What the hell am I doing with this stranger instead of being with you and grandma?"

"This was the only way we could think to keep you safe. Your mother's... This man, Petrov Dubrovsky, he will use us to get to you. He's been to see your grandmother. That's why her friend sent Mikhail to help. Then that other...man broke into your grandmother's house earlier today."

"Did he hurt anyone?" Nila didn't miss the way her dad avoided calling the man a tiger.

"No, no. Mikhail seemed to know he was coming and we got out in time. But that's when I decided we should split up. Petrov will expect us to run together. I can keep your grandmother safe. But I can't protect you both from...from someone like him. Mikhail can."

"How do I know you're safe? You just said Petrov could use you? What makes you think he won't go after you if he can't find me?"

"I'm taking precautions, love. No one, not even Mikhail, knows where your grandmother and I are going. I'm not going to tell you either."

"You have to tell me." A trickle of panic started in her gut.

"No. Not on cellphones. And I don't want to know where you'll be. In fact, I want you to keep your phone off unless you absolutely have to use it. We'll keep ours off, too. Just in case. I don't know if Dubrovsky has the resources to track cellphones, but I don't want to take any chances."

"No. Dad, I need to be able to reach you." The trickle of panic turned to a steady stream.

He paused then said, "I don't want to be out of touch either. Tell you what. As soon as you can, get one of those disposable phones. Leave me the number in a voicemail. I'll get a new phone after that, and we can keep in touch that way. I'm pretty sure those types of cellphones are impossible to trace."

"You watch too many cop shows."

"No precaution is too much when it comes to your life."

"But…"

"Nila, I would not be able to live if anything happened to you. I need you to stay safe and alive."

"I need the same for you, Dad," she murmured as tears pooled in her eyes.

"Trust me, love."

"You lied to me. My whole life has been a lie."

"No! Not a lie. You are who you are. Don't start doubting that." He sighed. "I'm sorry I lied, because you've been hurt, but I would do it again to keep you safe."

"How is this keeping me safe? I don't feel very safe at the moment."

"If I'd told you the truth, you would have tried to find your mother, maybe even others like her. Don't you understand? I never wanted them to know about you. And you would have ignored the danger to track down Anaya."

Hearing this story from her father was like a sharp stab to her heart. She wasn't even sure how to feel about any of it anymore, though betrayal and sadness and love for her father all tangled into the mix. She grabbed the wooden railing surrounding the porch and squeezed hard, trying to ground herself in a world that seemed upside down.

"They would have killed you, Nila. Don't you see that? Anaya's people would have killed you."

"They're still trying to kill me, even after all the deception."

"What do you want me to say? I don't regret what I did, and I would do it again. I'm sorry if that means you don't trust me anymore, but I did what I did for you. My only regret is that Petrov found out about you anyway. If I could, I'd kill him myself to keep you safe."

He sounded so fierce she actually smiled, though her lips trembled a little. "You're not a murderer. But thanks for the thought. We have a lot to talk about when we see each other."

"Yes."

She swallowed and released the porch railing. "I still think we should all stick together. I don't know why we're trusting this stranger to look out for me."

"Because he knows more about what's going on than any of us. Because my mother has promised me he'll protect you with his life."

She snorted. "Well, I can't risk Grandma's Evil Eye by not believing her, can I?"

"We'll see each other soon, love. Just stay safe. Whatever it takes." He took an audible breath. "I am sorry you're in the middle of this mess."

"Stay safe, too, Dad. Keep Grandma safe."

"I will. Talk to you soon. I love you."

"Love you, too."

For a long moment, she stared into the dark woods beyond the porch. She still couldn't wrap her mind around the whole situation. Her dad had said Mitch was telling her the truth. She just couldn't bring her logical brain to accept it. This wasn't a movie. Shapeshifter-anythings weren't supposed to exist in real life. Your supposedly dead mother certainly shouldn't be one.

But according to her dad, it was all true.

Now what the hell was she going to do?

Chapter Four

Mitch watched Nila through the front window while he waited for the water in the kettle to boil. Because he could hear both sides of her conversation, thanks to his tiger hearing, he'd tried busying himself with checking his cabin to give her some semblance of privacy. He gave up the pretense when he ran out of chores.

She didn't move for a long time after she hung up, and worry wound through his gut. He stretched out his senses to assure himself they were still safe. He could sense his own kind at a great distance even compared to other tigers, but more than that, he knew the night wildlife was still active and undisturbed. The area wouldn't be so active if a strange predator was in the area. Since this was his territory the wildlife was used to him.

Nila was as safe as she could be for now. Unfortunately, they'd have to leave again tomorrow, but they could rest here tonight and make plans. They still had a lot to talk about.

When he had two cups of English breakfast tea ready, he took them out to the porch. Nila looked up at him, her expression difficult to read. With only the light from the cabin shadowing her features she looked mysterious and vulnerable at the same time. He breathed her in, realized she'd used his soap, and had to swallow a growl of satisfaction that she had part of his scent on her skin. The instinctive reaction surprised him enough that he just stared for a moment. She raised her brows, and he remembered himself.

He held up a mug. "Tea. I didn't know how you took it, so it's just black."

"Thanks." She smiled, took the offered cup, and sipped.

He had to force himself not to stare as she licked her lips and sighed. She was in emotional turmoil. He knew this was all a lot to take in so suddenly. She didn't need him gawking at her and considering how she'd look with her hair down, mussed from his hands, the dark silk fanned out across his pillow…

He blinked and took a gulp of his own drink to wet his dry throat.

"You okay?" he asked quietly.

"No. No, I'm not. I keep hoping this dream will end soon. I don't even know how or what to think right now."

"Would you feel better if we sat down and talked? Or…do you want to be alone? I can show you to the guest room."

"No," she said, straightening. "I'd rather we talked, if that's okay?"

"Of course. Are you cold? I can start a fire?"

"I don't need a fire, but I wouldn't mind sitting."

He motioned her inside, watching her as she looked around the ground floor. He wasn't sure she'd even noticed her surroundings before, but he could tell she was taking in details now—the wide open floor plan, the sunken seating area surrounding a stone fireplace, the huge kitchen off to the right, the pool table and large entertainment center to the left. He couldn't help wondering what she thought of the place. Did she like his home? What did she see when she looked around?

This cabin was the closest thing he had to a real home. Most tigers lived in cities or towns but eventually bought second homes in remote, wooded places to serve as their retreats and territories, places they could shift and run freely in their animal forms. He was on the road so much for his job, he'd never bothered settling anywhere. He only had this place—his territory—and he loved it here so much it never mattered that he didn't have a main house anywhere else.

When she didn't say anything right away, curiosity got the better of him. "Well. Will this do?"

She glanced at him. "Nice. Just you?"

He nodded. "As I said, no girlfriend, no wife, no kids."

He motioned to the couch and she settled into the deep cushions.

"I know it's extremely personal since we just met, but…" She stared up at him. "But you said you weren't likely to have a wife or girlfriend or kids. Why? Is there anything…wrong?"

"No, nothing is wrong with me. I just don't think it's going to happen."

"You don't want them?"

"I'd love kids, it's just…" Among his kind, the only way to have children was to win a mate in the Mate Run and get her pregnant. The stain of his father's crimes hung heavily on him and his two older brothers. None of the rare tiger females were ever likely to take any of them as mates, so he'd resigned himself to never having kids a long time ago.

But before he could even begin to explain all that, he'd have to tell Nila about the Mate Run, and the serious trouble the tigers were in. As for the story of his mother's suicide and his father's mental break…

He frowned. "It's just that we have other things to talk about first," he finished because he wasn't sure he even wanted to tell her about his parents. Most of his people looked down on him, and he was loathe to see that same disgust from Nila.

She leaned back against the couch, cradling her mug in her palms. "I know. I'm just not sure what to ask or where to start."

He sat, keeping to the opposite side of the couch so he didn't crowd her—despite what his tiger wanted him to do. "Do you believe that tiger shifters exist now?"

"No. Yes. I don't know. I guess I have to, don't I?"

"You'll be safer if you accept they're real. Beyond Petrov's money and power, he's physically dangerous, too." Mitch had asked Rossa if Nila showed any signs of being able to shift. She confirmed Nila was as human as a human-shifter hybrid could be. That was part of the myths, too—that the offspring of a tiger-human mix could either be human or shifter. Because Nila had been born mostly human, she didn't have a tiger form to give her any protection in the shifter world. That made her infinitely more vulnerable.

"Fine," she said after taking another sip from her mug. "Weretigers—tiger shifters?"

He nodded at the preferred way his people referred to themselves.

"Okay. Tiger shifters exist. My mother was one. Petrov is also one. My mother managed to have me with my human father, which shouldn't happen. And now Petrov wants me dead. So far so good?"

"Yes."

"Does he want me killed because I'm a mix?"

"Those like Petrov consider you… They think you'll dilute tiger bloodlines and destroy the species. In fact, according to my grandmother, Petrov has been very vocal—and fanatical—in his opposition to even the idea of a tiger-human mix. Apparently, during a debate among a group of powerful tigers, Petrov announced he'd kill any 'abominations' he came across. At the time, everyone just thought he was talking. But over the years he's gotten even more fanatical in his beliefs, and his current actions prove just how serious his threat was."

"Why is diluting tiger bloodlines an issue? How could that destroy the species?"

"Tigers are in a lot of trouble, biologically. The sex ratio is extremely skewed—too many males, not nearly enough females. Female births continue to be rare. Tiger shifters are heading for extinction if a solution to the problem isn't found soon."

"Ah. So…a mix that produces an ordinary human is…bad?"

"It's a little more complicated than that. If your mother could have you, there's the possibility that you could have children with a tiger shifter, too. That possibility is…well, it's hope to a lot of the males that would otherwise never be able to have children."

"How is that a bad thing?"

"The tigers that think like Petrov believe those mixed matings will drive us closer to extinction, that they'll produce mostly humans and after a while, completely breed out the shifters."

"Will that happen?"

She asked with genuine curiosity— no judgment, no disgust—as if they were discussing a topic that didn't directly impact her life. He wasn't sure if that was good. On the one hand, it meant she wasn't running away screaming into the night. On the other hand, it was hard to tell if she even believed what he was telling her. He took in her scent, searching for clues, but there were too many layers of emotion for even his tiger senses to sort through.

"No one knows," he answered. "No one even believed someone like you could exist. Well, except my grandmother. She's done a lot of research into the possibility."

"Your grandmother… How did she and my grandma meet?" She narrowed her eyes and he could see she was starting to make some connections.

"Anaya went to my grandmother when she found out she was pregnant by a human."

"Why?"

"Elizaveta is an elder—a member of the tigers' governing body. She's the only female elder and one of the most powerful as well."

"Ah, so what better person to go to, then. When Anaya left me with my dad…?"

"Elizaveta befriended your grandmother so she could keep an eye on you. And protect you."

Nila snorted. "Right. Some protection."

"She doesn't know how Petrov learned about you. But as soon as she discovered he'd found you, she sent me to help, and she's got the Trackers—essentially our police force—after Petrov as we speak."

"Will they be able to catch him?"

"Yes." He spoke with more confidence than he felt. Petrov wasn't a tiger to take lightly. "But it will take some time. We'll have to get moving again tomorrow to stay ahead of him."

"Whoa, wait. I thought… Why do we have to go anywhere?"

She leaned forward, a move that brought her close enough he could feel her heat, and her scent washed over him in a delicious wave. He forced himself to pay attention to the conversation.

"That guy at the airport—the one who tried kidnapping you—he got a look at my face and took in my scent. It won't take long before they figure out who I am and were to find me. This is my primary home. I've never bothered hiding it."

"So Petrov will be able to find it."

"'Fraid so. It'll be the first place they look."

She released a loud breath. "Hell. How long do we have?"

"We'll be fine here for tonight, what's left of the night. Time enough to sleep and make plans."

She dropped back again, running a hand through her hair. "I'm not sure I'll be able to sleep now, but part of me wants to just shut down and hide in sleep or…"

She met his gaze and something he couldn't quite interpret moved through the dark depths. A delectable hint of desire flavored her scent, drawing his full attention. The attraction he'd been working hard to ignore pushed to the surface. He held perfectly still, afraid if he moved at all, he'd leaned in to her and take what he wasn't allowed to have. But he couldn't drag his gaze from hers, and the longer they stared at one another, the thicker the tension grew.

She blinked first and looked away. "I should sleep," she murmured.

He heard her reluctance but didn't trust himself to speak just yet. He was afraid he'd argue with her.

"You must be exhausted, too," she said with a light tone that sounded forced. "I shouldn't make you stay up keeping me company like this."

"I don't mind." He swallowed and cleared his throat. His voiced sounded rough and too deep. "I'm jetlagged, too, so I'm not that tired."

"Really? Where have you been?"

"Nepal on assignment with a detour to Moscow to meet my grandmother." Elizaveta didn't believe in relaying important information over the phone if she could avoid it, so rather than telling him about Nila in a call—even using their secret family language—and sending him directly from Nepal back to the US, his grandmother had ordered him on this side trip to

Russia, where she was looking into Petrov's background and resources. The side trip had cost a little time, but mostly it just screwed up his sleep patterns.

"Assignment?" Nila asked.

"I'm a freelance nature photographer—when I'm not rescuing hapless damsels in distress."

"Right." She smirked at his attempt at a joke.

Again that edge of desire curled through her scent, mixing with her natural essence, and catching him in a tight grip. His gaze dropped to her mouth without his permission. She had lush, beautiful lips that looked incredibly soft. Despite his best efforts, his imagination wandered to all the places he'd like to feel her sexy mouth. When she flicked out her tongue to wet her bottom lip, he had to swallow a groan.

She's not yours to have, Mitch, he reminded himself as he watched her. Not even for a little while. Not even for a single night.

Too bad his body wasn't listening to his brain.

CHAPTER FIVE

Nila swallowed hard and tried not to stare. Mitch looked so intense and so incredibly sexy, she was having a hard time remembering he was a stranger and she was in a lot of trouble.

Her gaze clashed with his before she forced herself to look away. That expression on his face said he'd happily fuck her if she asked him to. The thought was thrilling, filling her with a sense of power, making her acutely aware of her femininity. In a situation where she felt completely out of control, knowing at least in this she had some say in what happened actually helped.

Being alone with him made resisting the call to seduce him more difficult. The cabin smelled strongly of Mitch, which only spiked her need. He had a deliciously masculine scent, with hints of cedar and musk. She wanted to bury her face against his neck and breathe him in while she stripped him naked. Then she wanted to taste him, everywhere, just to see if he tasted as delicious as he smelled.

Bad idea, Nila. Bad idea. Hiding in sex wasn't going to get her out of her current predicament. Giving in to the amnesia of sex wouldn't help. She needed to stay clear-headed, which meant she needed to get off this couch and away from temptation.

"Either the tea is working," she said, very carefully setting the mug down on his coffee table, "or the jetlag is taking its toll. I think I should turn in."

"Good idea."

His voice cascaded over her skin, leaving a tingling of anticipation in its wake. Her body pulsed with need. Why wasn't she dragging him to bed? She bet there was a very serviceable bed in that guestroom. Without meaning to, she found her gaze wondering over his chest and shoulders, settling on the flexing muscles of his forearms.

She swallowed and stood so she wouldn't lean in and kiss him.

"This way." He gestured to the back of the house, behind the sunken sitting area, where a wooden staircase curved up to the second floor. She followed his lead.

On the landing, he turned right. "My bedroom is back that way." He motioned toward the opposite side of the hallway. "Here's the bathroom." He tapped a door as he passed. "And here's your room." Pushing open the next door, he leaned in and flipped on the lights.

When he stepped back, she walked past to get into the room and paused just inside the threshold. They hadn't touched, but she could almost feel the brush of his skin against hers, and the sensation made her shiver.

"If you're cold, there are more blankets in that closet."

She wasn't the least bit cold. In fact, she was overly warm. But she thanked him anyway. Without having to look, she sensed him moving closer, close enough she felt his heat along her spine.

"Is the room okay?"

His breath brushed against the side of her face as he leaned in. "It's fine," she whispered, her every nerve conscious of his proximity. All she'd have to do is lean back to be in his arms. If she turned her head, she could capture his mouth with hers. Her breathing increased right along with her heart rate.

Tilting her head to the side just enough to see him from the corner of her eye, she caught him staring down at her. The heat in his eyes dried her mouth. When she licked her lips, he growled softly. The sound sent a tremor of desire shooting through her body.

"I should really try to sleep," she murmured.

He nodded. "You should."

Neither of them moved for a long moment.

Finally, she faced the room and pulled in a long slow breath. She tried, again, to convince herself sleeping with him now would be foolish. She was in no state to make a wise decision about sex, and she was too old to go flying into bed with a man just because he was hot and she wanted to forget for a few hours. She had no idea what would happen in the next few days. The complication of sex with Mitch was more than she could afford right now.

Despite the rapid thump of her heart, she forced out a quiet, "Goodnight."

"Goodnight. If you need me, I'm just down the hall."

Oh, good. Being reminded of that would really help her sleep. With a silent groan, she firmly closed the bedroom door between them.

Nila woke with a start. She squinted against the pale light filtering into the room. For an instant, she didn't recognize her surroundings, then the whole horrible night came back to her.

Well, not entirely horrible. Meeting Mitch was almost worth the mess she was in.

She rose and opened the drapes, taking in the thick woods on the side of the house. Sparkling sunshine reached down through the branches, and a bright blue sky peeked out over the green limbs.

Her mother was a tiger shapeshifter.

In the light of day, the idea seemed beyond ridiculous. Thinking back, she could almost believe the conversation with her father had been a dream. The supernatural part of this mess was just a figment of her imagination. Mitch was real. The kidnapping attempt had been real. But the other…

It would explain a lot, though, she realized. Her excellent eyesight and hearing. Her nighttime vision was much better than those around her, and she always seemed to hear things several seconds before others. Her sense of smell tended to be on a par with pregnant women. She was also surprisingly strong for her size—nothing superhuman, but she shocked people with the things she was physically capable of doing. Being half tiger might also explain her affinity for big cats, particularly tigers, and that elusive something that drew her to the magnificent animals.

But ordinary humans had that kind of draw to certain animals, too. There was no reason to think there was anything unusual about her connection to cats.

Her excellent senses were a little harder to explain. Until now, she'd never thought much about them. None were so extraordinary that they hinted at a link to a supernatural creature. None of her differences were so extreme they made this shapeshifter business believable.

So why the hell did she believe it?

Groaning, she dropped her head against the cool window pane. What was she going to do? She had no idea how to deal with these revelations. She wasn't used to not knowing what to do. The sensation was awful.

Straightening, she shook her arms and then stretched them over her head until her spine popped, trying to work out some of the building tension. First things first. Bathroom, shower, and food. Then she and Mitch would come up with a plan. She needed it to direct her through the next few days. With direction, she could cope. Maybe in time, she'd learn to come to terms with the truth about her mother. But that could happen later. Right now, she just needed to take the next step and survive for another day.

By the time she got downstairs, Mitch was already in the kitchen. "Something smells good," she said.

He turned when she spoke and smiled. Nila's body reacted with a sharp thrust of lust. Her every nerve jumped with need and anticipation. For a moment, all she could do was stare. Early afternoon sunshine poured in through the windows, the light bringing out the sharp hazel color of his eyes and the broad cut of his features. He wore a t-shirt and jeans, nothing particularly special, but on his exquisite physique, the simple outfit was sexier than anything she'd ever seen a man wear. Her stomach tightened as a wave of awareness moved through her. Tingling chills covered her skin.

Get a grip, she told herself, breathing slowly through her nose. It's not the first time you've seen a handsome man.

Though she had to admit, she'd never met anyone quite as attractive as Mitch. She wasn't sure very many of them existed in the world.

"Are you hungry? I had some egg substitute in the freezer and the basics for an omelet. Not nearly as good without cheese, but I'm afraid it'll have to do. There's bacon, which I know you don't want but I'm having some, and since I left a loaf of bread in the freezer, we even have toast."

"I'm starved," she said as she leaned against the counter, remaining outside the open kitchen. Safer to keep some distance between them.

"Did the shower help with your jetlag?" he asked without looking at her.

"Felt great. So did brushing my teeth." She kept her toothbrush in her carry-on backpack thankfully. "Could have used a change of clothes, but washing off the grubby long haul travel feeling was nice."

He flashed her a grin over his shoulder. "Sorry I don't have anything here that would fit you. We can stop for fresh clothes on the way to our next stop."

She nearly groaned in relief. "Thank you. I really missed my duffle bag when I got out of the shower. Mostly, it was filled with dirty clothes, but there were at least a few clean t-shirts left."

And clean underwear but she didn't think mentioning her underwear was a good idea. She definitely didn't want to admit she'd decided to go without after the shower. The lack of that small, cotton barrier left her feeling a lot more vulnerable than she would have expected. She'd rinsed out the underwear she'd been wearing, but they'd take time to dry. In the meantime, her current commando state was going to remain her little secret.

As she watched Mitch move through the kitchen, focused on the muscles flexing along his forearms and the sure movements of his strong, sexy hands, she felt a thrill of wicked lust that would no doubt get her into whole heaps of trouble if she wasn't careful.

"Thanks for the eggs," she said in an attempt to distract herself from a fantasy of stripping him naked and fucking him on the kitchen floor.

"Pleasure. Not sure how you can go without meat, though."

"You cook a lot?"

"A bit. My older brother's the chef in the family."

"Really?"

"We went for a few years eating a lot of takeout—my uncle burned everything. I was too young to notice or care. In fact, I barely remember it. But Nick got tired of fast food and taught himself to cook."

"Wow. How old was he?"

"Must have been about twelve at the time, I guess. I was three when he started experimenting on us. We had some interesting meals those first few years."

She smiled. "How many siblings do you have?"

"Two older brothers. I'm the baby."

She snorted. "Spoiled?"

"Of course."

But a distant look filtered through his expression, belying the easy banter. Curiosity poked her. He'd mentioned his uncle but not his parents. What had happened to them? And why had his mood shifted?

Since they hadn't even known each other for a full twenty-four hours, she decided those questions might be too personal. Better to keep things light given how many other serious things they still had to discuss. "Was it fun growing up with big brothers?"

"Depended on the day. Sometimes they were great. Sometimes they were a pain in the ass."

"When I was a kid, I used to want a big brother. Mostly because I thought he'd have cute friends he could introduce me to."

Mitch laughed and Nila had to swallow her moan. That sound! His voice was husky and deep, and oh so sexy.

"You do realize if you'd had a big brother, there's no way in hell he'd allow you to date his friends." He plated up the eggs and slid them across the counter to her.

"How do you know? You have a sister?"

"Technically, no, but a family friend who's close enough she might as well be my sister. She's older than me, and I still gave her husband a serious grilling right after they got married. If I had a little sister, I wouldn't let my friends anywhere near her."

"I doubt that would stop your little sister." She grinned at his grunt of disbelief. She liked the way he talked about family—protective and close. Family was important.

She took a bite of her eggs. "Yum. Your brother might be the chef but you make a mean omelet. Thanks."

"You're welcome." He lifted his own fork then froze, his head going up and his gaze sharpening.

She frowned. "What's wrong?" A tingle of instinct shivered down her spine, a sense of…something, an awareness of… She couldn't put her finger on it, but it reminded her of the shiver she'd gotten at the airport just before she'd had a gun shoved into her back, a reaction she'd attributed to the air-conditioning. As she watched Mitch, her nerves twitched with a sudden alertness she couldn't ignore and a tremor of unease she couldn't blame on cool air.

He stood perfectly still for a long moment, his eyes unfocused, his head cocked to one side. His nostrils flared. Then he snapped his gaze around to the front door and dropped his fork. "Someone's here. We have to go. Now!"

He leapt over the counter which was so astonishing she gasped. An instant later, he had his arm around her waist and was pulling her toward the rear of the house.

"Wait. The car…"

"No time. He's out front."

Nila swallowed her panic and jogged at Mitch's side so he could stop dragging her. He led her to a panel near the first floor bathroom, hit a space on the wall, and a hidden door quietly slid open, revealing a wide staircase leading underground. Raising her brows, she squelched her questions. They had to get away first, then she could ask him why a seemingly normal man had a hidden escape route in his mountain cabin. As they navigated the dark steps, she realized the word normal wasn't quite right for Mitch.

"We have even more to talk about now," she whispered.

"Later."

"Do you have a plan?"

"It's progressive."

"Oh, good."

She nearly ran into his back when he stopped, and she realized they'd reached the bottom of the stairs. Glancing back at a noise, she watched the door above them close. Darkness engulfed them. "No lights?" she asked.

"Don't need them."

Which raised more questions, but they'd have to wait. Keeping a hand on his shoulder for both balance and reassurance, she waited while anxiety crawled over her skin. She heard the sounds of a lock turning, then bright light flooded the darkness.

"Come on." Mitch grabbed her hand and pulled her outside.

They came out a few hundred yards from the house, lower on the mountain so she could only glimpse the second floor from this angle. When the door behind them closed, she realized it was camouflaged from this end to look like part of the hill.

"Clever trick," she murmured.

He grunted in response while studying their surroundings, then pulled her to the right, away from the house. He moved quickly and easily through the trees and across the leaf strewn ground. Thanks to the summer heat and lack of rain, the dirt was dry and crumbly, so at least she wasn't worried about slipping in mud.

"Where are we going?" she asked quietly, though she wasn't sure why.

Mitch didn't have any trouble hearing her. "Neighbor's house first."

"How far?"

"About three miles."

"Shit."

He glanced back and gave her a sympathetic look. "You can do it."

"I know. I'm used to hiking. I just thought I'd get a break from it once I got back to New York."

He squeezed her hand but didn't slow his pace. They moved at a steady trot, but she had to concentrate to keep from stumbling over uneven ground. The tension and an empty stomach left her wobbly. A twisted ankle now would be a very bad thing, so she focused on where her feet landed and let Mitch lead the way.

Once, because she thought she heard something, she glanced over her shoulder. There didn't seem to be anyone following, but a tingle of anxiety crept down her spine again. She could practically feel something back there, liked she had in the airport parking lot.

At the same moment, Mitch picked up the pace so they were nearly running. She had no idea how far they'd come or how far they had left to go, but she knew their pursuer was catching up even if she couldn't explain how she knew.

This time, Nila did plowed into Mitch when he suddenly stopped, sending her stumbling and falling to her knees. She barely had time to feel the sting of scraped skin through her cargo pants before Mitch used his grip on her hand to lift her back up. As soon as she had her balance, she realized what had halted their progress.

Not ten feet away stood a huge Bengal tiger.

Chapter Six

Nila stared, unable to believe her own eyes. This wasn't possible. Who the hell kept tigers in this area?

A sneaky little voice in her head reminded her that the people after her were supposed to be tiger shifters, but faced with one of the huge cats, she preferred believing someone's pet had escaped and gone wandering through the woods.

Mitch shoved her behind him and stood facing the large animal, staring it right in the eyes. "Show yourself," he snapped.

Nila was filled with a horror so profound it turned to wonder as the tiger began convulsing, its body twisting, the hair along its spine rolling. She heard the snap snap of bone and the twang of tendons stretching, making her stomach roll with nausea. The tiger stood on its hind legs as fur receded, revealing human skin. The hind legs lengthened and narrowed, the fore legs elongated, the claws retracted, fingers and hands replaced paws, the face reshaped with terrifying and impossible movement of bone and muscle. Ears lowered to the side of its head, the nose lightened in color and became human.

Unable to look away, Nila stared into the animal's eyes as they changed from an almost glowing gold to the dark gaze of a man. He was tall and thickly muscled, with dark hair and dusky skin. He was also very naked, though he didn't seem to notice.

She had no idea how long the process took. Reality and sanity were distant memories by the time he'd finished. It was all she could do not to scream until her throat was raw. She'd just seen a tiger change into a human. Impossible. Her brain must have snapped, because this couldn't be happening.

"You're Petrov's oldest," Mitch said matter-of-factly.

The man flicked a glance at Nila, then nodded.

Over his shoulder, Mitch said to her, "This is your half brother, Vladimir Dubrovsky."

Nila's thoughts spun and she gripped Mitch tighter. She was so stunned, she couldn't think, never mind comprehend what Mitch had just told her.

Vladimir dipped his head toward her in a brief greeting. "Call me Vlad. I'm the reason our mother and my father were able to mate permanently...marry. I'm the reason they were able to marry."

She stared, unable to respond because she had no idea what he was talking about, and didn't have the ability to form coherent language at the moment anyway.

"I'm not going to let you kill her," Mitch said, breaking into the tense silence that followed Vlad's statement.

That got Nila's attention and her heart started racing. She blinked away her shock as another kind of panic crept in. She looked around, searching for an escape route, as every muscle in her body prepared to run.

But how could she escape something like Vlad?

"I'm not interested in killing her," the man said, drawing her attention back to him.

Mitch snorted. "Right."

Vlad held her gaze. "I don't want you dead," he repeated.

"Why?" she asked, the only word she could force through her dry mouth.

"I have my reasons." He looked back at Mitch. "I'm here to warn you. My father knows who you are. It won't be long before he and my brothers find this house. You have somewhere else to go? A place he can't find?"

"How'd you find this place before your father?" Mitch asked.

"He's not the only one with connections. I can't help you beyond this warning. My father would know. But you need to keep her alive."

"I intend to. Why are you warning us?"

Vlad was silent for a long moment. Then said, "Not everyone approves of my father's…methods, but there are more than a few who want him to succeed. And some…" He faced Nila again. "Some want you for themselves. They'll be just as dangerous as my father."

"I'll keep it in mind," Mitch said.

Nila blinked, shock still clouding her ability to think.

"You'll have to fight for her before this is done," Vlad said to Mitch.

Mitch remained silent, making Nila look up at him. His jaw was set, his expression grim, his gaze fixed on the other man. He didn't glance down at her, even when she squeezed his hand. There was more going on here than was evident in the words being spoken, leaving her lost. Which pissed her off.

"I have to go." Vlad started shifting again, the whole horrible process reversing itself before Nila's eyes.

She swallowed hard and forced herself to look away.

Fortunately, Mitch didn't wait around for Vlad to finish. He jerked her hand and pulled her forward, running once more. Nila did her best to keep up even as she felt bile rising in her throat.

Later, she thought. Think about this later. Just don't pass out now.

Easier said than done.

"Why aren't we going back to the cabin if they're not here yet?" Nila asked through ragged breaths.

Mitch didn't look at her. He was too busy concentrating on picking out an easy path for her through the woods. "I want them to think we abandoned the cabin suddenly, just before they arrived."

"If it takes days, the food will give away that we've been gone for a while."

"It won't take days. They'll be here in a few hours."

Thankfully, she didn't ask how he knew. He couldn't really explain his knowledge to a non-tiger. Deep seeded instinct wasn't something easily described. He'd grown up fighting his own kind, being attacked simply because of what his father had done. He'd honed the ability to judge an approaching attack better even than most Trackers. And that instinct was telling him they had three, maybe four hours before Petrov and his people arrived.

Vlad hadn't been that far ahead of his father. His scent carried his anxiety, and he was obviously in a hurry, a little desperate to make sure Mitch and Nila were gone. Those signals and Mitch's own instincts were enough to tell Mitch everything he needed to know.

"Vlad's given us a head start, but I don't want Petrov to realize we're that far ahead of him. He'll eventually figure it out, but first, he'll waste time and effort searching the area for us."

He jogged around trees, pushing her as fast as he thought she could go, to get to his neighbor's house. Tim Barnes had been doing some repairs on Mitch's spare truck while Mitch was away on his last assignment. He hoped the old machine was in working order now because he didn't have another immediate plan to get them out of the area. If the truck didn't start, he'd have to take Nila deeper into the woods and either find a good place to hide—not a great option since Petrov could hunt them out here—or another way to get back on the road to a new location.

By the time they reached the garage next to Tim's house, and his truck behind the garage, Nila was out of breath, but Mitch hadn't sensed the other tigers yet. His instincts still gave them a few more hours to get away. Without speaking, he handed Nila up into the cab of the old four wheel drive then he hurried to the driver's side.

He dropped the visor and the spare keys fell into his open palm. When he turned the ignition, the truck coughed and wheezed, but the engine caught and roared to life. He let out a breath and reversed out to the dirt path that wound back to a main road. As he passed in front of Tim's house, Tim stepped out onto his porch. Mitch waved to his neighbor who nodded back and raised a hand in greeting, though his brow was creased in a frown.

He'd have to thank Tim for getting the old machine running and explain all this—somehow—when he got a chance.

"Where to now?" Nila asked.

"Still working on that part."

He glanced at her. Her skin was waxy-looking and pale. She was covered in sweat from the run, and her eyes were wide with shock. No doubt seeing a tiger turn into a human had completely freaked her out. Yet she was holding up under the strain. He'd half expected her to start screaming and not stop after that abrupt and brutal confirmation with the reality of tiger shifters. The fact that she wasn't curled into a ball of quivery fright proved just how strong Nila was, and his admiration for her grew.

Hoping to focus her attention on something other than the process of a tiger shift, he said, "When I'm comfortable we've got enough space between us and Petrov, I'll stop somewhere so we can get clothes and supplies."

"I don't have any money. Everything, my passport, my wallet, is back at the cabin. The only thing I have is my cellphone. I recharged it last night, but the plug is still in your guest room. And my dad wants me to get a new phone anyway. You're sure we can't go back and get a few things? The gun you took from that man last night is still in your SUV. I hate guns, but it might be…useful given what we're facing."

"We can't go back. Petrov would know if we doubled back. He'd wonder why." And he might figure out that someone had tipped them off, sending them running far earlier than Mitch wanted him to think. Mitch had no idea what Vlad was up to, or why he'd helped them get away. But because Vlad had helped, Mitch didn't want Petrov finding out about his oldest son's betrayal.

Nila sighed, a sound so sad, it made his chest ache. He reached out and squeezed her hand where it rested on the bench seat. "Don't worry. I'll take care of everything."

"You have your wallet with you?"

"Yes. And I have resources."

"I really hate losing my passport. I have some good stamps in there."

She sniffed and a bolt of panic shot through him. But when he glanced at her, her eyes were dry. "We'll get it back. You'll get all your stuff back," he promised. He gave her hand one last squeeze then released her, because holding her hand was entirely too comfortable, too natural, and this was not the time to forget himself. From the corner of his eye he saw her squirm in the seat. "What's wrong?"

She snorted. "Oh, nothing."

He glanced at her again, but she was staring out the window so he couldn't see her expression. "Nila, I swear, I'll take care of you."

Inside, his tiger roared in agreement. Whatever it took, he'd make sure Nila was safe.

CHAPTER SEVEN

They were on the main road before Mitch broached the subject of Vlad shifting in front of her. "Nila, do you… Are you okay after seeing Vlad change?"

She snorted, a half-laugh, half-choking sound. "Not even a little, Mitch. I am pretty sure I'm insane now, and I'm wondering which hospital I'll wake up in when I come out of this delusion."

"You're not insane."

"I'm much more content thinking I am, you know."

He didn't quite know what to say to that. He was just grateful she wasn't crying.

"Vlad said something…"

Because he knew she was on the edge, he waited quietly for her to finish her question.

"He said he was the reason Petrov and my mother married. Is that true?"

Mitch nodded.

"Explain that, please. What did he mean?"

"You sure you're ready to hear this?"

"Of course not. But I just watched a Bengal tiger change into a man who then told me he was my half brother. Whether I want to or not, I need to learn more about what I'm facing."

Just then her stomach growled and he remembered they'd left their breakfast behind. "You're hungry."

"Start talking and we'll worry about food when we pass a drive thru."

"Fine," he said. But where to start? At the beginning. "Okay, you know how I told you the tigers are on the edge of extinction?"

"Yes."

"For reasons our scientists are still trying to figure out, the number of female tigers has dwindled down to only about ten percent of the population."

"At one stage, was it was closer to fifty-fifty, like humans?"

He nodded. "Males always outnumbered females to a certain extent. But the percentages were more like fifty-six to forty-four. There were enough of both to keep a healthy population."

"Now?"

"The drastic decrease in female numbers became obvious a couple hundred years ago. At that point, panic set in. The males got…carried away in their attempts to mate."

"Meaning?" She adjusted her position to face him.

"They started having death match fights over females. Groups ganged up on individual females and raped them— frequently killing the female in the process and making the situation even worse. The entire population descended into chaos."

"Couldn't they have found another way that didn't involve death matches and rape? I wouldn't particularly want to live this way, but was multiple…matings I guess you'd call it, polyandry, taking on multiple males for each female considered?"

"It was. Unfortunately, it didn't work as a consistent answer to the problem. A few polyandrous unions succeeded, but they were rare. Most tiger males are too jealous and competitive to share a female long term. And, like you, the majority of tigresses didn't want to live that way."

"In the wild, tigers don't mate beyond the time it takes to procreate, and the females are very territorial. I take it tigers shifters are different."

"Part human, part tiger. The human part wants a partner for more than just reproduction."

"Do they… Can they fall in love?"

"You're wondering if your mother loved Petrov?"

"Well, yeah, it'd be nice to know if she loved the man she left my father and me for."

He glanced at her and realized there was more she wasn't saying. He could guess, though. She was wondering if Anaya had ever loved Nila's father, Leo. Though whether that knowledge would make Nila feel better or worse… "Yes, tiger shifters fall in love. Once they mate, once they marry, it's as long term as a human marriage might be. Some last, some don't."

She sucked in a deep breath and blew it out. Finally, she asked, "So…is it still chaos? Rapes and death matches for mates?"

"No. About a hundred and seventy years ago or so, the elders instituted the Mate Run."

"Mate Run. That was one of the things we didn't get to last night. What is it?"

"Basically, a substitute for death challenges among the males, a way for them to compete for a female in a semi-fair way without everyone getting killed in the process. During a female's estrous cycle—"

"Wait, do the women have menstrual periods like human women?"

"No."

"Lucky bastards," she muttered.

He had to work not to grin. "A female's estrous cycle lasts for three days."

"Consistently or is there a range, like the three to six days for ordinary tigers?"

"They range by a few hours but not by days."

"How often do they cycle? Does it depend on the climate? Are there differences among the subspecies?" She frowned. "Are there subspecies?"

"Yes, there are subspecies. No, there aren't differences in how often females cycle among the subspecies. Shifters cycle about once every five weeks, give or take, and continue to cycle throughout the year."

She nodded, her gaze turned inward.

He wanted to ask what she was thinking. Instead, he continued explaining the Mate Run. "At the start of estrous, a female will run and all the males in the area chase her. Whoever catches her gets to…be with her for that cycle."

"Sex?"

"Yes."

"Does the female get any say in who catches her? Or does she just have to fuck whichever male happens to beat out the others?"

"It's completely female choice," he reassured, hearing the bite in her tone. "While the Run is designed to feel like a competition between the males to satisfy their need to 'win' a mate, in practice, a female allows the male she wants to 'catch' her."

"And then they have sex for three days?"

"Three days and three nights of little else but sex."

"Ordinary tigers do something similar." She was silent for a moment, then said, "Sounds like fun."

Mitch's pulse kicked at her comment and fantasies of spending three days fucking Nila instantly filled his imagination. Three hot, sweaty, erotic, lusty days of Nila naked, panting, coming as often as he could make her.

Swallowing, he held his breath for a heartbeat then let it out very slowly. The sudden onslaught of lust took him by surprise. Oh, he wanted Nila. Badly. He'd spent the dawn hours fighting the urge to join her in the guest room. And when she came down to breakfast, the smell of her was more delicious than the bacon he'd cooked. He'd been busy talking himself out of dragging her back upstairs to a bed when he'd sensed Vlad's approach.

Since then he'd been so worried about keeping her safe, he'd let his guard down. Now, with his fantasies taunting him, he noticed her scent again, the strong cinnamon-sugar flavor of it like a treat just waiting for him to taste. Very carefully, he flexed his fingers on the steering wheel and kept his gaze on the road. If he looked at her now, he wasn't sure his control would hold. He needed to focus. She was in trouble. He had to concentrate on the job of keeping her alive, not getting into her pants.

A road sign announcing food ahead provided a good excuse to change the subject. "You hungry?"

"Yeah, that'd be good."

Her voice sounded as breathless as he felt. He risked a quick glance at her. Her cheeks were a charming shade of pink, and when he allowed himself another taste of her scent, he realized he wasn't the only one affected by talk of sex.

Damn but that was dangerous. So very dangerous.

And oh so tempting.

Chapter Eight

Back on the road, Nila started where they'd left off. "So when a male catches a female, they're mated permanently?"

"Not that simple," Mitch said as he pulled back onto the highway. "The couple is only allowed to be together permanently if they get pregnant. Until a female conceives, she continues to run every estrous cycle."

"Can she choose a different male each time?"

"If she likes."

"Huh."

Her curious, interested sound caught his attention. "What?"

"Well, I was just thinking scientifically, in a strictly biologically sense, this Run is logical. It's like taking male competition to its purest level and yet still allows for female choice. Which I assume makes most tigers happy?"

"It's mostly worked since it was instituted."

"No more fights or rapes?"

"Tigers are aggressive, so there are still plenty of fights. But no more death matches, no more gang rapes and murders of females."

"And that's enough to keep everyone following the…is it a law?"

"It's a law. And yes, the fact that it somewhat keeps the peace, along with serious financial penalties for breaking the law, keeps most tigers in line."

"Most? Not all?"

"There was one recent exception—little over twenty years ago now. That was a unique situation, though. It was the woman who's like my sister. Her and her husband. And they only just finished paying back the fine."

"Twenty years later? Wow, some fine."

"As far as the elders were concerned, if it wasn't outrageously huge, it wouldn't be enough of a deterrent to others."

"But breaking the law only comes with a monetary fine? Nothing worse?"

He cut her a glance, trying to gage how she was taking all this information. "There would be worse punishments if the situation had been different. The circumstances around this particular breach only warranted the fine."

The elders had forced Alexis and Victor's hands, leaving them little choice but to break the rules of the Run. If the elders had imposed anything more serious than a fine, Mitch knew for a fact Alexis and Victor would have rebelled and gone into hiding. Since their second child turned out to be a girl, the elders made the right choice. Otherwise, the community would have lost a valuable female. Mitch smiled a little at thoughts of Alexis and her family.

"I understand the need for something to help control the chaos," Nila said, breaking into his thoughts. "And as I said, biologically speaking, it makes sense. But how does this work on an emotional level? You said tigers fall in love. Where does love come into all this?"

"Love and emotional ties definitely play a part in the Run, in the choices the females make, in the consistency of a pair to come together Run after Run until they conceive. But it can complicate things. Jealousy is still a difficult problem." He considered whether or not he should mention the growing discord among the young tiger males, but decided that could wait. She had more than enough to deal with at the moment.

"Getting married once a female is pregnant isn't a requirement of the Run," he continued. "She can select a new male for each child she wants to have, though she has to run again if she wants a new partner. But love drives most couples to get married, and then they tend to remain monogamous. This leaves a lot of males without mates or any hope of children. Still, the Run has kept the population from descending completely into anarchy and extinction, so overall it works."

Nila was silent for long enough Mitch started getting restless. What was she thinking? How did the Run affect her impression of his people? And most importantly, was the Run something that appealed to her? She'd liked the idea of three days of sex. Did that mean she'd want to take part in a Run if she had the chance? Although, how that would work, he couldn't guess since she wasn't physically capable of it.

Curiosity finally got the better of him. "Would you enjoy something like the Mate Run as a way of finding a partner?" he asked. He tried keeping his tone neutral and mildly curious, but he heard the hint of a growl creeping into his voice. He felt her stare on the side of his face and refused to look at her.

"I'm pretty sure I wouldn't survive the running part," she said, light and sardonic. "But I'm an old fashioned girl. I prefer meeting a man, deciding I like him, and going from there. I'm not knocking the process, necessarily. It sounds like the Mate Run serves its purpose and has probably saved a lot of lives."

He nodded.

"That's fair enough. But it wouldn't be for me. Does…does a female ever end up with a male she doesn't like?"

"Not that I know of. There are plenty of males to choose from."

She was silent for a moment. "Then Anaya at least liked Petrov?"

"They were married until her death and had four children together," he said softly. That didn't exactly answer her question, but he wasn't sure what to tell her. He'd never met Anaya or Petrov. He had no idea what kind of relationship they'd had behind closed doors. He only knew they'd been married for years.

"So Vlad was the baby Anaya and Petrov conceived during a Mate Run," Nila said. "That's what he was talking about."

Mitch nodded.

Nila fell silent again, and Mitch concentrated on his driving, allowing her the time she needed to consider everything he'd told her. He was used to this world, these stories, the intricacies and complications inherent in his people's struggle for survival. To Nila, this must be like entering an alien world, even given all her work with big cats. Her time with ordinary tigers couldn't have prepared her for something like tiger shifters and their much more complex social order.

Nearly half an hour passed before she spoke again. The sun was just starting to set.

"Where are we going? Or are we just going to keep driving until we run out of gas?"

He smiled. She was an amazing woman. He'd thought he knew strong women, but Nila's strength humbled him. "I have a friend in Baltimore. He just recently married. He'll help us."

Elizaveta had warned him to avoid the elders' compound in West Virginia and to stay away from other tigers if he could, without explaining in much detail why. He could guess, though. They had no way of knowing which tigers would support Petrov in his efforts to kill Nila. Better to avoid all tigers, just in case. But Max was his best friend. Mitch knew he could trust Max and his wife with Nila's life.

"Human or tiger shifter?" she asked.

"Tigers."

"Will we stay in Baltimore?"

"We'll have to move on. Cities provide good cover in some ways. There's a lot of anonymity. But there are also a lot more humans who might see and report your location to Petrov's people. We'll have to stay in more isolated locations and hope Petrov is captured before he finds us."

"If others are hunting him, how is he still able to come after us?"

"He's clever and an extremely efficient predator. He's also wealthy, and money can buy a lot of secrecy."

"Can he bribe the people your grandmother sent to capture him?"

Mitch didn't respond at first. That thought had crossed his mind on more than one occasion. The Trackers enforced tiger laws and went after those who broke the laws. Alexis was a former Tracker, the only female Tracker in recent memory, and she'd been training new Trackers since she retired, so Mitch had a lot of respect for the office. But they weren't infallible. A corrupt Tracker, or Trackers, was possible.

"There are enough tigers who disapprove of Petrov trying to kill you. They will want him caught," Mitch finally said, mostly confident he was telling her the truth. "But he won't be easy to find. Our only hope is that we're more difficult for him to find than he is for the Trackers to locate."

"You don't make that sound easy."

"It won't be."

CHAPTER NINE

Nila studied Mitch's friends with a great deal of curiosity. Maxim Rudikov was a large, well-muscled man with dark hair and eyes. His features were broad and sharp, giving him a rugged handsomeness. His wife, Irina Gorban, was a beautiful woman with long, light brown hair and green eyes. She wasn't nearly as tall as her husband but was still several inches taller than Nila.

Though Mitch had told her Irina was pregnant, the woman had only a slight bump. If she were human, Nila would guess she was less than five months along but had no idea if tiger shifters carried children the same nine months as humans or closer to a normal tiger's four months. She found herself incredibly curious about everything to do with tiger shifter reproduction, and having a pregnant one sitting across from her made it hard to resist asking all her questions. This didn't really seem like the right time for that kind of conversation, though. They had more important things to discuss.

Unfortunately, they weren't actually discussing those things yet either.

They'd arrived a little after eight in the morning, driving most of the night with one break at a truck stop to sleep for a few hours. Since knocking on Max and Irina's door, they'd gone through the niceties: coffee, tea for Irina, an exchange of small talk. They settled in the couple's comfortable living room and chatted about innocuous thinks like Max's new car and their new house extension. The process nearly drove Nila insane. She was running for her life for god's sake.

Finally, they took mercy on her.

Max asked, "Okay, Mitch, what's going on?"

"You know how my grandmother's been researching the legend?"

Irina and Max nodded without comment. Mitch had told Nila the story of the ancient couple on the drive down. Apparently, the tigers had a myth of a human woman being able to have children with a tiger male. They'd had a bunch of kids—both tigers and humans—and according to Mitch the story was wreathed in romantic "crap". His disregard of the romance had made her laugh. The name of the couple, even the origins of the story, had been lost to time, so most tigers didn't believe it could really happen.

Obviously, they were wrong.

"Nila's mother, Anaya Pujari, was likely a descendant of that first couple," Mitch said, "because Nila's father is human."

Silence rang loudly in the cozy room as all eyes turned to her. Nila squirmed in her seat and set her coffee aside. Their stares made her feel like a bug under a microscope. The silence stretched on so long she very nearly stood and left the room.

Irina was the first to look back at Mitch and break the tense, uncomfortable moment. "You're sure? There's no mistake about her parentage."

Nila scowled. "No talking about me like I'm not here."

Irina cringed. "Sorry. It's just… If what Mitch says is true, you shouldn't exist."

"Yeah, so he keeps saying. But my dad is definitely not a tiger shapeshifter."

"You're sure about your mother?" Max asked.

"No. I never even knew my mother was alive until two days ago when I was almost kidnapped at JFK."

Irina's gaze snapped back to Mitch. "What happened?"

"It's complicated, but my grandmother has known about Nila all along. After Nila was born, Anaya returned to the Mate Run as soon as her cycle started again. She ended up mated with Petrov Dubrovsky. About three weeks ago, no one is sure how, Petrov found out about Nila. My grandmother is pretty sure he killed Anaya because she was discovered dead right before Petrov started hunting for Nila."

Irina gasped. When Max growled, the sound made the hair on Nila's arm raise.

"Petrov killed his mate?" Max asked, his voice deep, his anger a tangible thing in the room.

"We think so. There's no proof so the elder's haven't been able to take measures, but there's no doubt he's after Nila now. And he's made no secret of the fact that he wants her dead."

Mitch paused and met her gaze. "Yesterday, she met her half brother, Anaya and Petrov's oldest son, Vlad."

Irina faced Nila. "What did he do? Did he try hurting you?"

"Thank you for talking to me," Nila said, trying to hide her irritation. "No, he didn't hurt me. He warned us that Petrov was only a few hours away."

"He shifted in front of her," Mitch said quietly.

It was the first time he'd broached the subject since right after it happened. Nila still did not want to discuss what she'd seen. She'd blocked the whole thing to avoid going completely insane. When her life was no longer in danger, she'd allow the nightmares and terror to take her, but now she didn't have time.

"You weren't prepared, were you?" Max asked.

"I'm not ready to talk about that. We need a place to hide. That's all."

Max nodded in understanding. "He knows who you are, Mitch?"

"The man who tried taking Nila from the airport got a good enough look and was in contact long enough to hold my scent. Vlad confirmed Petrov knows who I am."

"Then Petrov also knows who your grandmother is. He'll know the elders have sent the Trackers after him."

"With his resources, I wouldn't count on the Trackers getting to him quickly. They haven't even been able to prove he killed Anaya."

The statement made Max growl again.

"We can't take any chances with Nila," Mitch finished.

The couple nodded in unison and glanced at her again, a strange sort of awe filling their expressions.

After another uncomfortable moment, Max said, "He'll look for you with your friends, but you can stay here if you want. I'll help you keep her safe." He looked directly at Irina when he said, "You can go stay with your father."

"Oh, no, Max, don't even think of sending me away. I might not be able to shift, but I can still help."

"You know how I feel about this. You keep the baby safe. I keep you safe."

She smiled, a gentle expression filled with so much love Nila's chest ached to see it. Did people really love each other that much? Was this what it was like for mated tiger shifters? That thought reminded her that her mother's mate was trying to kill her. She didn't want to think that Anaya had loved Petrov this way, but what if she had? And he'd killed her. Nila shuddered.

"Max, I can protect myself and help you both protect Nila. She can't shift either." Irina paused and faced Nila, her eyes wide. "You can't, can you? I mean, seeing Vlad shift…"

"I never even knew there was such a thing as real shapeshifters until that guy tried to kidnap me. And I didn't fully believe Mitch until I saw it with my own eyes yesterday. No. I can't change into anything but new clothes."

Irina grinned. She faced Max again. "See? I can help even in human form. In fact, it might be better that I can't shift. I'll be able to protect her while you two hunt."

Mitch raised a hand before Max spoke again. "I am not here to put you two in danger. Especially not you, Irina. Don't argue. You know how we all feel about this. There's no way

I'll allow you to risk that precious new life. We're not staying. I was just hoping you'd be able to point us toward a hiding place. Somewhere isolated. And not in either of your names. I need to use cash, so cheap is good, too."

"Do you have enough cash? We'll give you what we have here." Irina rose and hurried down the hall.

Nila noticed Mitch didn't argue and wondered how tight their budget was. She couldn't even help, despite the fact that she had plenty of money sitting in her bank account, because she didn't have so much as a driver's license on her anymore. She made a mental note to pay Mitch back everything he had to spend keeping her alive. That was, if she managed to stay alive.

"Petrov will be able to find mine and Irina's retreats," Max said. "Irina's in particular. Every male on the east coast knows her territory."

Irina came back out at that moment and said to Nila, "My territory is where I go when I need to…be my other self and can have privacy from the males. They aren't allowed there without my permission. Which means every single one of them knows exactly where my cabin is located. All female territories are common knowledge."

"All territories? That must be a lot. Do you mean here in the US? How many are there?" Nila knew females were rare, but knowing all the female territories in an entire country were well known started to put the limited numbers into perspective.

"All female territories around the world are known," Irina clarified.

Nila felt her mouth drop open and had to consciously close it. "That can't be good. How many females are left?"

"Worldwide, exactly five hundred and sixty-seven—including young, mated, and old."

"In the entire world? How many here in the US?"

"A hundred and forty-seven in total. Of those in the US, ninety-one are unmated."

"And how many males?"

"Around three thousand in the US. Very roughly fifty-five hundred to sixty-five hundred worldwide. But male numbers aren't monitored as precisely."

"Holy shit."

"Exactly," Mitch said with feeling. "You see the problem."

Nila let out an audible breath. "Yeah. Not even six hundred females to six thousand males worldwide? That really isn't good. Is this creating a genetic bottleneck?"

Even if they managed to keep making babies, limited genetic diversity could make extinction unavoidable. Real tigers were facing a similar problem—though their decreases in numbers were the result of poaching and habitat loss. And real tigers were down to just over three thousand in total. But given the low numbers of tiger shifter females, the shifters might actually be closer to extinction.

"Our scientists think we're okay for the moment." Max answered her question. "But…well, there's debate."

Nila's stomach hollowed out. This species she'd only just found out about were struggling against extinction, and according to Mitch, she might be their salvation—or at least a new hope for alternative ways to breed—if she was able to have kids with a tiger shifter.

The possibility was so mind blowing, so overwhelming she couldn't even comprehend it. She was an ordinary woman—or had thought she was just two days ago. How the hell did this happen?

Mitch leaned closer and put a hand on her shoulder. "We need to get on the road again soon. I don't want to stay too long and risk Petrov coming here. Thanks for your help."

"Where will you go?" Irina said as she handed Mitch a handful of bills.

"How about John's place?" Max said.

"John's place." Irina drew out the words as if she should have thought of that answer sooner.

Max faced Mitch. "I have a human friend who has a hunting cabin at the edge of Green Ridge State Forest. He travels a lot so I keep an eye on the place when he's gone. We have spare keys. You can stay there."

"He won't mind? I'm assuming he's away now?" Mitch said.

"He's out of the country and not due back for another two months," Max said. "The place is pretty basic, but there's an indoor bathroom, a bed in the bedroom, and a couch in the living room. Enough room for the two of you. He's also got a couple of hunting rifles stored there. Might come in handy."

Nila blew out a breath. She hated guns, but given the circumstances, having a weapon like that seemed prudent.

"I'll give you the key to the gun cabinet," Max continued. "You can stay there the full two months if you need to."

"Perfect. That'll give us time to find somewhere to go after."

"Wait." Nila held up a hand. "You don't think we'll be on the run for two months do you?" She turned in her seat to look up at Mitch. "I'm supposed to be in Texas in a week."

"Why?"

"One of the zoos has a female leopard due to give birth soon. She's had trouble in the past—lost a few cubs—so the resident vet has asked me for help." She leaned forward in her seat, a move that dislodged Mitch's hand from her shoulder. "I've made a commitment. I have to be there."

"A week?" Mitch frowned. "Nila, Petrov is smart and has a lot of resources. And he's avoided the Trackers this long. We could be on the run for months."

"No. I have too many people depending on me. I have a life and an important job. At least to me and the animals I help. I can't just disappear for months. What about my grandma and dad? They can't stay in hiding indefinitely either. No. If this goes on for more than a week, Petrov and I will just have to meet and settle this."

"Christ, Nila, he wants to kill you. Do you not understand that? He's not going to bother talking to you to settle anything. He sees you, he catches you, he kills you."

She felt the tension radiating from Mitch even though they were no longer touching. Irina stepped closer, worry making a crease between her brows. Max remained where he was standing near their fireplace, but he studied her thoughtfully.

"I am not staying in hiding for months, Mitch. One way or another, this thing needs to be settled before I'm due in Texas."

"What good will you do anyone if you're dead?" Mitch hissed and paced away from her. "This other vet will just have to do without you."

"And what about the others who are expecting me at some point? I have work to do."

He whipped around and faced her, his eyes glittering with heat and emotion. "It will have to wait, damn it. We're talking about your life."

Mitch's words hung in the air, followed by a ringing silence. She held his gaze, despite the difficulty of staring down all his righteous anger. She didn't want to be stupid with her life. She definitely didn't want to die. But these people had to understand she was also not prepared to hide in some isolated cabin for the rest of her life just to survive. She would run for now because it gave her time to learn more about her situation. But if this stretched on too long, she was fully prepared to turn and fight to finish things.

As she stared at Mitch, an image of Vlad shifting from tiger to human flashed through her mind. She forced back a shudder, but her resolve wavered. She'd faced down many big cats before. But these weren't just any animals. These were something mythical, something that shouldn't even be real. She realized with a growing dread that she didn't know how to fight a tiger shifter. Did you need special weapons to kill one? Like a werewolf? Could they be killed?

She hated this, hated not knowing, hated even more the knowledge she did have because every little bit she learned made her want to shut down. She wanted this to end, to be a nightmare she'd wake up from, a coma induced hallucination she'd eventually come out of. Anything would be better than this.

She finally broke eye contact with Mitch, not wanting him to see her uncertainty. She realized with no little surprise he was the one thing about this mess she actually hoped was real.

But if he was real, then the rest was, too.

Where the hell did that leave her?

Chapter Ten

They didn't speak again until they'd left Irina and Max's home, keys in hand to their friend's cabin. Mitch wasn't even sure how to start. He was so angry she might take any chances with her life that he could barely see straight. Yet the sane, rational part of his brain recognized that on some level she was right. If he were in her position, he wouldn't want to go into hiding forever when he had a life to live. He'd turn and fight, too.

But he was one of thousands. She was rare. Special. And the thought of Petrov getting anywhere near her made him insane.

He clenched the steering wheel and took long, slow breaths until he had his temper under control.

She'd never listen to his reasoning if he shouted or bellowed orders. Her grandmother had made that very clear. Nila was stubborn and strong minded. She was not the kind of woman he'd be able to intimidate or bully into doing what he wanted her to do. A fact he'd concluded for himself over the last two days.

So far, she'd held up under the strain. She was cooperating and allowing him to help her. For the moment. But he had to convince her to let him continue helping her until the Trackers found Petrov and his people. He just wasn't exactly sure how he was going to do that.

"You can't fight Petrov," he blurted. Then grimaced. Not exactly a diplomatic opening. But once he'd started he couldn't stop. "You don't know what you're facing. He's stronger, faster, more vicious, and that's in human form."

"I know," she murmured.

He opened his mouth to continue his rant then realized what she'd said. "What?"

"I said I know." Turning in her seat a little to face him, she said, "I know I can't fight him one on one. He's…nothing I've ever experienced before. I don't even know how to fight him. Can he be hurt? Are tiger shifters…I don't know, it sounds silly to even ask, but are they immortal, or do you need silver bullets or…? Would a gun work? I hate the things, but… Anyway, I know I don't know enough or have the skills to go head to head with him."

Mitch took a deep breath and let his shoulders relax.

"Yet."

That single word tightened his muscles again.

"Mitch, I can't hide forever. Neither can my father and grandmother. They won't have the funds, and I'm sure neither of them expected this to go on very long."

He tried keeping his tone reasonable but an edge of panic taunted him. "I realize this isn't easy, and I understand that you don't want the situation to continue indefinitely. We'll think of something. Maybe a trap to lure Petrov out, if I can coordinate it with the Trackers. But you won't be involved. You have to stay alive and safe. I promised my grandmother. I promised your grandmother." And he'd promised himself. "We can hide for a while before we need to do anything more drastic. Give the Trackers time to do their job. Petrov is focused on coming after you. That means he'll be more likely to make mistakes covering his own tracks. They'll find him."

She sighed. "It better be soon."

But she didn't sound confident. At least she wasn't running off to find Petrov on her own. That gave him time to do… something.

He glanced in the rearview mirror, about to switch lanes and get onto the freeway, then paused, frowning. That blue car had been behind them for a long time. Could just be his imagination, but…

Rather than get on the freeway, he took the surface roads and headed in a very roundabout way to a chain store where they could buy supplies. He kept his gaze jumping to the cars behind them. No sane person would take this route to get to this particular store, so if the blue car was just coincidentally behind them, it would turn off somewhere before the store, or continue on after.

"We need to pick up some stuff," he said aloud.

"Will I be able to get a change of clothes?"

She sounded desperate enough that he smiled. "Sure. Have to be cheap."

"That's perfect. I just need…a few things. I'll pay you back when I can get at my money again."

"Don't worry about it." He checked the traffic behind them again. The blue car was still there. "Money's not a problem for me, but the elders can pay me back since I'm doing this for them. They have funds."

"Is there a tax the tigers pay to the elders? Like income tax to a government? Or is it just that the elders have their own money?"

"Most of them have their own money. My grandmother got very good at manipulating opportunities over the years."

"Do I want to ask about the legality of that manipulation?"

"It's nothing morally objectionable. Let's just say she's a very clever woman and leave it at that."

Mitch checked behind them again to confirm the car was still there and only realized Nila had fallen silent when she hadn't spoken for several blocks. He glanced over to see her staring out the side window, her shoulders and back looking both stiff and hunched.

"What's wrong?"

"I've been avoiding thinking of something, and I'm having trouble ignoring it now."

"Vlad?" He'd wondered when she'd want to talk more about what she'd seen.

"Not exactly."

"What then?" His gaze flicked to the mirror as he changed lanes and prepared to enter a parking lot. Blue car moved lanes but continued past them as they pulled in. Frowning, he watched the car disappear up the street. When it was out of view, he found a place to park near an exit.

"You're…you're a tiger shifter aren't you?" Nila murmured.

At first, he wasn't sure he'd heard her right. He put the truck into park and faced her. "Of course I am. What did you think?"

She shrugged and gave a soft snort. "I told you, I was avoiding thinking about it. You never actually said."

"I assumed you realized. How else would I know what I know? And my grandmother is one of the elders. I haven't been trying to hide anything from you."

"I know," she muttered, still staring out the window. "I guess I've been hiding the knowledge from myself."

"Does it bother you that I'm a tiger?" He held himself perfectly still while he waited for her answer. His pulse pounded as discomfort settled into his chest and gut along with something a little like fear. Did she find him repulsive now? She hadn't flinched when he touched her at Max and Irina's, but maybe even then she wasn't facing the truth about his nature.

"It's just… I was hoping to have a friend in the middle of all this that was, well, like me."

"Nila, there is no one like you."

"I mean human. Not able to do all the shape shifting stuff."

His jaw tightened and he had to force out the next sentence. "Are you afraid of me?"

"No. No. Not you. I'm just… I don't know. Overwhelmed seems a little mild for how I'm feeling."

She finally faced him and Mitch held his breath, searching her eyes for revulsion. When he found only confusion, relief loosened his jaw. He forced himself to suck in some air.

"I'm still adjusting." She shrugged and forced a smile. "Let's go get our supplies."

He nodded, afraid to say more, afraid to damage her already fragile balance. She wasn't disgusted by him, didn't find him repulsive. That was all he could ask of her right now.

On their way back to the truck with their newly acquired gear, Mitch spotted the blue car again, parked along the side of the road behind a bus stop so it was hard to see. If he hadn't been looking, he might have missed it. As subtly as he could, he tried to get a glimpse of the driver, but there was too much blocking his view. He couldn't sense a tiger. Even at this distance, he'd be able to tell if that car was driven one of his kind. So, who was it?

Hurrying Nila into the truck, he stowed the bags behind the seat then climbed in on the driver's side. He headed out of the parking lot at a reasonable pace. The blue car pulled out too, following at a discrete distance. Again, if he hadn't been looking, he might not even realize it was there.

"Petrov must have had Max's place staked out," he said. "We're being followed."

"What?" Nila resisted the impulse to look behind them, but she still glanced in the side mirror. "Are you sure?"

"I am now. Damn it. I should have known Petrov would station someone near Max's house. I thought we were far enough ahead of him… But he's probably been watching Max this whole time. Fuck."

"What are we going to do?"

His gaze narrowed as he checked the traffic around them. "Lose them before we head toward John's cabin."

"If they know about Max, do you think they'll know about his friend's cabin?"

"They'll search Max and Irina's places first. Then dig into Max's friends. And they'll assume tiger friends first before human friends."

"You're sure?"

"It's what I'd do. Our human friends generally don't know our true natures, and we don't like to expose them to possible involvement in tiger politics. Too risky. If we can lose the tail, we should be safe enough at John's cabin for a few days anyway."

Nila sighed. "I feel like I'm living in cars."

"Sorry about that."

"Don't apologize. It's not your fault. If we didn't have to run from a crazy, homicidal tiger, this wouldn't be an issue."

The corner of his lips lifted in a half grin, the expression charming and sexy all at once. Nila found herself staring at his mouth and had to look away before she got distracted by more fantasies of that mouth moving across her body.

She glanced into the side mirror again. "Which car is it?"

"The blue four door. Three cars back and in the right lane."

"You're sure? They're putting on their turn signal."

He fell silent for a long moment, his gaze flicking back and forth from traffic in front of them to the rear view mirror and the cars behind them. She watched what she could from the side mirror. The blue car did turn, but Mitch continued to study the traffic.

Finally, he said, "Must have realized I spotted them. They've traded cars. Now it's the gray sedan."

"How can you be sure?"

"There's a tiger in the sedan."

"Two things. One, you can tell that at a distance? And two, there weren't tigers in the first car?"

"Yes, I can tell at this distance. I can sense my own kind at distances greater than most tigers—which is why my grandmother sent me to help you. And no, there weren't any tigers in the blue car. I warned you Petrov had connections in the human world as well as among tigers. Didn't think he'd go this far…"

"He must be desperate."

"He's insane is what he is."

"Since he wants to kill me, I tend to agree, but why specifically do you say that?"

"He killed his mate. That's a pretty good indicator of insanity in the tiger world. If you're lucky enough to get a mate in the Run, you should treasure her. All females are precious. Killing one is just… The Run was instituted to stop that kind of thing. Most males consider killing a female beyond repugnant, despicable."

"Got that impression from Max. But people kill without being insane. You even told me tiger males used to kill females. It might be repugnant to most, but it doesn't make Petrov crazy."

"If he's utilizing humans this way, risking exposure like this, he's not in his right, logical mind. Unfortunately, that doesn't diminish how clever and resourceful he is."

He muttered something under his breath, but Nila managed to catch a few words and gasped. "You think he'll kill the humans when he's done?"

Mitch shot her a sharp look. "You heard that?"

"I have excellent hearing."

He raised his brows. "Guess your mother's genes are showing." Then he glanced behind them again.

"The guy at the airport…was he a tiger or one of Petrov's humans?"

"Tiger."

"Why didn't he know you were one at first? Or can't all tigers sense other tigers?"

"We can all sense each other, some better than others. Petrov's man was distracted and not expecting me. There were a few other tigers at the airport—other associates—so he probably thought he was sensing one of them."

"Wait, there were others?"

He nodded. "I assume backup."

"Sonofabitch," she breathed, a tingle of panic for what might have happened crawling over her skin. "Can you guys sense humans like you sense tigers?"

"No. Only works with other tiger shifters. We have to pick up humans the old fashion way—through scent, sight, and hearing."

She glanced behind them again. "Grey car's still there. What are we going to do? We can't go to the cabin with them following."

"I know the Baltimore streets pretty well. I spend a lot of time down here with Max when I'm not traveling. But if they're using humans, then they've likely got locals who'll know the streets better than me. I need to get somewhere where I know the terrain better."

"We need a new car. They'll have this license plate number now."

"Probably have Max and Irina's cars, too." He checked the mirrors again, then changed lanes.

As far as Nila could tell, he was just driving around town, testing their followers.

"Don't suppose you have any friends in town?" he asked, without sounding too hopeful.

"Wouldn't Petrov already know about them if I did?"

"Are you saying you do?"

She shrugged. "Acquaintances. I've done work at the Maryland Zoo."

"There aren't any tigers in the zoo."

She chuckled. "I work with all the big cats, not just tigers. And I get called in by the resident vets of zoos a lot to help when there are issues beyond general care. Like the leopard in Texas."

She saw him flinch at the reminder, but otherwise he ignored it.

"You don't really stay in one place for long, do you?" he asked.

"Nope. Closest thing I have to a permanent home is a room in my grandmother's house."

"Would these acquaintances from the zoo help you if you needed it?"

"Bill would. He's the head vet there, and we got to know each other pretty well when we were working together."

"How well?"

The sudden growl in his words made her glance at him. He stared straight ahead, but his jaw was tight and his hands clenched the steering wheel enough to turn his knuckles white.

"Pretty well," she said, frowning. "Let me see if I still have his number in my phone."

"When did you last see him?"

"Year, year and half ago."

"You're sure he's still here?"

"No. But we need help Petrov isn't likely to know about, right? It won't hurt to try. Ah, here's his number."

She glanced at Mitch again to see his hands had relaxed, but his jaw was still clenched. She rang Bill's number on the new disposable cell they'd picked up, and waited for an answer, wondering how well connected Petrov really was? If he'd researched her past, he'd know she worked in Baltimore. Would he think to stake out the zoo's personnel in case she went to someone there? Did he even have the resources for that?

When Bill answered, he was both surprised and pleased to hear from her, which made the conversation much easier. "I know I'm asking a lot without being able to explain much, Bill. I'm really sorry about this. But if there's any way you can help, I'd really appreciate it."

"My old Jeep is pretty beat up, but it runs like a charm so you're welcome to borrow it."

"Thank you so much. I don't know how to pay you back."

"Don't worry about it, honey. For you, anything."

She grinned, double checked his home address and disconnected with another round of thanks.

"What did he say?" Mitch asked, his voice clipped and hard.

She frowned at his tone. "We can borrow his Jeep." She gave him directions.

"This is his house?"

"Uh huh. He's not on duty today."

"Lucky us."

"Actually, it is lucky. Now how are we going to get there and change cars without letting the bad guys realize what we've done?"

Without warning, and without signaling, Mitch moved across three lanes and made an abrupt right turn. A few blocks down, he turned again, and then again until she was so disoriented she had no idea where they were anymore.

"You might have warned me about that first turn," she grumbled as she studied the traffic behind them in the side mirror. "But looks like you lost them."

"For the moment. They'll find us quick enough if we stay on the streets."

"We'd better get to Bill's then."

Nila wasn't entirely sure, but she could swear Mitch growled.

Chapter Eleven

It took them until late afternoon to ditch the truck at a safe distance from Bill's, make their way to his house with their new gear, collect the Jeep, and get on the road again. Mitch was growly and irritable the entire time but she couldn't get him to talk about it.

The drive to the cabin was quiet and uneventful. Mitch slept while Nila drove, which pleased her since he'd barely slept since they met. She had no idea how much sleep a tiger shifter needed, but he had to need more than six hours over two days.

John's place was tiny compared to the cabin Mitch kept. It was a single story and from the outside looked big enough for only one room. If she was here alone, the place would seem cozy and comfortable. But the idea of being in such close quarters with Mitch made her edgy.

The lust lurking between them hadn't eased. In fact, every time they happened to touch, another zing of electricity moved over her skin and she had a hard time not reacting. She'd been avoiding thoughts of spending time alone with him in the middle of nowhere. Now, staring at the small structure, her pulse started pounding as she faced the inevitable.

She slid out of the Jeep once Mitch decided they were safe and headed into the cabin to investigate their temporary home. The place wasn't much more impressive inside. Though there was a separate bedroom off the back, it was barely big enough for the double bed and chest of drawers that were the only furnishings. As promised, there was an indoor bathroom with a tiny shower stall. The main part of the cabin contained a living room with a couch and coffee table, an open kitchen, and a huge fireplace taking up most of one wall.

Though it was small, the place was comfortable. A bookshelf lined with books stood beside the fireplace, and a radio sat on top of the mantel. Out of curiosity, she turned it on to see if they got any channels. Soft music wafted out, filling the room with life.

"It's nice," she said with a half smile. "Not huge, but nice."

Mitch nodded without comment and went back to the Jeep for their supplies. Well, at least she liked the place.

By the time they'd finished unloading the car and unpacking, it was full dark, and Nila found herself yawning despite the low level buzz of energy in her system. She kept glancing at Mitch, expecting…something.

They hadn't been alone, outside of a car, since his cabin two nights ago, and she'd been trying not to jump his bones then. Now…now, she still wanted to seduce him. The longer they were together, the less it felt like she was trying to hide in sex. She'd accepted her situation—as much as she was able—and wasn't trying to forget. She just wanted Mitch, a lot, and it was getting more difficult to keep her distance.

It was very obvious there was only one bed in this place. They were going to have to discuss sleeping arrangements soon.

She stood uncertainly in the middle of the living room. She still had a lot of questions that needed answering, but she wasn't sure where to start. And the tension hovering between them made thinking about anything beyond the solitary bed difficult.

Mitch stood near the fireplace staring back at her as if he couldn't decide where to start, or what to start, either. He had his hands on his hips and a frown creased his brow.

Finally, he said, "I'm going for a hike around the area. I want to check the territory."

"Now? It's pitch dark."

"I won't have any trouble seeing."

She blinked. "Are you going to…to change?" The idea was both fascinating and horrifying. She wasn't even close to being ready to see that again, especially not with Mitch. But a part of her was curious about the whole shape shifting thing. Did it hurt? Was it hard to do or easy? What happened with his clothes? Vlad had been naked when he changed to human. Would Mitch have to be naked to become a tiger?

The idea of Mitch naked was a little too distracting, so she immediately shut down that line of thinking.

"I'll have an easier time studying the terrain as a tiger," he answered. "You'll be safe here. But lock up and stay awake until I get back. Don't…don't take a shower. You should be ready for anything."

"Okay." She hadn't been thinking about a shower, but now that he brought it up, she wondered if she stank. With a half laugh, she realized she probably did and with his sense of smell, it was no wonder he wanted out of the cabin. "You be careful. Don't go too far if you can avoid it. We can explore more tomorrow morning."

He smiled, giving her a soft quizzical expression she couldn't quite interpret. "I'll be fine. You stay safe. I'll be back soon."

Once he left—still fully dressed she noted—she locked the door and went to the bookshelf to see if there was anything interesting to read. She might as well keep herself occupied.

Mitch returned several hours later, just as she was starting to worry. She launched off the couch to face him when he walked through the door. Fully dressed, she noticed, but his hair was a little mussed, like he'd been running. He looked sexy as hell and the closer he got, the harder her heart pounded.

"Everything is okay? You're okay?"

"You were worried?"

"Well, of course. There are homicidal…people out there trying to kill me and that means you're in danger, too."

"Actually, Petrov will have to think twice before killing me since my grandmother is one of the elders."

She dropped her shoulders and rolled her eyes. "The guy is probably crazy. You said so yourself. You think he'll be bothered about who your grandmother is?"

He raised his eyebrows as he crossed to the couch. "You're right. Petrov won't care if he kills me. But anyone with him will have second thoughts. That's one of the reasons I'm a good bodyguard for you."

"You're not indestructible, though, are you?"

"No."

"Then I have a right to worry."

He gave her another of those soft, quizzical looks she couldn't interpret.

"Did you find anything?" she asked to get past a growing sense of awkwardness laced with an embarrassingly desperate need to throw herself into his arms.

"Nothing. The last tiger in the immediate area was Max and that was several weeks ago."

"You can tell... Wait, don't tell me you guys...mark the territory?"

"Tiger instinct." He shrugged.

"Fair enough. So, we're safe for the moment."

He nodded. "You should try getting some sleep now. I'll take the couch."

She wasn't entirely surprised by his offer. Still. "We can rotate who takes the bed. If this goes on for more than a few days, you're going to get really uncomfortable sleeping out here, given the size of you. I'm small. I'll be more comfortable out here. And really, I should take the first night on the couch. You've barely slept since I met you."

"I'd rather the couch tonight. I can monitor things better from out here."

"You are going to sleep, right? You aren't planning on staying on guard all night?"

"I'll sleep."

She narrowed her eyes. "Promise?"

He tilted his head to one side. "You're so funny."

She wondered whether she should be insulted or not when he reached out and ran a finger down her cheek. The brief contact stopped her breathing for an instant, then her heart started thumping hard again.

"I promise to sleep. Better?" he said, his voice lowered to a quiet, deep octave.

A shiver raced across her shoulders and down along her arms. That voice was going to follow her into her dreams. "Good," she said.

Even after he dropped his hand back to his side, she stood where she was, staring, knowing she should move away and not able to make her feet cooperate. He smelled delicious, like fresh air and woods and something very male. How was it he could smell so good, even after a long hike?

She wet her lips and pulled in another deep breath, trying not to be too obvious but unable to resist leaning a little closer to him. She'd never been so grateful for her heightened sense of smell. But then she wasn't sure she'd ever come across any smell as delicious as Mitch.

"You want the bathroom first?" he asked.

She blinked. This was ridiculous. She was acting like a high school girl with her first crush. She smiled tightly and moved toward the bathroom, stopping to collect a few things from the closet on the way. She hadn't bought a lot of clothing, a few t-shirts and a pair of shorts, but she'd splurged on a pair of cotton pajamas and made sure to get a supply of clean underwear. The last of which was probably the most important thing she'd purchased all day.

She closed the bathroom door firmly and tried very hard not to indulge in a fantasy of Mitch joining her in the shower. A few wet and naughty thoughts still managed to sneak through, though, leaving her restless and edgy by the time she was finished.

When she emerged, she left the door open and motioned him toward it. "All yours. You sure you want the couch tonight?"

"Positive."

He brushed passed her on the way to the bathroom, and Nila's entire body reacted, her muscles tightening and her nerves jumping. She wanted to lean into him and taste every single inch of his very hard, very sexy body. Swallowing hard, she forced herself toward the bedroom.

When she heard the bathroom door close, she released a loud breath. He hadn't locked the door. That was a temptation she wasn't sure she could resist. She should warn him to lock the door since he couldn't trust her to stay out. But even starting that conversation might lead to places best left unexplored.

As she sprawled face down across the bed, she tried to remember why she wasn't going to jump Mitch the minute he exited the bathroom. There were some very good reasons, she was sure, but damned if she could remember any of them now.

Flopping over onto her back, she stared up at the ceiling. This was going to be a long night.

Chapter Twelve

Nila woke blurry, restless, and exhausted the next morning. Despite having the bed, she'd still slept badly. Her dreams alternated between sexual fantasies of a very naked Mitch and horrific nightmares of half-man, half-tiger things chasing her through the woods. The combination left her out of sorts and in desperate need of coffee.

A glance out the window confirmed the day was cloudy; a nice change of pace from the glaring late summer sun. But the muggy heat was already creeping in past the noisy window air-conditioner.

Rolling out of bed, she stumbled into the main room still wearing her pajamas, intent on making coffee and determined to ignore Mitch until after that first cup—even if he was awake and looking sexy and disheveled. What she didn't expect to see was an empty cabin. He wasn't in the kitchen, the bathroom, or outside on the narrow front porch. Frowning, she stood barefoot on the steps leading to the front yard, scanning the area. The Jeep was still parked where they'd left it the night before.

But no sign of Mitch.

Both annoyed and worried, Nila went back inside to look for a note. He'd hardly have gone anywhere without letting her know. He had to realize she'd worry. Was he that thoughtless?

Then she spotted the fresh pot of coffee in the kitchen. And beside it, a note scribbled on a paper napkin.

"Studying the terrain in the daylight. Back by 10:30. Mitch."

She glanced around for a clock and saw the time on the small microwave oven above the stove. Ten twenty. Ten minutes before she had to start worrying. She poured herself a cup of coffee, took several reviving sips, then went to take care of her morning business.

Mitch was standing in the kitchen when she came out of the bathroom.

"Anything new?" she asked, crossing to her abandoned cup. The coffee was still warm enough to finish, thankfully. She cradled the mug in her hands as she tried not to stare at Mitch.

Damn but the man was handsome. His hair was mussed again, as if he'd been running. His eyes were bright and intense, more green than hazel in the morning light. He was fully dressed in jeans and a t-shirt, and he smelled of the woods again, like fresh air and trees. She tried not to scowl. It seemed wrong that he looked so good when she felt like shit.

"The area is still clear," he said, leaning against the counter and crossing his arms over his chest. "Looks like our nearest neighbors are about six miles away, so we're very isolated here."

She swallowed a groan as she watched his forearm muscles flex. What the hell did he just say? Oh. Isolated. "Is that good?"

"Absolutely. I don't want Petrov getting innocent humans involved in this."

"I'm an innocent human. Tell him to leave me alone."

Her snarky comment earned her one of Mitch's adorably charming grins. "Sleep well?"

Grimacing, she went to the couch with her coffee.

"First night in a strange place. That can make sleeping difficult."

"Never had the problem before," she said. "I rarely have the same bed for any length of time."

He pulled a coffee mug out of the cabinet. "I'm the same. Still, a new place can take some time."

"You have trouble sleeping in strange beds?"

"Sometimes. Depends on where I am. And what I'm sleeping on." He grinned as he poured his coffee.

To keep her mind off Mitch sleeping on her, she asked, "What made you take up nature photography?"

"I like it. I started taking pictures when I was a teenager. Turned out I was good at it. And the freelance aspect suits me. Gives me the kind of flexibility with my time a nine-to-five job wouldn't."

"Do you need a lot of flexibility?"

"It helps when I have tiger business to take care of. Or if I participate in a Run, I need to be able to take a few days off without raising suspicion."

Her stomach bottomed out and for a few seconds she had trouble thinking. Why hadn't she considered this? Once she'd come to terms with the fact that he was a tiger shifter and not just another human caught up in this weird world, she should have realized he'd participate in Mate Runs. He was young and healthy, and of course he'd want a mate, wouldn't he? After seeing how happy Max and Irina were, how could she expect Mitch to want anything less for himself?

"Have you done many? Runs, I mean." She asked with her face in her mug.

"A few." He leaned against the kitchen counter again his mug in one hand, his other resting on the countertop.

"Ever been successful?" She couldn't quite bring herself to look directly at him. After days of lusty fantasy about him, confronting this reality was a little embarrassing. And sobering.

"I'm not mated. I've already made that clear."

"You said the females might have several different male partners during their cycles, before one of the males gets them pregnant. That's how the permanent mating happens, right, the female has to get pregnant. But you also said it took Max and Irina several years of running before they conceived. Some females don't stick with the same male every season, right?"

"True."

When he didn't say anything more, she risked looking at him. She couldn't read his expression. She dropped her gaze back to her mug. Fine, he didn't want to tell her about the number of times he'd caught a female and had a chance to mate permanently, he didn't have to. She was acting silly anyway. Jealousy didn't make a lot of sense, given their situation. And he'd met one of her previous lovers just yesterday! She could hardly be annoyed by the fact that he'd undoubtedly had many previous relationships, too.

But the Mate Run… That was serious. That was an attempt to find a wife, a life partner, a woman who would have his children. He'd chased that possibility when he'd participated in a Run. That was a lot more serious than her two week fling with Bill.

Since she didn't want to talk about this anymore, because then she'd have to admit how much she cared, she changed the subject. "So, what's the plan for the day?"

"Keep an eye on the area." He shrugged. "I'll try calling my grandmother for an update this morning."

"And beyond that?"

"Relax. Read a book. Take a nap. You can do whatever you like so long as you stay close enough for me to hear you if there's trouble."

"Sounds like a vacation. I don't get a lot of those."

He grinned. "Now you have a good excuse."

"Yeah, except I'd have preferred the beach this time of year."

"Next time you're running for your life, we'll go to the beach."

She laughed over a funny little twist in her tummy. His comment hit her hard. Not at the thought that she might have to run for her life again, but the idea that he'd be there if she needed to. Swallowing more coffee, she forced down the giddy sensation. She didn't have long term, permanent relationships.

She traveled too much, she worked too hard. She'd never even considered settling down.

But beyond that, she had no idea how her current predicament might change her life. Her mother was a tiger shifter. No matter what her father said, that changed things. She just didn't know how yet. She couldn't predict what her future might bring—if she managed to survive—or what the tigers really wanted from her.

Given the story of the mythical couple, she knew Elizaveta, at least, would want to see if she could have children with a tiger—that "hope" Mitch had talked about the very first night they met. Nila had no intention of being used as a brood mare or having kids before she was damned good and ready. But she had a feeling that even after Petrov, her life was going to be chaotic for a while. What man would want any part of that?

She shook off a vague sense of melancholy at the idea that she'd have to say goodbye to Mitch once all this was over. She had bigger things to worry about.

"Can we talk more?" she asked.

"About?"

"This…situation. I want to know more about my mother, Vlad, the whole…thing."

"You're ready to hear more?"

"I think I've had enough time to process what you've told me so far."

"Okay. After I shower and call my grandmother, we'll have breakfast and talk."

"Thanks." The thought of Mitch in the shower was a little more than her overactive nervous system could take, so she said, "I'm gonna go sit on the porch, stare at the scenery."

"Enjoy. It's getting hot out there."

She hurried outside to avoid the temptation of following him into the bathroom.

She'd opened the door to more information. Now she had to settle herself so she could listen. Absorbing what she'd learned so far had been tough. She still didn't want to think too closely about the sight of Vlad shifting shapes, but she could no longer avoid the full story. She had her suspicions, and now she needed to know what her mother being a tiger shifter meant for her.

She stayed on the porch as long as possible, watching the morning light contrasts between the open yard and the shade under the trees. The growing heat seeped into her, soothing her.

When she finally went back inside, she felt ready to face what Mitch had to tell her. Or at least she thought she was ready.

Until she saw Mitch fresh from the shower, his hair damp, his skin glowing with warmth, his clean t-shirt clinging tight to his muscled torso, his jeans hugging his butt to perfection. With that view, trying to concentrate on anything but getting him back out of his clothes was going to be almost impossible.

She appreciated a handsome man as much as the next woman, but this was ridiculous.

"Good shower?" she asked, hoping to unglue her tongue from the roof of her mouth.

"Great. I needed it."

His grin nearly made her swoon. To keep from an all too undignified reaction, she sat on the couch where she wasn't able to stare at him easily.

"Yeah, it was nice to get out of the clothes I'd been wearing since India. Actually, I'm just grateful to have underwear on again." She muttered the last sentence with a great deal of feeling. Walking around without underwear for the last two days had been…well, she wouldn't have cared if she wasn't constantly daydreaming about a certain very sexy man.

A clatter sounded from the kitchen and she turned to see Mitch swiping a handful of silverware off the floor.

Mitch concentrated on picking up the mess he'd just made as he asked, "Again?" He wasn't entirely sure he'd heard her correctly. Because if he had, he was pretty sure he was going to go a little bit insane. He couldn't resist glancing at her when she answered.

She grimaced and her cheeks turned pink. "I've been commando since your cabin. No spare pairs in my backpack."

That was it. He was insane. The woman had just robbed him of whatever reasonable brain cells he had left. He couldn't tell if she'd done it on purpose or not, but for several moments, it didn't matter. As he straightened to face her, his every nerve ending screamed out to cross the room, strip her naked, and fuck her until she cried out his name again and again.

She glanced away, the blush in her cheeks deepening and mumbled something about needing to brush her teeth. In the next instant, she'd disappeared into the bathroom.

Mitch took a series of slow breaths, and finger by finger relaxed his fists, though he continued staring at the bathroom door as he forced himself to calm down. He couldn't remember the last time he'd wanted a woman this badly. And he knew from her scent and actions, she wanted him, too. That only made matters worse. He wasn't entirely sure how they were going to get through this without landing into bed together, but he knew for both their sakes it would be better if they didn't. He couldn't have her. He wouldn't be allowed to keep her.

But for a few long minutes, he didn't give a damn about any of that.

His only consolation was that she seemed to want to resist the attraction between them as much as he needed to. Scowling at the door, he stopped to wonder about her resistance. What made her hesitate?

Maybe the fact that they'd only known each other for three days, and in that time, she's been running for her life?

He shook his head, feeling like an idiot. Of course she didn't want to fall into bed with a virtual stranger, especially given the circumstances. Stupid to think attraction would overcome all that.

With one last deep breath, he turned back to the stove. Breakfast. They needed breakfast.

He had the ingredients for a good omelet now and was determined to feed her something other than fast food. Her vegetarian sensibilities were probably screaming at her at this point. He pulled the eggs out of the fridge and promised himself that if he couldn't give her a multitude of explosive orgasms, the least he could do was make sure she ate well.

By the time she reappeared, breakfast was well underway, with omelets on the stove, toast in the toaster, and fresh cups of coffee poured. He kept his back to her, though, so he could concentrate on cooking and not injuring himself in the process.

"Food will be ready in a few minutes. We're gonna try the omelets again."

The sound of her chuckle tickled the nerves along his spine.

"Thank you," she said. "You didn't have to cook for me."

"Least I can do." He decided not to mention this was a trade-off for the orgasms he'd like to give her instead. To keep his errant body on track, he started the conversation they'd been avoiding. "What's your first question? I'm sure you have a lot after the last few days."

He glanced at her long enough to see her settle on the couch, a slight frown turning her beautiful lips down. He focused on his cooking again.

"I've been considering the mythical couple," she said. "They had both shifter and human children, right?"

"Right." He flipped the eggs out onto two plates, added a couple slices of buttered toast, and put the entire meal on a tray to carry to the coffee table in front of the couch. He handed over her food, still trying not to look at her while at the same time trying not to make it obvious he was avoiding looking at her. He felt like an idiot. But he couldn't think of another way to keep his hands to himself.

"So…does that mean the human children were ordinary? Did they have any…I don't know…special skills?"

He leaned back against the armrest to eat, keeping as much space as he could between them. "The legend is vague, and it's been passed down through so many generations it's hard to say what was even part of the original story and what was made up in the intervening years. Are you worried about something specific?"

"No, but I do have better senses than other people. I'm strong for my size. I have really good instincts…most of the time. But is that part of being half tiger or just me?"

He shrugged. "I'd guess because you're half tiger, but I really don't know for sure. The scientists my grandmother has working on human-tiger theory and the legend might know. They'll want to meet you."

She frowned. "I'm not going to be someone's science experiment."

The growl in her tone made him raise his brows.

"I'm serious, Mitch."

"I believe you. But my grandmother will want you to…help in their research."

"How?"

"Provide blood samples. Submit to medical tests…" He hesitated to say more, given Nila's mood. How would she feel about the fact that his grandmother wanted her to mate with a tiger, to try and produce more tigers?

"She wants to know if I can have tiger children? I've guessed that part already."

He sighed. "She's…hopeful. But Anaya gave birth to a human, so despite my grandmother's hope, matings between acceptable human-tiger shifter pairings might only result in humans, and that won't save us."

She set her fork on her plate and stared at the fireplace. As she absorbed the information, he couldn't stop himself from studying her expression.

"So, outside of me," she finally continued, "have you found the descendants of this couple? Do they exist or was I just some sort of freak anomaly?"

"The researchers have found some genes in the mitochondrial DNA that might trace back, and genealogical research has led them to believe they've found one possible line of descendants—if the couple came from India. The couple's origin is still debated, though, so India could be a false lead. Fact is, it's been impossible to say if any of their findings carried much merit because, until you were born, they'd found no evidence of another human-tiger mating. There are a few elders who've been pressuring my grandmother to stop her research because of this. With you..." He let the implications hang in the air.

"The supposed line of possible descendants...are they tigers or human?"

"Both."

She nodded, still staring at the fireplace. "The fact that I'm not a shapeshifter is bad, isn't it?"

"Not necessarily. You're an only child. If Anaya and Leo had other children, one of them might have been a shapeshifter."

She turned back and faced him. "What exactly does Elizaveta expect from me? Specifically."

He swallowed and set his plate aside. He didn't want to tell her this part, to admit that she'd be offered her choice of any tiger male she wanted, but she deserved the truth. "Those like her will want you to consider taking a tiger mate, a husband. They'll encourage you to have as many children as possible from that pairing."

"What if I don't want to have children?"

The question startled him. Of all the possible problems with this situation, that hadn't crossed his mind. "Don't you?"

She shrugged. "Actually, I do want kids, one day, but not now. Not any time in the near future." She glanced down at her plate, then set it on the coffee table, her eggs only half-finished. "What if I can't conceive with a tiger shifter? I mean, just because Anaya was able to, doesn't mean I can. And I doubt one of your males will want to be stuck with a human who can't give him children in the end."

The fact she was even discussing mating with a tiger should have given him some relief. The conversation had just the opposite effect. His muscles tensed with some unnamed emotion and his chest tightened uncomfortably. "Our scientists have been working on DNA and blood tests they hope will help them determine ahead of time if a mating will be successful. Anaya's DNA was the only they've had from a proven mating between the two species to work from, though. Just the fact tigers and humans can procreate will be worth the risk to many of our males. They have so few other options."

She nodded but her gaze was distant. "And then there are the tigers like Petrov who want me dead so I don't destroy tiger bloodlines?"

"Yes."

"Where do you fall in all this?" she asked, shifting to hold his gaze.

"I wasn't sure. I've never subscribed to Petrov's extreme beliefs, but I didn't really believe the legend either. I thought it was a fairytale, like so many others did for so long." He held his palms up in a kind of surrender. "But you exist. I can't deny the possibilities anymore."

"Do you think it's a blessing or a curse?"

Without looking away and without hesitating, he said, "Blessing."

Nila was a blessing, even if he still wasn't sure how he felt about his grandmother's research. What he knew without any qualms whatsoever was that Nila was going to be important to his people. She was hope, possibility, and no matter what happened, he considered her a miracle.

Chapter Thirteen

Nila wanted desperately to stop this conversation again, to go back to blissfully imagining all the wicked things she'd do with a naked Mitch and ignoring all the implications of her birthright. But she told herself she would face the full story now. She couldn't afford her ignorance any more.

Holy hell, did she want it, though.

"Okay," she said, "so, Elizaveta is expecting me to take a tiger shifter husband."

"She'll want you to, but you have a choice. She would never force you into a relationship you didn't want."

"She couldn't even if she wanted to," Nila said sharply. She bit her bottom lip to keep quiet for a few breaths. She was having a hard time controlling the chaos of her emotions and she was going to take out her temper on Mitch if she wasn't careful. She softened her tone when she said, "I obviously can't do a Mate Run. Does she intend on trotting out all the eligible males and let me pick my favorite, like a weird preternatural The Bachelorette?"

Mitch wouldn't meet her gaze. "I don't have any idea what she intends. Introducing you to some of the important, unmated males is probably on her list of ways to coerce you into doing what she wants."

"You're making your grandmother sound very manipulative."

"She can be when she wants to be. She learned a lot under Stalin."

"She wasn't still in Russia during the war, was she?"

"She and her family moved to Zurich just after the end of the war. My father immigrated to the US in the sixties. My grandmother followed after my grandfather died in '67. She still keeps a place in Russia and travels back and forth a lot, mostly for business."

Nila was very tempted to follow the digression away from the topic at hand—his family history was fascinating—but she forced herself to ask more questions. "What if I don't want anything to do with the tigers? What if I want my normal life back and all this other business to go away?"

Still without looking at her, Mitch said, "It's too late. The community knows about you. There's no going back. Even if you don't want a tiger mate, even if you refuse to deal with us, tigers will continue coming after you. The males willing to mate with a human will try seducing you. Those who think you're a liability will try killing you."

"Are you telling me I'm going to be on the run for the rest of my life? That even after Petrov gets brought before your elders, others will still be gunning for me?" Panic and disbelief overwhelmed all other emotion in that moment. She did not intend to spend the rest of her life running from these crazy people.

"If you don't take a tiger mate, then yes, you will probably continue to be in danger."

"What the hell good would a tiger mate do me?"

"Offer you his protection and the protection of his family, his wealth. If you choose a powerful enough male, you'll be safe."

"Are you powerful enough?" The question was out of her mouth before she knew she was going to ask it and the minute she spoke the words she wanted to take them back. The last thing she wanted Mitch to think was she intended to pressure him into a relationship just to keep her safe. She didn't know what he wanted for his future, and for that matter, she had no idea what she wanted for her own future, but she did know she would never force him into anything he didn't want. "Sorry, forget I asked that. It was rude."

"I'm not powerful enough," he said, ignoring her apology. He finally met her gaze, his expression oddly blank. "My grandmother is an elder and she is influential. But my immediate family…our position is…we don't have enough power for me to be an option."

That pronouncement left her cold and depressed, and she wasn't entirely sure why. It wasn't like she was in love with Mitch. She wanted him, wanted him more than she'd ever wanted another man in her life. But she didn't do long term relationships, and she didn't intend to marry or have children any time soon. She had bigger things to worry about.

She was not going to be forced into anything because of someone else's agenda, especially not marriage and children. This was her life they were talking about. She'd always had full control over her choices and decisions. She owned her mistakes and her successes in equal measure. She was not giving over control of her life to anyone. She was not choosing a husband because someone else said she should or because he could keep her out of trouble.

She decided who she committed herself to.

The fact that Mitch took himself out of the running pissed her off, and an instant later, the reaction embarrassed her. To be mad that he didn't want to saddle himself with a human was ridiculous.

"Is there any way for me to avoid any of this?" she said. "Anything at all that will stop the crazy tigers from trying to kill me?"

"A DNA test might prove you can't have children with a tiger. That would help a little."

"But?"

"But your mere existence is offensive to some. They're the ones you'll have to worry about."

She launched off the couch and started pacing the room. "I'm stuck? No matter what I do, you're telling me my life is no longer my own?"

"It's still your own. You'll just have to make some adjustments."

"And my grandmother? And my dad? What happens with them? I can't have psychotic tigers trying to get to me through them. This cannot continue."

"Then I suggest you choose a very powerful tiger mate."

She stopped in mid-circuit to stare at him. "I can't believe you just said that to me." Was he really telling her to choose a husband based on political influence and strength? What the hell century was this? "I thought I could deal with this, but…I need to go for a walk." His sardonic expression did not help her mood. She narrowed her gaze. "What?"

"Just stay close to the cabin so I can hear you if you need me."

With a firm nod, she stalked to the bedroom, dressed, put on her shoes, then stomped back out the front door, all without looking at Mitch again.

She couldn't believe the situation she was in, through no fault of her own, just because she existed.

And the one man in this entire mess she actually did want to be with had just told her he was not an option.

Mitch waited in the cabin, quiet and still, listening to her stomp around muttering to herself. He couldn't blame her. She was in a terrible position through no fault of her own. At least she was staying near.

He'd almost stopped breathing when she'd asked him if he was powerful enough to be her mate. By all that was holy, he wanted to be. Physically, he was strong enough. That's why he was here. He had plenty of money now, too, since his father had left him and his brother's everything when he moved to South America a few years ago.

But among the tigers, he was at the lowest end of the social spectrum. So, despite his physical strength and money, Mitch simply didn't have the social and political power to keep the crazier tigers from coming after Nila. He'd known from the beginning he couldn't have her.

She had broached the possibility, though, and he was having a very hard time remembering he couldn't just take her, the rest of his people be damned. Being alone with her was painfully difficult. He sure as hell hoped the Trackers caught Petrov soon.

Nila returned ten minutes after she'd left, her face flushed, her hair mussed, but her breathing steady and even. She gestured at the kitchen counter where he'd left the new disposable cellphone they'd picked up in Baltimore. "What did your grandmother say when you called her?"

Understanding her need to change gears, he said, "The Trackers almost had Petrov in Baltimore. Using humans is complicating things for him, making him easier to find. But he got away."

"And his sons?"

"They're all still out there."

She pursed her lips and put her hands on her hips. "Including Vlad?"

Mitch nodded. "I'm not sure what game he's playing, but he'll be close to his father."

"I want to call my dad and grandma. Will it be safe?"

"Should be. Especially with the new phone." He didn't think Petrov could actually track their cellphone use, but like Nila's father, Mitch didn't want to take chances. Petrov did have some serious connections and resources. Mitch was glad Leo had suggested getting the disposable cell.

She snatched up the phone and went onto the porch to make her calls.

He was tempted beyond measure to go to her and offer comfort, but he didn't think she'd accept any from him at the moment. Besides, if he took her into his arms now, he wasn't sure he'd be able to let her go, no matter the consequences.

Chapter Fourteen

Nila wandered onto the porch with a cup of tea, breathed in the clean air, and listened to the quiet hum of a soft breeze blowing through the trees. She leaned against the porch railing, still trying to figure a way out of this mess. Even if she refused to have children with a tiger, there was still the possibility her kids would be capable of having children with a tiger—if she carried the gene Anaya had—which meant, no matter who she married, her future children would be in danger, too.

She could always refuse to have kids, but then she'd be allowing others to dictate what she did with her life. If she was physically able to have kids, she wanted them. One day. She didn't want to throw that option away. She just didn't want to be forced into something she wasn't ready for and with someone she didn't love.

A noise from behind the cabin caught her attention and she straightened. Mitch had left after lunch, nearly two hours ago, and she hadn't so much as heard his footsteps since. When he appeared around the side of the cabin, she caught her breath. He was shirtless, carrying the t-shirt in one hand and wearing only his jeans and boots. For the first time since they'd met, she got a very good look at his muscled, bare chest and it was all she could do not to drool.

He wasn't bulky, but he was finely chiseled and well proportioned. His shoulders were broad and strong looking, his arms nicely muscled, his stomach rippled with a six pack. He was sweating, the beads of perspiration dripping over his torso and through the hair covering his chest and arrowing down his abdomen. His face was flushed, his hair damp, his eyes sharp and dangerous.

Life was just not fair, she decided. No man should be allowed to look so good. Without meaning to, her imagination taunted her with what he must look like naked and she nearly dropped her mug. He paused on the porch beside her, forcing her to take in his sexy male perfection up close.

"Anything?" she asked, before she attempted to wet her dry mouth with another sip of tea.

"Still clear. The neighbors have dogs. That's a good thing. The dogs will pick up the scent of tiger and alert us if any get near."

"The neighbors are six miles away."

He shrugged. "I'll hear them."

"Wow. And I thought I had good hearing."

"My hearing only works that well outside the city," he said with a smile.

The expression made her knees weak. This close, his scent washed over her, and what should have been stinky male sweat was having the same effect as deliciously scented cologne usually had on her. Her heart beat rapidly, her breathing rushed in and out of her lungs, her stomach danced, and her muscles clenched in anticipation of a touch. The longer she stood there, the stronger the effect grew until she could barely see straight. Lust, need, desire, passion, whatever the hell this was, it was strong enough to rob her of all sense.

"I'm going to shower," he finally said, breaking the long silence.

She blinked, only then realizing how long she'd been staring at him. She waited for the cabin door to close behind him then allowed herself a sigh. He was pulling away from her, she felt it, putting distance between them that wasn't there before, even when they barely knew each other. She should probably be grateful for his actions. Sex would be an even bigger complication than she'd originally thought. For both their sakes, keeping things platonic was the wisest choice.

So why did she still want to throw caution to the wind and go join him in the shower?

Three days of watching, three days of staring, three days of smelling him and seeing him and hearing him, talking, sometimes laughing, and mostly just being with him. Three days of nothing to do but study his movements and anticipate the brief moments of physical contact, a brush of his hand, an accidental bumping of bodies in the small space. Three days of fantasies and sleepless nights. Three days alone with Mitch, and Nila was ready to burst.

Sometime over the previous days, she'd forgotten why sleeping with him would be a bad idea, and when her conscience tried reminding her she didn't need the complication, she ignored it. What the hell did her conscience know anyway? She'd never denied her desires like this before, and the waiting and anticipation were killing her.

To make matters worse, Mitch had been so damned controlled. If he had to touch her, he did so respectfully and quickly. He frequently cooked for her, because he claimed he liked cooking, but he never got too close or lingered too long in her company.

She was at the end of her rope.

Flopping onto her back in the bed on the fourth sleepless night in a row, she decided enough was enough. She just couldn't take the tension anymore. If she didn't at least talk to him about this desire between them, she was going to scream.

Once the decision had been made, however, she found herself hesitating at the bedroom door, listening for movement from the main room. It had to be past midnight. He was bound to be asleep. He wouldn't thank her for waking him when he got so little sleep as it was. Even for what she intended. She remained where she was for several minutes, trying to talk herself into going back to bed.

When that didn't work, she opened the door, promising herself that if he was asleep, she wouldn't wake him. On quiet feet, she crossed the wooden floor to the couch. She was about to lean over and check on him when his eyes popped open. The suddenness of his actions made her straighten with a gasp.

"Is everything okay?" he asked, sitting up.

His lower body was covered by a sheet, but his upper body was bare and beautifully displayed in the faint moonlight drifting in through the cabin's front windows. She tried speaking, but for a long moment, all she could do was stare.

Finally, she said, "Nothing's wrong. Exactly. But…" But he was gorgeous and frowning with concern. His mouth was just too perfectly made for kissing, and she couldn't stand the tension any more.

Without a word, she straddled his lap, braced her hands on his shoulders, leaned in close, and kissed him. For a painfully long moment, he didn't react. He remained perfectly still, his hands pressed into the couch behind him, his mouth motionless, his muscles tense beneath her touch. She softened her lips against his, allowing herself a brief moment of bliss before embarrassment made her pull away.

Before she could, though, Mitch flew into motion. His mouth opened against hers, his arms came up to circle her waist, tightening her against his chest, and his tongue delved between her lips, turning the kiss into something serious and molten hot. She clung to him then, answering the sudden onslaught of passion with relief and need and desperation. She wiggled closer, swallowing his groan as she devoured him. He tasted so good, felt so wonderful. The frustration she'd been feeling before was nothing to the passion she felt then, the thought that if she didn't get her pajama bottoms off and get his cock inside her in the next few minutes, she might not survive.

Rubbing her pajama-covered breasts against his bare chest was both torture and triumph. But the barrier was too much.

She released her hard hold on his shoulders long enough to shrug out of her top. She pulled her mouth from his to jerk the shirt over her head and before she'd finished, his lips closed over her nipple. Moaning, she flung the shirt aside and gripped his head, holding him close to her breast as he sucked the sensitive flesh. She dropped her head back and ground herself more firmly against his erection. There was still too much material between them, but she wasn't ready for him to stop his delicious assault on her breasts.

He scrapped his teeth over her nipple none too gently, then swirled his tongue around the area to sooth the burn. Leaving one breast, he moved to the other, once again sucking and teasing her until she groaned, fisting her hands in his hair.

"Yes," she murmured, not even sure if she spoke aloud. "More."

He answered by tightening his grip on her waist and sucking her harder, sending delirious jolts of lust right to her core. She was wet and ready, and a little worried she'd come just from his mouth on her breasts. But she could have more than one orgasm in a row and she intended on having as many as Mitch would allow her tonight.

When his lips left her breast, she brought her head forward, intent on capturing his mouth with hers again. Before she knew what was happening, though, he'd lifted her off his lap and set her on her feet beside the couch. Blinking in surprise, she waited for him to rise and join her, assuming he wanted to move this to the comfort of the bed. But he didn't move. He sat perfectly still, breathing hard, staring up at her.

"What's wrong?" she asked.

"We can't do this."

"Why not?"

"You are not mine to take," he murmured.

The statement made her frown.

Before she could ask what the hell he meant, he said, "I can't do this. Not with you."

"What's wrong with me?"

"Nothing," he said with a great deal of feeling. "Nothing is wrong with you. I just can't."

She held his gaze for a long moment, until she was certain he was serious. When she realized he was, a knot settled in her chest. She swallowed hard, nodded, and returned to the bedroom, walking with as much dignity as she could muster given how devastated she was by his rejection. She gave a passing thought to collecting her pajama shirt but decided against going back. She needed to get away from him before he saw her hurt.

In her adult life, she'd rarely worried about rejection. She only ever made a move on a man she knew wanted her in return. Mitch's rejection brought up feelings of insecurity and inadequacy she'd thought long set aside. She'd been too different looking, too unique in school to be considered pretty. Her strong senses and strength got her labeled weird early on and that label followed her through high school, no matter what she did, making dating even more impossible.

But when she got to college, she discovered unique had its advantages and strength was admired. Many men actually loved the blend of Indian and Italian that made up her heritage and formed her features. She'd come into her own in her early twenties and had never looked back.

Or so she thought. Having a man like Mitch, a man she'd thought wanted her, turn her away pricked her self-assurance and hurt far more than a simple rejection should have. As she closed the bedroom door, she assured herself it was only her pride that hurt so much. Pride and maybe vanity. This had nothing to do with deeper emotions.

She walked the few paces to the edge of the bed before she stopped and simply stood there, staring at nothing. She wasn't in love with him. She wasn't. Lust was simple and easy, and if the person she was lusting after didn't want her as much as she wanted him, so be it. There were reasons she'd been trying not to sleep with him anyway, though she couldn't think of any at that moment. She was sure by morning, she'd remember why this was a foolish decision and be glad he'd put on the brakes.

Her oddly strong reaction to him was probably just a result of their situation and the danger she was in anyway. Once Petrov was caught, she still had to face an uncertain future. She couldn't blame Mitch for not wanting to get mixed up with her.

She was still standing by the bed when the door burst open behind her, slamming loudly against the wall. With a screech, she spun to face the intruder. Mitch stood framed in the doorway looking dangerous and intense. A shiver of something close to fear tickled her spine.

In three strides, he closed the space between them, took her face in his hands and muttered, "Fuck the consequences."

Then he was kissing her, hard and hungry and desperate.

Chapter Fifteen

He couldn't taste her enough, feel her enough. His hands actually shook as he stroked down her neck and over her shoulders, taking her breast in one hand and wrapping the other around her waist to hold her as tightly to his body as he could get her. She tasted like paradise and promise and need. Her desire drove him completely out of his mind.

He nudged her backward until she tumbled onto the bed. Following quickly, unable to stand being separated from her for more than an instant, he kissed her deeply. Not gently, and not with any sort of finesse or attempts at seduction. He was too far gone. He kissed her hard, devouring her soft murmurs of pleasure with such fierce hunger he barely recognized himself.

When she'd walked out of the bedroom in her pajamas with her hair loose and her eyes heavy and dark, he'd nearly swallowed his tongue. She looked ethereal, beautiful, and forbidden. Then she'd straddled him, kissed him, and his need rose up like a hungry animal, wanting nothing more than to devour every inch of her. He'd gone hard in seconds, insane with the taste of her. Only the barest hint of sanity remained and his conscience reared its relentless head.

She wasn't his. He couldn't have her. He couldn't keep her. This should not happen. She was hope for his people, not some random woman. There would be consequences, serious consequences if he allowed this. She was destined for someone else and they'd both be hurt if he didn't keep that in mind. His people wouldn't allow him to have a relationship with her—not given his status, not given her value. Sleeping with her would only make things worse, at least for him.

And what if she could have tiger children? What if he got her pregnant? According to tiger law, she'd be his then, but he would have broken tiger law by being with her outside a Run—except she couldn't run. Her situation was unique, she was special, and how the law treated her could change everything among the tigers. The only thing he could be sure of was that none of his people would want him to be her mate.

He didn't know where the strength came from to set her away from him, but he'd done it. And regretted it even before she closed the bedroom door.

Now, with her in his arms again, her soft body pliant under his touch, he didn't give a damn about the consequences, what his people wanted, or what tiger law would allow. He'd worry about that when the time came. Now she was his, hungry for him, and he couldn't resist her.

He slipped his hands beneath the band of her pajama bottoms and cupped her ass, squeezing, delirious to realize she wasn't wearing underwear. Stripping off her remaining clothing should have been easy, but his need to keep his hands on her skin made the process awkward. Giggling, she wiggled free of the garment then rolled into him, pressing the full length of her body against his. When she moved her hips, rubbing his rigid cock, he groaned and tightened his hold on her ass.

Later, he would explore her more fully, learn every inch, discover every sensitive spot she had. Right now, he had to be inside her. He slid one hand around her hip, across her lower abdomen and down, cupping her heat, sliding a finger over her sensitive flesh. When he slipped between her folds, he found her wet and ready. A brush over her sensitive clit brought her hips up off the bed. The reaction and her little cries of need overwhelmed him. One taste, he needed one taste.

He hadn't thought he could delay being in her, but the scent of her, the promise of her drove him. Sliding farther down the bed, he settled between her legs and had his mouth on her before she could react. Her hands clenched in his hair, her body tightened as she cried out his name. The sound of his name from her made him wild. He licked and sucked, tasted her fully, winding her tight. Her grip would have hurt if he wasn't so distracted by her flavor.

When he focused on her clit, she writhed beneath him, panting and moaning. Then she stiffened and her whole body jerked. He held her hips, continuing to apply a steady, relentless pressure as she came with a breathless shout.

Before she could recover, he moved up her body and slid into her wet heat. Closing his eyes, he savored the feel of her as her inner muscles still clenched from her release. She was perfect, hot and snug and so wet. When he looked down at her, she was staring up at him with her dark, beautiful eyes, her lips curved in a faint smile.

He was lost.

He moved slowly, sliding in deep, then nearly pulling all the way out before pushing forward again. Her eyelashes fluttered as she tried to hold his gaze. When her legs wrapped around his hips, he increased his rhythm, still trying to move slowly, to savor her.

He leaned down and kissed her, and his restraint shattered. He needed her too much, and he couldn't maintain a slow rhythm a moment longer. She moved with him, taking his hard, pounding thrusts with moans he swallowed. His muscles tightened, his body tensed, and he came with a shout.

He collapsed on top of her for a moment, stunned by the strength of his release, sated and content to be exactly where he was. After a few deep breaths, he rolled to his side, taking her with him, unable to release her just yet.

Her natural scent mingled with the smells of sex and the cedar bed, a combination so delicious he wanted to bath in it.

She smiled at him and cupped his cheek in one hand. The gesture sent a wave of deep satisfaction through him, and an equally strong sense of dread. This felt right. Perfect.

How the hell was he going to give her up to another man?

She leaned close and brushed her lips against his. He closed his eyes and held her close, kissing her deeply. He didn't want to think about the future or consider how complicated he'd just made both their lives. For tonight, she was his and he intended to take advantage of that.

CHAPTER SIXTEEN

When Nila woke a few hours later, Mitch was sound asleep beside her, his arm heavy across her stomach. Dawn was still hours away, but a question had nagged her in her dreams, making sleep difficult. She rolled over to study him in the faint light. Looking over his handsome features both eased her disquiet and made it worse.

She ran her hand over his chest, savoring hard muscle and crisp hair. He'd barely given her time to explore his body all night. Now, she enjoyed the freedom to simply gaze and touch. She stroked his torso, her fingers dipping and rising over muscle ridges that hadn't relaxed in his sleep. The sheet covered his hips so she nudged it down to trace her fingers over the thick cord of muscle above his hip. She loved that particular muscle on men—it was just so sexy and male.

"What time is it?" he murmured.

She glanced up. His eyes were still closed. She smiled and continued her exploration. "No idea, but early. Probably still a few hours to dawn. Sorry to wake you."

"Not complaining."

She pushed the sheet down his thighs, then stroked her fingers over his erection, savoring the contrasting hardness and silky texture. He pulled in a deep breath and his hips shifted toward her.

"Does that feel good?" she murmured.

"Like torture."

She chuckled. "Would you like me to stop?"

"Absolutely not."

She glanced up again to find him staring at her, his eyes glittering and full of heat. Holding his gaze, she shifted positions and took him into her mouth. She'd wanted this for days and the freedom to finally indulge made her greedy. She sucked and licked, reveling in his groans and rapid breathing, the tension in his muscles, the way he fisted the sheets. She heard the material rip and a shiver danced down her spine. Holy hell but the man was strong. The idea of having all that strength at her mercy only fed her need.

She pushed him to near breaking with her mouth, then straddled his hips and guided his cock into her, sliding down slowly. She watched him tense, his jaw clench and his eyes squeeze shut. He made her feel powerful. Strong and sexy. When so much else was out of her control, when she faced creatures stronger and faster and more dangerous than she could comprehend, when she felt so completely powerless to control her own life, Mitch gave her a chance to find herself again.

And that sense of rediscovering her inner strength, of finding her own center again, pushed her closer to emotions for him she wasn't sure she should feel so quickly.

In that moment, with only the sounds of their harsh breathing filling the small room, with his masculine scent rising up to mix with the smells of sex and cedar, she felt completely like herself, and knew her heart was beating faster for this man. Watching his orgasm take him, seeing his neck muscles tense, his jaw clench, feeling the pulse of his cock deep inside her, she knew love was only a few dangerous, foolish breaths away.

Then her own peak demanded her full attention and she let go, allowing the climax to wrap her up in heat and thorough release.

She dropped down to hug him, trying to catch her breath, and smiled when he wrapped his arms around her, holding her tight. The moment was quiet and perfect.

Too perfect to last. The realization of how easy it would be for her to fall in love with Mitch crept in past her contentment. The question that plagued her dreams came back to poke at her.

She had to ask, had to know the truth. But she was so loath to disrupt their embrace she kept quiet as long as she could stand to. Then she rolled off him and sat up.

He didn't relinquish contact though, and she was grateful for his warm palm stroking along her hip and waist.

"What's wrong?"

She smiled. "That transparent, am I?"

"You're frowning. This doesn't feel like a frowning moment. Something is bothering you."

"I have to ask you something, and I'm afraid to."

His hand stilled, but his expression was open. "Ask."

"Why aren't you an option? Why aren't you…powerful enough? I don't understand. If your grandmother is powerful…" She trailed off and blew out a breath. "I don't know. I don't want you to think I'm trying to force your hand, or that I seduced you for any underhanded purpose. That was lust pure and simple."

He smiled. "Same here."

"But…we both know this complicated things. And I want to understand why, from your perspective. I want to know why you've pushed me to pick a 'powerful' tiger if you want me yourself." She raised a hand when he opened his mouth. "Again, don't think I'm trying to coerce you into anything. I know sex doesn't mean a relationship, and I'm not trying to push you into one. I just… I just want to understand."

He held her gaze for a long moment, his hand once again stroking her skin. She took the contact as a good sign. But discomfort made her want to squirm. The darkness was a blessing. Somehow it was easier to have uncomfortable conversations in the dark.

Finally, he let out a breath that sounded resigned and he sat up, leaning against the headboard. "I hate talking about this. But you deserve the truth. Especially after…" He gestured at the bed. He ran a hand through his hair and said, "It all starts with my mother's suicide."

She sucked in a breath. Oh, god. This wasn't a good start.

"I was only six months old at the time. I don't remember her or anything that followed. That part was a lot harder on my two older brothers than on me."

"What…why did she…?"

"Depression before my birth tipped into a severe post partum depression after. No one realized how bad it was, though, until after. In fact, according to my grandmother, my mother seemed to be in fine spirits in the days before. They all thought she was doing well."

Nila's heart broke for him and his family. "How?"

"Poison. Arsenic. One of the few poisons that works on my people and humans."

Part of her wanted to ask more about that, but she held her questions for another time. She didn't want to interrupt what had to be a difficult story for him to tell.

"My mother's death…broke something in my father. He went tiger and stayed that way for weeks. He slaughtered cattle and just left it, not killing for food, just…killing."

She couldn't control her gasp.

"We were living in Montana at the time. The ranchers obviously noticed what was happening. My father killed too often for the slaughter to be ignored. That wasn't good. It risked exposing him, as a tiger on the loose, which risked exposing us all. But the elders could have forgiven it, paid off the affected ranchers, found a way to quiet the rumors. Then he killed a human. The man was beating a woman who bore a very vague resemblance to my mother. But killing a human violates one of our most fundamental laws. We can't afford attention from human authorities when our population is barely avoiding extinction as is. Because of that, killing a human, especially in tiger form, is almost always an automatic death sentence."

"Oh, Mitch. I'm so sorry. Was your father…?" She couldn't say it, it was too awful and tragic.

"No. My grandmother bargained for his life. Everyone recognized the extenuating circumstances. This was more than thirty years ago, before forensic science improved so much. But the woman told authorities the truth, that a tiger had killed her boyfriend. They couldn't find a rogue tiger, of course, but the damage had been done. That combined with the cattle slaughter was too much. The elders confined my father."

"Like jail?"

"Our equivalent."

"How long?" She shifted a little closer to him, not touching because she wasn't sure if he'd want physical contact, but she wanted desperately to comfort him.

"Only eight years the first time."

"First time?"

"Despite the counselling, he never really recovered from my mother's death. He blamed himself for not recognizing the severity of her depression, that it would push her to suicide. He was out for…seven, almost eight years, and then he started stalking a human woman who looked like my mother. Before he could do anything, the Trackers brought him in, and he agreed to another confinement."

"Agreed?"

"He didn't trust himself either. He's never said so to me, but I think he recognizes how close he is to…instability. When he was confronted about the stalking, he asked to be confined."

"How long that time?"

"He stayed five years before my grandmother finally talked him into leaving."

"Where is he now?"

"He moved to South America."

"South America?"

"Lot of open spaces for a man, and a tiger, to disappear."

"Why not someplace where other tigers, non-shapeshifting tigers, live? He'd blend in better."

Mitch snorted. "Poaching mostly. My father spends more time as a tiger now than human. He runs less risk of being killed by random poachers in the jungles were hunters aren't expecting to see him."

"That… That must be really hard on you."

"Probably be worse if he'd raised me. But I barely know him. He's always kept his distance. Hard to miss what you've never had."

She wasn't sure what to say. Condolences and sympathies seemed hollow in the wake of his story. Her heart ached for him. He'd been essentially orphaned at six months old. She might not have known her mother, but she'd had her father, steady and strong, in her life.

"Who raised you?" she asked.

"Mostly my Uncle Erik. He's the third of five boys. My dad was the baby in the family…but the only one to find a mate."

"But you have a nephew."

"One of Alexis' kids. She not just like a sister, she's also my grandmother's adopted daughter. So her kids may as well be my nephews and niece."

She couldn't resist touching him any longer so she snuggled up next to him against the headboard. To her relief, he wrapped an arm around her and held her close.

"So…a lot of family tragedy, but…I'm not seeing how this answers my question."

"The bargain my grandmother had to strike to prevent her youngest son from being executed involved a serious financial payment to the elders' coffers and a drop in status for her entire family. In the tiger world, mental lapses like my fathers are viewed as detrimental to the entire community. His sons were labeled as defective, too, making us free game to any tigers who wanted to challenge us."

"Challenge?"

He shrugged. "We got beat up a lot. Or at least others tried. We all became very good fighters, very quickly. I grew up looking over my shoulder."

"That's awful! Why was that allowed?"

"Because there was nothing to stop it. My grandmother wasn't allowed to interfere, and kicking the ass of an elder's grandchild is a treat a lot of males couldn't resist."

Nila scowled at the sheets. He wasn't making tiger society sound like a very nice place. In fact, the more he said, the more she didn't want anything to do with tigers beyond Mitch.

His arm tightened around her. "Hey, it is what it is. Not so bad as all that. My brothers and I are pretty tough. We survived. And the elders didn't take away our option to mate."

"Wait." She faced him. "What does that mean?"

"Usually, when a tiger is deemed unfit, he's forbidden from taking part in the Mate Run. The community doesn't want him potentially passing on his 'weakness' to his children when we're already so close to extinction. The one concession my grandmother was able to get from the elders was that her grandchildren still be allowed to run for a mate. But we're considered bottom of the barrel among the tigers. Even though we can run, none of us were ever likely to be chosen—despite my grandmother's hopes."

Nila wasn't sure how to feel about that. Mitch had run so he'd gone after a potential wife, even knowing he wouldn't be chosen. Why had he done it? Did she really want to know?

"My grandmother insisted we run," he said, as if reading her mind. "All three of us have taken part in at least a few but none of us run now. My oldest brother, Nick, hasn't run in… ten years. Dom is pretty close at almost eight. I did a few Runs about three, four years ago because my grandmother nagged me until I did."

"Ah." Relief seemed a weird reaction to have, but there it was, and she couldn't really explain why she was relieved.

He shifted to face her, making sure she met his gaze when he said, "So you see, I'm considered weak and powerless among my kind, even if my grandmother is an elder. I can physically fight off any tiger that comes, but no tiger will be deterred from coming after you if I'm the only thing standing in the way."

She stared into his eyes and hated. She hated the situation. She hated that he'd been through so much. She hated that his people treated him so badly. And most of all, she hated that, despite everything, he still tried convincing her he wasn't the right man for her, that she shouldn't even consider him as an option.

"Thank you for telling me all this," she forced out around a churning mix of emotions too tangled to clearly sort through. "Now I need you to know something."

He nodded and straightened away from her, taking a deep breath as if he was bracing himself for whatever she had to say.

"I don't give a fuck about any of it."

He frowned.

"I don't give a fuck about your position, or that the others think you're weak even though you're not. I don't give a fuck about status. I only care about your father's crime in so far as it's negatively affected your life. I have little sympathy for a man killed while he was beating a woman, so I can't be outraged by your father's crime. I am…heartsick to think how you and your brothers had to grow up. But as far as your bottom of the barrel position in tiger society…I don't give a flying fuck."

She held his gaze as he stared at her for a long moment, not flinching despite the fact she couldn't read his expression. Then suddenly he swept her up into his arms and kissed her, hard, with a fierceness that matched the kiss when he'd slammed open the bedroom door earlier. But there was more here, not just lust, something…something she was afraid to dissect. Something with emotion and power. She tunneled her fingers through his hair and held him tight, answering his passion, pouring all her tangled, chaotic feelings into their kiss.

She had no idea where this conversation left them, what would happen when the sun rose, but in that moment, he was hers, she was his, and the rest of the world could wait.

Chapter Seventeen

Nila woke hours later to a bright morning. She was sated, a little sore, in desperate need of a shower, and feeling warm and fuzzy down to her toes.

Mitch held her, his arm around her waist as she snuggled her back to his front. The pillows and tattered sheets smelled like him. And sex. She rubbed a hand along his forearm, loving the strength and muscle.

Her emotions weren't any more settled than they had been the night before, but for one thing—she still wanted Mitch. She had no idea where this would lead, or what he wanted from her in the end. She just knew she wasn't prepared to give him up. Not yet. Not because of idiotic politics.

Her stomach rumbled and she had to stifle a groan.

Gently, she disentangled herself from his hold and slipped from bed. She brushed a finger over his temple. He looked gorgeous in sleep. The last time she'd woken up next to a man, her mind had been on the job ahead of her that day. Mitch was completely different. It wasn't just sex with him. It was something more. Something more was a scary prospect. Especially because she was a little afraid of what more meant.

Nibbling her bottom lip, she scooped up her clothing and headed to the bathroom. She took her time in the shower, trying not to put too many expectations on the day ahead. They'd broken the tension, and she understood him a little better now, but there was a lot unsaid between them.

Mitch was still asleep by the time she was dressed, so she made herself a cup of tea and went onto the porch to savor the morning. Things would heat up over the course of the day, but this early, the air was both warm and inviting. Taking a deep breath, she swallowed the smells of woods, earth, and the steaming floral scent of her tea. A musky addition caught her attention, something vague, just at the edge of her senses that she couldn't quite identify. She frowned out at the trees, wondering what it was. It didn't stink like badger or skunk, it wasn't pungent enough, and it wasn't bad, just…

A sense of awareness curled through her, something vague and insistent. It reminded her of the feeling she'd had that afternoon in Mitch's cabin, just before he'd realized a tiger had found them.

She released a slow breath. Probably just an animal she wasn't familiar with skirting around the edge of the cabin. The possibility of a bear made her move closer to the door.

Her stomach jumped and her nerves tingled. What the hell? She was suddenly edgy and felt…hunted. They hadn't seen evidence of a large predator, but that didn't mean they weren't in the middle of one's territory. She narrowed her gaze as she studied the sun dappled ground under the trees. Mitch would have picked up a dangerous predator in the area, wouldn't he?

Her screaming instincts assured her she was in danger, though. That weird sense of awareness told her threat was coming from all around the cabin. Swallowing a panicky need to call Mitch's name, she eased inside and locked the door. The feel of a hunter's gaze followed her. Trying not to scream or hyperventilate, she set her tea down and backed to the bedroom, keeping an eye on the front door as that sense of awareness centered in that direction.

What the hell was she sensing?

She heard the bedroom door open but didn't turn to face Mitch. "Something's out there," she said quietly.

"Yes. Tigers."

"More than one?"

His hands clenched her shoulders. "I'm sensing five."

As he said it, she realized she felt five different points of danger with that weird sense of awareness. Was she sensing them, too, or was she just imagining things? "This is so not good. We can't outrun them if they're in front of the only exit."

"You can't run fast enough anyway. They'll shift. If I changed to a tiger, I could get away, but…"

"But I don't have that option. Now what?"

"Barricade the door for what it's worth. Then we'll try slipping away."

Mitch moved around her to the couch. She followed, helping him move the heavy piece of furniture without discussion.

"Will this help?" she murmured.

"Not for long."

Just as they got the couch in place, a huge thump shook the door. Nila squealed in surprised shock, despite her best efforts to remain quiet.

Mitch pulled her away from the door, scanning the small cabin. "Let's get the rifles?"

Nila tried not to wince. Having an actual weapon in her hands should make her feel better when facing down tiger shifters, but she hated the damned things so much they still gave her the willies. Since arriving, Mitch had made sure they both knew how to use the two rifles John had stored here: one lever-action and one bolt-action. They hadn't actually fired the guns because they only had one box of ammunition per gun, and Mitch didn't want to waste any—even to get used to the rifles' recoils—but she at least knew how to take off the safeties, load them, and pull the triggers.

"You want the bolt-action?" he asked as they backed toward the bedroom again.

She was much more comfortable with that rifle since it was similar to the tranquilizer guns she'd used, but it wasn't as quick to fire a second round and it carried one less cartridge. Still, given her nerves, sticking with what she was comfortable with seemed the better idea. "Yeah. You've got faster reactions anyway."

At the bedroom door, he took her face in his hands and stared at her, hard. "You will have to shoot to kill. Can you do that?"

She swallowed and took a moment to really consider if she could or not. She'd had to put wounded animals out of their misery before, but this was a different kind of killing. Not mercy. But definitely self-defense. If she didn't shoot to kill, those shifters out there would tear her apart without any hesitation.

She nodded, though she couldn't actual say the words aloud.

He studied her for a moment, a moment she wasn't sure they had, then he dropped a swift kiss on her mouth and moved into the bedroom.

"Be prepared," he said as he unlocked the gun cabinet in the bedroom closet. "I might have to shift to hold them off. It won't be pretty. Don't look, and if I tell you to, keep running and don't look back."

"I can't just leave you."

"You might have to. Don't argue and don't get heroic. I won't be distracted during a fight if I know you're away and safe."

She knew he was right. These were creatures she couldn't even comprehend. Seeing her half brother shift in front of her, knowing the strength, speed, and deadliness of a regular tiger, she knew she didn't stand much of a chance against five shapeshifters, even with a gun.

"Fine. But I don't like it."

The corner of his mouth tilted up in a half smile as he pulled out her rifle. She tried not to flinch when he handed her the weapon. Another loud thud sounded from the living room. Nila shivered. That front door wouldn't hold against the pressure for long. In fact, she was surprised it had held this long. She suspected they were toying with her and Mitch, not really hitting hard enough to shatter the wood. Maybe they were attempting to drive them into a trap.

When she voiced the fear, Mitch nodded. "They have the cabin surrounded. There's no way to get out without encountering one of them." He handed her the box of ammunition for her rifle, then pulled out his own gun.

"Is it Petrov?" She checked the guns safety and loaded the cartridges. Her rifle would hold three rounds in the magazine and one in the chamber. She had four shots against five shifters before she had to reload. She hated those odds.

Mitch loaded his own rifle with quick efficiency then put the rest of the cartridges into his jeans' pockets. "Smells like Petrov and two of his sons," he said. "Not Vlad, though."

"You can tell? You're sure?" She filled the side pockets of her cargo pants with the remaining ammunition from her box.

"Scents carry a shared familial…element. I memorized Vlad's scent. Three of those outside the cabin are related to him by blood."

"Could it just be Vlad's other brothers? He's got three."

"Maybe. But Petrov would want to be here, so I'm betting he's out there."

Her gaze flicked toward the front door. "If we're surrounded, how are we getting out?"

"Front door. I'll lead."

"Why the front door?" Her heart hammered so hard she was afraid she might pass out. She worked at slowing her breathing and calming her pulse. Panic wouldn't help now. She needed to maintain some semblance of rational thought so she could help

Mitch get them out of this trap. But her hands still shook as she hoisted the rifle into a position that would make bringing it to her shoulder and firing easier.

"The weakest of the tigers is there. The brothers and Petrov are around the back of the house. The fifth is to the west of the cabin, near the bathroom window. He feels as strong as Petrov and his boys."

"You can tell that? How?"

"I don't know. Instinct. I'm told not all tigers can pick up as much as I can about others. Probably got it from the years of fighting. Their scents also tell me a lot, even without this other instinct." He studied the front door from his position in the bedroom. "They can tell a lot about me, too."

"Will they know you'll go to the front, then? Maybe we shouldn't do that."

"They'll assume we'll try escaping through the back, which is why Petrov and his boys are back there. Going out the front is our only option."

"Jesus," she whispered. She took off the safety and settled her finger alongside the trigger without touching it. "Are we shooting our way out?"

"Yes. But don't waste ammunition. We need to put some distance between them and us so we'll have time to reload."

She let loose a steady stream of curses under her breath to release some of the fear and tension building in her blood. The colorful array earned her a raised brow and another half smile from Mitch.

"Better?" he asked.

"Kind of. It does help."

"Keep it up." He pumped his rifle's lever, cocked the hammer, and pressed his hammer block safety to the fire position, then he settled his shoulders.

Though she'd noticed he only had on jeans and no shirt, for the first time, she realized he wasn't wearing any shoes. "Can you run without shoes?"

"Better than with them," he murmured, his gaze still on the door. "Are you ready?"

"Absolutely not. Let's go."

They eased out of the bedroom, Nila following his lead and moving as quietly as she could manage. She was wearing the same hiking boots she'd had on since India, not easy to run in but they'd have to do. She couldn't run better in bare feet, even though she was part tiger.

The thought of trying to outrun something that moved at least as fast as a tiger made her stomach flip flop. All her training screamed that running from a predator was a bad idea. She had a lot of experience with ordinary tigers and had always taken extreme precautions so she wouldn't have to try outrunning one, even to get to the nearest tree, because running only triggered their hunting instincts—prey runs, predator chases. Her instincts had also helped her avoid being in dangerous positions with any large cats. Was that part of being half tiger or just training?

At the moment, she hoped like hell, whatever it was, it aided her with tiger shifters, too, because she needed all the help she could get.

She did not want to die, not now, not yet. Especially not this way, by someone who hated her just because she existed. Fear wouldn't help her if she let it rule, so she tried with all her will to push it aside as they neared the front door. She focused on opening her senses so she could be ready for what lay outside that flimsy wooden barrier. Again, she noticed those five points of danger—in the exact positions Mitch had told her the others were located. That wasn't her imagination. She was sensing the shifters. She'd never felt that with normal tigers.

She'd have to ask Mitch about that later—if they survived.

Fear continued trickling in despite her efforts, making her stomach clench and her adrenaline race. By the time they reached the door, her hands were shaking so bad, she clenched the rifle tighter in an attempt to steady herself.

Another loud bang shook the frame. This time the wood gave, splintering down the middle. Nila swallowed the screech scraping her throat and edged the barrel of the gun up, settling the rifle into position against her shoulder so she could fire. Mitch held his weapon by his thigh as he stared at the damaged door. The couch was still in their way, Nila realized. They'd have to move it to get out and that would leave the door wide open. They could get trapped inside.

She was about to mention this snag in their plan, when Mitch reached out with one hand and faster than she could blink, shoved the entire couch to the side, sending it tumbling away. Before she could even begin to process the strength it must have taken to do that, he flung open the door and fired one shot. The sound of a high pitched yowl filled the early morning.

The next thing she knew, Mitch had her by the arm and was rushing her toward the cover of the trees. She glanced around but didn't see the tiger Mitch shot. He let go of his hold on her as soon as he knew she was following, which freed her to use her own weapon if necessary. She let her peripheral vision pick up any movement and concentrated on following Mitch's lead.

A sound to her left and the flash of orange striped fur caught her attention. She swung the gun and fired in the direction of the tiger without thinking and without aiming, absorbing the surprisingly light recoil through her shoulder. Another hissing yowl confirmed she'd at least hit something, which surprised her. The flash of fur fell back as she and Mitch picked up speed.

Her worst fears were confirmed, though. The others were chasing them in tiger form. Which meant they were faster, and stronger, and she only had three shots left until she had to reload. She didn't know if her first had done more than distract that particular tiger anyway. Mitch had assured her the ammunition they had would slow the animals down, but he hadn't said whether they'd kill a tiger shifter or not—or how many shots it would take to stop one.

Afraid to think too closely about the overwhelming odds against them, she raced as fast as her feet would allow over the uneven ground, keeping Mitch's back at the fore of her attention while still trying to maintain an awareness of her peripherals. She stumbled, more than once, but terror brought her upright faster than she might have expected, and she managed to stick close to Mitch without him having to drag her.

She still felt the hunters around them, but the faster her adrenaline pumped, the harder it was for her to concentrate on their locations. Her lungs burned and her muscles screamed, a stitch clawing at her side.

Mitch must have known because he started weaving through the trees, leading them on a more erratic, slower path. The tigers loped fast enough to keep pace, but they hung back outside shooting range. That was something at least. They were wary of the guns now.

Unfortunately, even with Mitch's new tactic, Nila couldn't run long enough to get away from their pursuers. Her human legs, even if they were trained and prepared to race through the woods, wouldn't hold up against the strength and stalking persistence of a tiger. And she knew the enemy scented them. The shifters didn't even have to keep up. She and Mitch were leaving behind a trail, like it or not. All the tigers had to do was follow, wear out their prey, and attack when they were vulnerable.

Sucking in a breath, she forced herself not to look back. Even a glance would risk another fall, and she really didn't want to see five tigers coming for them. She only hoped Mitch had a plan, because she had nothing.

They ran past the point when Nila thought she might collapse. Her thighs and calves screamed at her, the stitch worsened, and she sucked in rough gulps of air that were just barely enough to keep her upright. Her fingers loosened on the gun, making her afraid she'd drop the valuable weapon. She didn't even have enough oxygen in her lungs to call Mitch's name and warn him she couldn't continue much longer.

When she tripped over a root and fell face first onto the ground, the gun nearly flying from her grip, she knew she'd reached her limit. She struggled to her feet as Mitch hurried to help her up.

"You hurt?"

"No, but I can't run anymore." She panted, struggling for enough air to speak. "My body won't let me keep up."

Mitch looked behind her, still with a hand on her arm. "They've fallen back. They're staying beyond the range of our guns."

"Figured. What now?"

"We get to high ground and defend from there. Try finding a place where we can see them coming, a clearing or something."

"Have a spot in mind?"

"Maybe."

He tugged her back into motion. She stumbled along beside him, working desperately to keep the now heavy rifle firmly in her grip. The thing weighed less than eight pounds but felt like a ton to her tired muscles. She was trembling so hard from exertion, she wasn't sure she'd even be able to fire it now, but she was safer with it than without it, so she held on for dear life.

Though Mitch continued moving them as quickly as possible, they no longer ran. All Nila could manage was a weak trot and even that slowed into a drunken walk after ten minutes.

She had no idea how far they'd gone or where they were. She had to trust Mitch's sense of direction entirely. Again. The trust wasn't as difficult as it might have once been. She had complete faith in his ability to get them out of this disaster. She just had to keep up and do her part. Working together was their only hope.

Finally, they pulled out of the cover of the trees into a meadow which angled up. From the top of the small hill, they'd be able to see the tigers coming out of the tree line. Once they reached their vantage, she realized they could see 360 degrees and there was at least ten yards of grass between the hill and the trees in all directions.

"If they have guns, this is not a good idea," she muttered, squatting down to make herself a smaller target. She chambered another round and held her rifle at the ready.

"They're all in tiger form. Where would they carry a gun?"

"What if one of them followed in human form? Just in case."

"I'd know it. And they would have fired at us already."

"Even from the cover of the trees?"

He kneeled down low beside her. "Maybe," he admitted with reluctance. "But I doubt they have guns. I'd have sensed a tiger in human form."

He frowned and she remembered he couldn't sense humans, only tiger shifters. Petrov had already used humans. If he'd brought one or more with him, Mitch would only be able to pick them up when they got near enough to smell or hear.

"Tigers prefer to kill up close and personal," he finished. "Petrov will want to kill you the old fashioned way."

Since she knew exactly and in great detail how tigers killed prey, she didn't ask for more information. "I trust your instincts and knowledge, Mitch. If you say they don't have guns, they don't. But we should stay low while we're up here. Just in case."

"Fair enough."

"By the way, why didn't we do this from the cover of the house?"

"Too many ways in that we couldn't cover simultaneously." He shrugged. "Plus, they could always just set the place on fire and force us out."

"Shit." She sucked in air, trying to replenish her deprived oxygen levels, and studied the tree line back the way they'd come. Mitch swiveled to watch their backs.

Movement in the trees made her raise her gun. She caught a faint flash of striped fur in the shadows, but it disappeared in the next breath. The tiger camouflage worked well in this setting, tricking her eyes so seeing them was difficult even for a trained observer like herself. She'd never actually had a tiger hunt her before, but she'd had to pick them out of dense forest. Allowing her long honed instincts to guide her, she pinpointed two of the animals pacing just inside the trees, crossing paths as they guarded the direction back to the cabin.

"Two are there," she murmured, nodding toward them.

"I've spotted the other three. I smell blood on two of them. They're wounded. That works for us."

"How many shots will it take to kill one? Is it just a matter of aiming better? How much damage can they take?"

"A lot," said a deep voice from off to the left.

Chapter Eighteen

Gonna come out in the open, Petrov?" Mitch called.

Nila swallowed loudly and flicked a glance in the direction of the voice, but she kept her concentration on the two pacing tigers in front of her.

She wasn't sure if Mitch was guessing or if he knew what Petrov sounded like. But the idea that the man who wanted her dead was just a few yards away was terrifying. Somehow having the attackers in tiger form had made this easier, less personal. She'd seen tigers hunt and kill. It was natural and part of their survival in the wild. But hearing Petrov's all-too-human voice brought home the otherworldliness of the situation, the impossible odds of trying to go against five enemies who could hunt and kill like tigers, think with the logic and cunning of a human, and were stronger and faster than either species.

"Did he shift or has he been in human form?" she murmured to Mitch. If he'd been human this whole time, he might have a gun.

"Shifted," Mitch whispered back, his voice so low she was grateful for her excellent hearing.

Shivering, she readjusted the rifle so the barrel was more firmly pointed toward the two tigers she watched.

The sound of the man's laugh made her skin crawl.

"Would you like to see my human form?" he called out. "Come down. And I'll make your death quick, easy."

"No," Mitch answered for her.

"If we have to come and get her, we'll kill her slowly and painfully. Over several days. After I've let my boys have her a few times."

She resisted another shiver of revulsion. The taunting man really was Petrov. Which meant two of those "boys" were her half brothers. Yuck. Her stomach turned and bile rose in her throat. Mitch's answering growl was quiet, so quiet she wondered if Petrov heard it, even with his excellent senses.

"Ignore him," she murmured. "He's trying to upset you."

Mitch stiffened beside her. Though she wasn't looking, she felt his muscles tensing and releasing in a slow, rhythmic way.

"You're not changing are you?" she hissed. "You can't use a gun as a tiger."

"Just reigning in the anger," he whispered, his voice harsh.

"Oh, Nila, won't you talk to me?" Petrov said, his voice singy-songy. "I was your mother's mate after all."

Nila refused to rise to his goading. Petrov had heard enough from her already. She had to concentrate on the other tigers because it was obvious, even to someone like her, that Petrov was acting as the diversion. She knew Mitch recognized the same thing because he didn't answer Petrov either. She felt him swiveling as he studied the area around their perch.

"What, no more conversation? Pity. But pointless. You're both dead. It's just a matter of time."

She held still, trained by years of waiting and watching large cats in both captive and wild environments. With effort, she concentrated on slowing her breathing, focusing her senses, and ignoring Petrov's continued attempts to distract them.

Her focus on the two cats she watched saved her from having to take a wild shot. She saw the animal change directions abruptly, sighted down the barrel of her rifle as it charged their position, and fired in the general direction of the huge animal's head. Chambered another round, and fired again.

The tiger dropped. She didn't look too closely at the damage she'd done. She'd seen the results of poachers, which was why she hated guns, but she worked hard to turn off her inner revulsion and fear. Now down to a single round left in the rifle, she carefully reloaded, in case she didn't get another chance. She concentrated on breathing in and out so her hands wouldn't shake and opened her senses to the remaining tiger so she could keep track of him.

There were growls and chuffing barks from the trees, the sound of Petrov and the sharp retort of Mitch's rifle, but she didn't turn to see what he'd fired at or if he'd hit his target. On the gentle breeze, the scent of blood mixed with dry earth carried to her.

The tiger below hadn't risen, but she couldn't tell if it was dead or not. She didn't really want to know or think about that yet. Hell, what if that had been one of her half brothers? She forced down a distressed whimper. She'd break down, probably throw up, and cry about all this later. If they survived.

The animal in the woods started convulsing and horror washed through her. "Damn it, this one is shifting," she muttered, hoping Petrov didn't hear her. She'd had a hard enough time shooting a tiger—awful and painful to shoot one of the animals she'd spent her life trying to heal—but she balked to near immobility at the thought of shooting a human.

"Remember they will kill you if they get up here," Mitch whispered, his tone so low she was sure no one else heard him. "He will happily rape you, and torture you, and then slit your throat. If you're lucky."

Nila swallowed hard. Well, that put things into perspective, didn't it? Shooting a man out to hurt her that badly didn't seem quiet as impossible as it had a moment earlier.

She lifted the barrel and braced her arm on her raised knee.

The wait felt interminable but finally, the shape that had been a tiger stood taller and stepped into a patch of light so she could see the man. He was naked, tall, muscled, with dark hair. She couldn't make out his features clearly, but something about his baring reminded her of Vlad.

"You wouldn't kill your brother, would you, Nila?" the man called, confirming her fears.

She didn't answer, though his comment made her think the tiger she'd shot actually wasn't one of her brothers. There as more relief in that realization than she should feel for a man trying to hurt her.

Behind her, Mitch whispered, "You okay?"

She nodded, then realized he probably wasn't looking at her. "Fine. I'll fall apart later."

Tracking the new man as he angled closer, moving just up the edge of the hill, she wondered how close she'd let him get before firing. Swallowing, she rested her finger against the trigger.

Not very close at all, she decided.

"I suggest you tell your son to back off," Mitch shouted. "She has no tie to him, Petrov."

"Even if you shoot him, Nila, he'll just keep coming," Petrov said, amusement in his tone. "It takes more than you have to kill a shifter. He'll reach you and after we kill Mitch, we'll make you suffer. A wounded tiger is a terrible thing."

She actually knew that part already as she'd seen her fair share of wounded cats. But she was prepared to keep firing as much as it took to keep these men away from her. The tiger below, the one she'd hit twice, still wasn't moving.

Unless he's playing dead, her traitorous mind thought. Shit, shit, shit, shit. Cursing in her head didn't do as much as cursing out loud, but she didn't want Petrov knowing she was upset. The less he knew about her mental state the better.

The man below her took another long stride up the hill. Nila fired.

Her first shot hit something because he screamed. She chambered another bullet, the sound of the bolt dropping reassuringly powerful, and fired again without looking too closely at the details of her target. Her ears rang as she readied her third round, but before she could fire again, a new sound rose from around them. The shouts of men and the roar of tigers filled the area.

Not more! They were already surrounded and outnumbered. Now, it sounded like more than a dozen animals circled them. They'd never survive, not against those odds.

Nila raised her rifle, prepared to go down fighting because she'd rather die fast than fall into Petrov's hands. Then another sound reached her.

The growl and roar of a tiger fight.

"Mitch?"

"The others are fighting Petrov's allies," he said.

"Who are 'the others'? What do they want?"

"No idea, but they're helping us."

"Are they the Trackers your grandmother sent?"

"We'll know soon. Don't relax your aim."

She looked back to where her half brother had fallen. There was nothing there but some blood on the grass. The other tiger was gone now, too. Damn it, how had they moved away so fast? Had she killed the one or not?

"They're both gone," she hissed at Mitch. "The two I shot. They're gone."

He gripped her shoulder with one hand, the awkward angle proving he still wasn't looking at her.

"They're wounded. They aren't a threat to us now," he assured.

"How did they get away? I looked away for a few seconds."

"We can move fast. Really fast."

Not entirely sure how to respond to that without sarcasm, she held her tongue and searched the trees for new threats. The sounds of fighting, both man and beast, surrounded them, loud in the otherwise quiet summer morning.

And then it was over. The noise cut off abruptly. She heard movement in the trees. A moment later, three tigers and a naked man moved into the clearing.

The man held up his hands. "Don't shoot," he called. "We drove off the others."

"Who are you?" Mitch said.

"My name is Sanjay," the man said. "We're here to help."

"Who sent you?"

"No one. We heard about Nila and wanted to help you protect her."

"You're not Trackers." Mitch stated that as fact rather than a questioned.

"No," Sanjay said.

"How did you get to us and the Trackers haven't?"

The man shrugged then must have realized Mitch didn't see him because he said, "News travels faster than people. We were already in this area. Our territory is nearby. We heard the fight and gunfire and came to investigate. We realized what was happening when one of us recognized Petrov."

Mitch held silent for a long moment. Nila wanted desperately to ask him what he was thinking but now was not the time. She kept her gun aimed toward the three tigers and one man below and waited for him to make a decision. He knew this world, these people. She had no idea if they could trust the newcomers or if this was some complex ploy.

Finally, Mitch said, "We'll come down. I'd prefer to see everyone in human form. But Nila...hasn't seen a lot of shifting."

Without hesitating, the three tigers moved back into the trees and just out of sight. She, Mitch, and Sanjay remained where they were. Waiting.

Chapter Nineteen

When the three others finally re-emerged from the trees, they were in human form, and all of them were completely naked. No one seemed aware of the general state of undress, however. Nila decided they must be used to it. Or maybe tiger shifters just didn't have a sense of modesty.

Sanjay shouted up to them, "Are you prepared to talk with us?"

"We'll come down to you, but I want you all grouped together first. No one coming up behind us."

Another three men appeared from around the hillside. Seven tiger shifters. They were more outnumbered now than they'd been facing Petrov.

Mitch touched her shoulder and she glanced up at him. He stood beside her, his gaze focused on the small group of men.

"Are we safe going down there?" she whispered.

"For the moment. Sanjay is telling the truth. At least what he's admitted out loud is the truth."

"How can you tell?"

"His scent."

Reaching out a hand, he helped her to her feet. Her leg muscles quivered, still exhausted from the run. She held the rifle in front of her, the barrel pointed toward the ground, her finger still close enough to the trigger to raise and fire if she needed to defend herself again. Side by side, she and Mitch eased down the hill until they stood in front of their rescuers.

Nila tried reading their expressions, taking a beat to look at each one, but each face was neutral or openly friendly. Two of the men smiled broadly at her and nodded in greeting. Two others actually winked. That startled her into doing a double take. Well, they didn't seem to want to kill her. At least, they were making an effort not to frighten her.

Unfortunately, their efforts were only freaking her out more.

She caught one of the men looking her over and narrowed her eyes at him. He had the good grace to look away.

The impact of what had just happened, of what she'd had to do, washed over her as her adrenaline ebbed. For a long, scary moment, she thought she really would throw up. She leaned forward a little and took several slow breaths through her teeth as she tried holding back the rising bile.

"Nila, what's wrong?" Mitch put a hand on her shoulder and tried to turn her to face him.

"Wouldn't do that. Feel like I'm gonna barf."

"We should get her someplace comfortable," Sanjay said. "She looks very pale."

"We can't go back to…where we've been staying," Mitch said.

"Our place isn't too far from here."

"Does she need to be carried?" one of the other men asked.

He sounded genuinely concerned, which surprised Nila.

"We can take turns if she's not able to walk," a third man said.

"No," Nila finally spoke up. She continued breathing deeply, and closed her eyes for a brief moment to settle herself, then straightened. "I'll stay on my feet. Thanks anyway."

"Which direction?" Mitch asked Sanjay.

When Sanjay pointed off to the right, Mitch took her by the elbow and motioned for the others to lead the way. His hold didn't interfere with her grip on the gun, yet his touch was comforting and reassuring. She smiled up at him. He nodded in acknowledgement then focused on the others, watching intently.

They walked for an hour and a half, and more than once during the journey, Nila thought she might pass out. So much for not too far.

Mitch shifted from a loose grip on her elbow to holding her around the waist, practically carrying her after a few miles. She hated putting so much burden on him—incase he needed to fight—so she stayed on her own feet, but barely and with only will keeping her upright.

"You sure you don't want me to carry you," Mitch murmured into her ear after she let the barrel of the gun slip and hit the ground. Again.

"No. If you have to fight, it'll be easier to just let go of me than it would be to drop me." If Mitch could move and shoot, she could always just lie down and fire her rifle at anything that got close. At this stage, that was all she'd be capable of.

One of the leading tigers dropped back to walk next to them. When he fell in beside Nila, Mitch growled and the young man jogged around to walk next to Mitch instead. Nila would have been amused if she wasn't so worried about something else going wrong.

"We're almost to our cabin," the young man assured her, his tone friendly. "I'm Richard, by the way." He looked directly at her when he introduced himself. "You'll be able to rest there, and eat."

"I'm a vegetarian," she muttered. She'd always found it a good idea to warn people about that before they tried feeding her.

The news earned her a surprised frown from Richard and for the first time he glanced at Mitch. "She doesn't eat meat?"

Mitch shook his head.

"But, how is that possible?"

Nila gaped at the young man. "It's possible by me not actually taking meat into my mouth and swallowing it."

She paused after she'd made her claim and realized with growing embarrassment that if he were so inclined, Richard could take that statement in an entirely different way than intended. Heat crawled over her cheeks. She glanced away, hoping no one noticed her blush. Given the state of her, a red face could easily be attributed to the day's heat.

Mitch chuckled and she knew he'd picked up the accidental double entendre. Her cheeks warmed further.

To Richard, Mitch said, "She's not like us, even if her mother was a tiger."

"But…but she's still…"

When Richard trailed off, Nila glanced at him. He was frowning at the ground. "I'm still what?" she asked.

"Well, it's still possible, right? For you to mate with a tiger?"

Being asked outright left her flummoxed. She didn't know what to say.

But maybe it was better if all these men didn't believe she could give them children. She was very outnumbered here, and according to Mitch, and Irina and Max for that matter, most males were not likely to get a mate. Their desperation wouldn't work in her favor.

Richard's nostrils flared and his chest expanded as he breathed in deeply. Then he smiled. "I'm sure everything will work out," he said.

She knew the smile and tone were meant to be reassuring, but since the expression never reached his green eyes, Nila remained wary. Richard trotted back to join the others several yards ahead.

When he was gone, Mitch's arm tightened around her waist. "Stay near me. I don't trust these guys."

"You're not the only one."

They finally reached a huge multi-story cabin near the edge of a small lake. Nila took in the area, noting the beautiful setting and the luxury of the house. But she was too exhausted to really appreciate any of it. If she didn't get some food soon, she'd move past hunger into that nauseous place where she wouldn't be able to eat. Or she'd pass out.

Sanjay dropped back to them, stopping just in front of Mitch and gesturing at the cabin. "Welcome. This is our shared home. You can stay here as long as you like. Whatever we have is yours."

This last he said directly to Nila, a very slight smile curving his lips. She decided to ignore the possible innuendo and instead said, "I just need something to eat. Then Mitch and I have a few things to discuss."

Like what they were going to do now. Did they dare go back to John's cabin, or did they have to find a way to a new safe house now? She still had the phone. They could call someone to come help them. But who could they trust? And how would they avoid Petrov finding out where they were again? She was sure he hadn't left the area.

"You can stay as long as you like," Sanjay said. "We'll help protect you, Nila. Petrov and his followers won't dare attack you here with so many males to defend you."

"Uh, thanks. I appreciate the offer." She wasn't about to commit to anything, but she didn't want to reveal her distrust too blatantly.

"I'm sure you'll find the place to your liking. You won't ever want to leave." Sanjay smiled broadly.

Nila was sure he was still trying to be reassuring and friendly, but all she could think about was serial killers and cults. Did tiger shifters have cults? Or serial killers?

Shit.

Chapter Twenty

Sanjay led them into the house. The others had already gone inside. They reappeared fully dressed shortly after she and Mitch stepped through the front door. The clothing was something of a relief. She wasn't used to feeling quite so overdressed just having clothing on.

Nila stopped just inside the front door and stared. The house was as luxurious inside as it appeared outside. Thick rugs covered hardwood floors. Two circular stairways at opposite ends of the large main room lead to the upper levels. Off to the right, a bright open plan kitchen took up an entire corner of the house.

The living room boasted a giant fireplace against one wall and floor to ceiling windows looking out over the lake. The room had high ceilings, making the first floor feel even larger. To the left a hall led into other parts of the house.

Nila was nearly overwhelmed. The house reminded her of the kind of places you saw in architecture or interior design magazines. Everything was so clean and neatly arranged.

There were even flowers in a glass vase on the coffee table in the middle of the sitting area in front of the fireplace.

Flowers?

That wasn't the only detail that struck her as…well a little odd for a cabin retreat for a collection of men. There was no television in the living room, no radio, no technology of any kind. Even John had a radio in his place. Maybe they just didn't like technology, but still…

There weren't any empty beer cans, no random food containers or cups left behind. The place was spotless. The throw pillows on the couch were fluffed and perfectly arranged. The rugs covering the floor were angled to accent different areas.

They either had a maid who looked after things for them, they were an unusual collective of men, or there was a woman living here somewhere.

The whole thing felt very…strange. The place was not consistent with her preconceived notions of men out camping in the backwoods.

Maybe you should dump preconceived notions when it comes to tiger shapeshifters, she thought.

Sanjay showed her and Mitch to the couch. She set her gun on the floor at her feet, since the weapon would be unwieldy in close confines anyway, but noticed Mitch kept his gun close to hand. They'd barely sat when platters of food started appearing before them. She smiled when she noticed the only plate with meat on it was set in front of Mitch.

The men were all very polite and solicitous. Would you like something to drink? How do you take your tea? Do you need more cheese? We can make a full brunch if you're still hungry.

They'd set enough food in front of her to feed three people, so she assured them she was fine. Once Mitch confirmed he was satisfied, each of the men finally introduced themselves.

She was trying to focus on one man at a time, and failing miserably at remembering names, when a handsome Asian man stepped forward. He had short cropped black hair and deep brown eyes. Bowing his head in greeting, he introduced himself as Dr. Ryan Yin.

His mention of being a doctor piqued her interest. "Where do you practice? What's your specialty?"

Ryan smiled. "I'm a surgeon. I work in Boston, but I'm on leave at the moment."

She was about to ask another question when he was nudged aside by yet another man, this one blond-haired and blue-eyed who introduced himself as Jim.

She smiled and nodded as each man made a play for her attention. There were more than the original seven she realized, looking around the large sitting area. At least ten, maybe twelve men hovered near. The realization made her swallow hard.

After the rush of introductions and attempts to stand out from one another, Nila finally held up a hand and asked for a break. "Just a little fresh air. I'm so full now I'm getting sleepy."

"You can take a nap if you like," one of the men, she thought his name was Pat, pushed close to say. "We have plenty of beds. You're welcome to any of them. Mine is just down the hall there." He pointed to show the way.

"No. That's fine. I don't really need a nap. Just some air." She turned to face a scowling Mitch. "Will you walk out onto the porch with me?"

She considered picking up her rifle but was afraid the males would view that as a threat so she left the weapon on the floor. When Mitch left his gun leaning against the side of the couch, he confirmed her thinking. They had to be careful here. Antagonizing the group would be bad. She wasn't sure how much use the guns would be against so many shifters anyway.

As she and Mitch headed toward the glass doors leading to the balcony, the entire group followed them, but Mitch kept the tide back with a glare and a growled, "She'll be safe with me."

Once they were outside, Nila noticed the multi-layer wooden porch up the back of the house led down to the lake. Mitch walked her to one of the lower levels. She knew the others could still see them from the house if they made an effort to look, but the distance provided a little breathing space.

"This is overwhelming and scary," she murmured, knowing the others probably heard her anyway. "Why are they being so…attentive?"

"You're a female who can give them children. At least that's what they think. Hope. All the males in the area will be courting you soon."

"Oh, god, I hope not."

It was on the tip of her tongue to ask if she couldn't just tell them she was with Mitch and put an end to the attention, but she didn't want to force him into anything. They'd had one amazing night together, and they'd gotten a lot out on the table. But she hadn't even had time to fully process her feelings for him. She needed more time to talk with him about his situation and where that left them. She just didn't want to do that here. Until they talked more, she didn't feel she could lay any claims on the man.

And she was scared.

What if he didn't want more than sex? What if, despite what she'd said about his status, he felt it was a wall between them that couldn't be breached? What if he didn't want to breach that wall for her? Sex and lust didn't translate into deeper feelings. She might be falling, but that didn't mean he was.

She'd deal with that when the time came, though she was afraid the news might break her heart. In the meantime, she didn't want to rush the conversation. They had more than enough to deal with at the moment.

"They'll keep a respectful distance," Mitch said. "For now. But this is something you'll eventually have to deal with. You'll probably need to establish a territory. They'll respect that and stay away unless invited."

"A territory? How the hell do I do that? And more importantly how do I do that when I'm currently on the run?"

He pulled in a deep breath, his chest expanding and drawing her attention. Swallowing back a little rush of desire, she looked out over the lake in an attempt to keep her mind on the conversation. Oak and hickory covered the area, the oak coming close to the water's edge near the cabin, leaving a small beach below the porch. A wooden dock stuck out into the lake, but no boats were tethered. The water sparkled in the hot August sunshine, making Nila crave a dip as sweat dripped down her back from just the few minutes she'd been outside.

"For now," Mitch said, "we'll worry about keeping you alive. Once Petrov is out of the picture, you can figure out the territory thing. It shouldn't be too hard. You just need a base, a house or cabin or something, and then let it be known that's your space. No one is allowed in unless invited. Then don't invite anyone."

Would you come if I invited? But she couldn't say that out loud. As far as she knew, he intended to go back to his life after Petrov was captured. He'd told her he wasn't in the running as a possible mate. He'd explained why she shouldn't even consider him. She was torturing herself imagining the what-ifs.

"Would the males just stay away? What keeps them from… ignoring my territorial boundaries?"

"Custom, law, tradition, instinct."

"Can I ask an odd question?" She looked up to see him grinning at her.

"Given what's been going on the last week, I doubt what you have to ask is as 'odd' as what you've learned."

"True." She smiled and looked back at the lake to avoid getting lost in his gaze. "Tigers in the wild are solitary and only come together to mate, while tiger shifters obviously aren't so solitary since they get married. But, this place… Is it…?" She was going to say "normal" but given none of this was normal, her question seemed absurd.

"You're wondering if it's usual for this many tigers to live in one cabin?" Mitch finished for her.

"Yeah."

"It's not normal at all. We don't gather up in groups and live together like this. Families, parents and children, live together, and sometimes those families are large. But even extended families tend to leave space between their homes. Uncles and aunts, cousins and grandparents won't live next door to one another, nonetheless in a single home. We're an independent species, and we like our space."

"So, if this is odd, then we might have gone from the frying pan into the fire?"

He glanced over his shoulder back at the house. "For now, you're safe enough. They all want to make a good impression on you, and they definitely don't want you dead."

"Which is a step up from Petrov."

"But we're seriously outnumbered."

"I noticed."

"And I'm worried their attention might get a little too… aggressive."

"Fantastic," she muttered with no little sarcasm. "So what do we do? Safe for now isn't all that safe. But Petrov knows where we were staying. He's probably watching the place."

"Don't suppose you have the cellphone?"

She patted her hip pocket.

"I think we can risk a phone call."

"Who?"

"Elizaveta. She can send someone else to help."

"Why her? Why not Irina and Max? They're closer and they know where we are."

"I'd rather not get Irina involved. I don't want her risking her pregnancy."

Nila frowned up at him. "Why is everyone so worried about her pregnancy? Is it difficult for tiger shifters to carry to term?"

"No. Once we conceive, we generally have the same success rate as humans in bringing healthy children into the world. We're so protective of Irina because her scans have shown she's having a girl."

Nila straightened. "Ah. Now I get it."

"The female tiger who can conceive a female child is also considered extremely valuable. We not only want Irina's baby safe, we want her safe."

"And if Max tries helping us, Irina will follow."

Mitch chuckled. "I doubt he'd be able to stop her. She's very strong willed."

"Who do you think your grandmother will send, then? It'll have to be someone you trust."

"I have a few friends on this coast that can help if they know where we are. She'll contact one of them."

"One? Maybe she better send in the cavalry." Nila glanced back at the house then met Mitch's gaze.

He pursed his lips, frowning in thought. "The only problem with sending more tigers to protect you is that it might spark fighting with this group. I don't know why they're gathered here, I don't know what's going on with them, but adding too many additional males to the mix can only complicate things.

One trusted friend coming to give us a lift out of the area will be less threatening."

She conceded his point with a shrug. "Should I call my dad?" she asked as she pulled out the phone. "I'm still worried Petrov will go after him and my grandma."

"You'll worry your father if you call before we have a safe place to stay. Petrov knows where you are now. He'll continue coming after you directly. He doesn't need your family."

She stared at Mitch without responding.

He sighed. "Will it make you feel better to talk to him?"

"Yes."

"Okay. I'll call my grandmother. Then you call you father. But be brief." He nodded toward the house. "They're hearing some of what we say."

Worry made a fist in her stomach as she waited for Mitch to finish his call. She stared at the lake, trying to let it sooth her, but she practically felt the looming house behind her like a hunting animal crouching in the tall grass. The hairs on the back of her neck rose, and she shivered despite the summer heat.

CHAPTER TWENTY-ONE

When Mitch finished his call, he handed Nila the phone, a pensive expression on his face.

"What did Elizaveta say?"

"She's worried about us being here. There are rumors of young males gathering in groups. The elders are…leery. The young males haven't actually done anything yet."

"Yet being the operative word?"

He nodded. "There've been rumblings, dissatisfaction, issues with the Mate Run. She doesn't want us staying here. Since we have no way to leave just yet, though, we'll have to take the risk. At least for tonight. Sanjay was right. Petrov won't try attacking this place with so many males. Hopefully, my grandmother can get someone here by morning."

His frown deepened as he glanced up at the house.

"What's wrong now?" she asked, though there was already so much wrong, she couldn't imagine what else might worry him. Her nerves were lit up with the anxiety crawling over her skin. She wasn't sure she could take any more.

"I'm wondering why I didn't pick up signs of them before. I didn't smell any of them in the territory I explored around John's place. Only Max and Irina."

"Maybe they've been avoiding that area because of Max and Irina?"

"Possibly. But I went through the woods beyond where Max normally goes when he's here. Not that much farther, but enough I should have scented…something."

"How far are we from John's? Quite a ways, right? You never explored too far because you never wanted to leave me alone for long. Maybe you just didn't get far enough out in the right direction. Maybe they spend most of their time in the woods in the complete opposite direction from John's."

"Why would they, though? John is human. Max isn't here all the time. It's not Irina's territory. Why avoid that direction?" He put his hands on his hips and his frown turned into a full scowl.

She wanted to shrug off his concern, but she was too nervous about the situation to believe her own excuses. If Mitch was worried, she was sure the reasons were valid. "Whether it's coincidence or not, we'll be safer somewhere else."

"Agreed."

"Did your grandmother say who she was going to call?"

"My grandmother never says anything over the phone. I'll know I can trust the person she sends when I see him."

"How did you let her know where we are?"

"I gave her the rough distance and direction from John's cabin. She knows were that is already."

"From when you talked to her earlier in the week?"

"We haven't been that detailed on the phone. I gave hints for her to research. Things only she would pick up on. She confirmed her knowledge in ways only immediate family would understand." His dark expression finally softened. "We actually have a secret family code. My grandmother is… Well, she's a little paranoid and very sneaky—don't ever tell her I said that." He pointed a finger at Nila in warning.

She raised a hand, palm facing him. "Swear I'll keep that to myself."

He almost smiled as he held her gaze. "I can't wait for you to meet her."

"I'm looking forward to it." Though she had mixed feelings about Elizaveta, she really was looking forward to meeting the woman face to face. It was obvious Mitch loved her, and her own grandmother had spoken fondly of her Russian friend for years. Nila's curiosity was peaked.

But Nila knew Elizaveta intended on pressuring her into marrying and having children with a tiger shifter. The only tiger shifter Nila wanted anything to do with had already made it clear he wasn't an option, despite what had happened last night.

Nila shook off this line of thought. She couldn't worry about the future when she was worried about the here and now. They were surrounded by all these tigers she couldn't trust. In fact, she'd yet to meet a tiger besides Mitch, Max, and Irina who didn't give her the creeps. Even her own half brother—the one not trying to kill her—had freaked her out. That didn't bode well for Elizaveta's plans of marrying Nila off to a tiger shifter.

Unless the elders let Nila choose Mitch…

She let her gaze roam over his handsome face, down across his beautiful body as thoughts of their night together teased her. If not for their current predicament, she'd find it so easy to drag him into the woods, strip him naked, and fuck him until they were both boneless heaps of satisfaction. The temptation of his heat and scent drew her a step closer to him.

She considered the way he'd protected her today, the way he was still protecting her and had been since they'd met. Strong and independent as she was, it still gave her a little feminine thrill to have such a powerful man guarding her back. There was so much about him she admired, so much she liked, even without the phenomenal sex.

Nila sighed and looked back at the lake. While she might not be in love with Mitch yet, she was definitely falling.

"You going to call your father?" he asked, breaking into her thoughts.

Before she could answer, though, a deep voice rolled down to them from the top level of the porch.

"Hello. May I join you? I'm Gregory."

Mitch stared up at the man standing above them. His every instinct shuddered at the vulnerable position he and Nila were in, but he tried not letting it show. Instead, he studied the newcomer. The man was young, strong, with short-cropped brown hair and dark eyes.

There was something strange about him, too. Gregory descended the steps, approaching them slowly and openly to avoid any appearance of threat. Mitch pulled in a deep breath. Something wasn't quite right about Gregory's scent signature.

The young man held out his hand to Mitch, his grip firm but not aggressive. "I'm very glad to meet you. Any male who protects an unattached female the way you have is a worthy man to call friend. I hope my associates have been making you comfortable and at home."

"Everything's been fine. Thanks." Mitch tried pinpointing what was wrong with the young man's scent but couldn't place it. Something was just…off.

Gregory turned to Nila and smiled. "Nila De Luca. It's a great pleasure to meet you. I'm very glad you've chosen to take refuge here with us."

Mitch watched Nila's expression closely. She gave the young tiger a tight, closed lip smile and quickly pulled her hand away from his friendly handshake.

"Are you enjoying the scenery?" Gregory asked her, gesturing toward the lake.

"It's lovely here. How long have you all had this place?"

Mitch wanted to hug her for that question. From her, the curiosity would seem harmless. But knowing just how long all these males had been collected here was important.

"I've owned the cabin for a couple of months. We're still getting to know the place ourselves."

"Well, it's beautiful," Nila said. "If I had a home like this, I'd want to spend the entire summer here. Do you live far?"

"This is actually my primary home now."

"Lucky you."

A hum of unease curled through Mitch's blood, adding to his already edgy state. They had to get out of here. Soon.

Gregory continued exchanging small talk with Nila, leaving Mitch to study his scent. A tang of unpleasantness that he couldn't find human words for wove through it, like the sharp bite of sour chemicals coating a piece of overripe fruit. The combination left a bad taste in Mitch's mouth.

Their situation just kept getting worse. Maybe he should take Nila and run tonight, hide in the wilderness where no other tiger could get to her. The need to get her away from Gregory was almost overwhelming, and without thought he moved closer to her so their arms touched. The contact with her calmed some of his unease, but he still wanted to scoop her up and take off into the trees.

Gregory finally turned back to Mitch and said, "You made a call. I hope there isn't a problem."

"No problem. Just needed to check in with my grandmother to arrange a ride out of the area and let her know about Petrov. The Trackers should reach him soon."

"You're welcome to stay as long as you like. Or we can arrange something once Petrov is taken care of." Gregory's head tilted very slightly to one side. "I heard the elders had sent Trackers after him. Who's your grandmother?"

"Elizaveta Chernikova."

"The female elder? I didn't realize. You must be…Mikhail? Or Dmitry? You're too young to be Nikolai."

"Mikhail." He didn't bother giving Gregory his more commonly used and preferred nickname. Best this cub remembered exactly who Mitch's grandmother was, even if his own status wasn't all that impressive. Most of the tigers were, if not in awe of the elders, then at least respectful of their authority and cautious of their wrath. And Elizaveta's wrath was the stuff of legend. If Mitch was lucky, Gregory was too young to realize that wrath couldn't protect her grandsons.

"It's a pleasure to meet one of the infamous Chernikov brothers," Gregory said with a slight bow of his head.

So much for luck, Mitch thought. The "infamous Chernikov brothers" tale almost always included the fact that their grandmother wasn't able to protect them.

"Mikhail," Gregory continued, his tone thoughtful. "You're close with Maxim Rudikov and Irina Gorban, aren't you?"

There was a sharp tension in the question that made Mitch narrow his eyes. "I've been friends with Maxim since we were kids. You know them?"

"We're acquainted." Gregory forced a tight-lipped smile that didn't reach his eyes. "Well, I've taken up enough of your time. I'm sure you two are still discussing a lot. Make yourselves comfortable here. You're welcome to stay as long as you like."

He held Mitch's gaze for a moment. The sour chemical smell seemed to intensify. Mitch swallowed an instinctive growl of warning, even as he moved to stand just in front of Nila, protecting her from whatever was wrong with the young male.

When Gregory faced her again, his smile took on a more genuine air. "Please, consider this your home. We'll do whatever it takes to make sure you're content and safe here."

Mitch watched him stalk slowly back up to the house, waiting until he was sure the young tiger had gone inside before looking away.

"What the hell was all that about?" Nila murmured as soon as he faced her again.

"There's something wrong him. I'm not sure what. His scent is off."

"I could have told you that. There's something a little, I don't know, desperate in his eyes. A little feral maybe? I couldn't pinpoint it either, but he gave me the creeps. This whole house gives me the creeps. And what was all that undertone when he mentioned your friendship with Max and Irina?"

"I'm guessing he knows them and for some reason doesn't like them. Which means he isn't inclined to like me either. But now that he knows who I am, I'm hoping he'll be cautious about me."

She nibbled her bottom lip a moment. Then she frowned up at him. "You said your grandmother can't protect you, so why would he be cautious?"

He flinched inwardly at her comment. He'd hated telling her the story of his father's crimes. He hated talking about the whole situation, especially since his own knowledge of it came from other people.

But another part of him was relieved. She understood his position now. She would have to accept he wouldn't make a good mate.

That thought tightened a knot in his chest and his tiger growled in protest. He wanted to be a good mate for her. He wanted her to consider him.

His conscience wouldn't allow him to encourage her, though, despite what had happened last night. He gave in to his own weakness. He'd suffer for it later, when she went to another man, but he could be strong now and make sure she was safe.

"All that fighting my brothers and I had to do made us formidable," he finally said. "We ended up with a reputation that's made our adult lives a little easier. A little."

"So you think they won't want to start a fight with you because you'll kick their asses?"

"Exactly."

When she smiled, Mitch wanted to puff up his chest with pride. The reaction made him feel like a fool but what the hell. He wanted to impress her. His tiger wanted her to know how strong he was—even if that strength wasn't the kind she needed.

Her smile fell away when she asked, "These young men, knowing who you are, they won't consider you a…contender for me, will they?"

"No one will. I can't command the necessary influence to keep you safe long term."

She tilted her head to one side. "And they think they can? Who are they?"

"All the unmated males will still try courting you, Nila, even if they aren't powerful enough. You need to choose someone strong, though, because of those who think the way Petrov does."

She shook her head and faced the lake. "Stupid."

"What?"

"This. Whole. Thing. I am not a commodity, and I am not choosing a husband or whatever based on power."

"Then you and your family will be in danger for the rest of your lives. And you will always be on the run."

"No."

She said it so matter-of-factly, he didn't actually know how to respond. "Nila, you can't avoid the situation. It is what it is."

"I don't give a fuck, any more than I give a fuck about your status. I'm not running for the rest of my life, and I'm not going to choose a life partner just because of his power base. I'm just not. I don't know how to get out of it, but this cannot be the state of my life."

What could he say to that? He didn't have any answers. He hated that he couldn't fix this mess for her. Hated more than anything that he couldn't wave his hand and make her world right again. He'd give up a lot to do that for her.

He gestured back toward the house. "We have other things to worry about at the moment."

She followed his gaze. "I do not want to go back into that house."

Her voice was so low he barely heard her. He gave in to his weakness again, just a little, and squeezed her hand. The brief touch sent a wave of possessiveness through him. He ignored the sensation and said, "Why don't you call your father? You'll feel better."

He moved off a few feet to give her a little privacy but stayed near enough to reach her in a few strides.

The problem of Gregory and the other young males gnawed at him.

He absolutely did not want to take Nila back into that house.

CHAPTER TWENTY-TWO

Since they were in agreement about the house, they stalled and stayed outside as long as they could. They took a walk down to the dock once Nila finished talking with her father. She was aware of the house behind them, looming and watching. She never could see the men near the windows, but she felt them staring, waiting, following her movements.

"We'd be safer disappearing into the trees," she said when they stood at the very edge of the dock. The water lapped gently at the wood pilings, a cool, tempting retreat from the day's heat. The sun beat down on them, but clouds piled up along the distant hills.

"They'd be able to track us. And so would Petrov. I'm sure he's sent someone to find us while others watch John's cabin."

"And the elders' Trackers? Where the hell are they?"

"Circling in on Petrov as we speak."

"So shouldn't he be running?"

"He's too determined. And he's too close to our location."

"But he won't attempt to get at us here? Out here on this dock?"

"Not with all those males back their watching your every move."

She shivered. His words echoed her thoughts. "They are watching us, aren't they?"

"Of course."

Without consciously deciding to, she took a step closer to Mitch, near enough to feel his body heat and soak up a little of his strength. She couldn't remember ever feeling so vulnerable. She hated it. Hell, even having a gun pressed into her back hadn't made her feel this exposed.

She wanted to wrap her arms around Mitch and hide in the security of him. She was standing close enough. All she'd have to do is turn a little to her right and raise her arms.

She didn't. "I hate this," she said aloud. "I hate being hunted and stalked and watched."

"I know," he murmured. "I'm sorry."

"Why? You haven't done anything but help me."

"I just mean, I don't like that you have to go through all this either."

"I resent that my choices are being determined by things that have nothing to do with me," she hissed as the anger found root and grew with each word. "I am really pissed off that people I didn't even know existed until a week ago think they can kill me just for being born. I hate that others have decided I'm some sort of prize to be won. And I refuse to be a martyr or a messiah to the tiger shifters. I want my life back."

"I'd give you that if I could," Mitch said, his voice low and deep.

"Then do." She turned to face him. "I don't give a damn about your status."

"So you've said. But you need to care."

"Shut up and listen to me. I don't care about your status." She closed the space between them so they were a breath apart, chest to chest, thigh to thigh. She tilted her head up so she could meet his gaze. "You are the only person I have felt safe with since this mess started. You're the only one I've felt normal around. Like myself and not some genetic freak."

"Nila…"

"No. No excuses. Last night I finally found myself again, and being with you felt right. So no more 'I'm not an option' bullshit. I refuse to buy it."

"It's a fact. You might feel safe with me, but I can't keep you safe the way another male might be able to."

"I don't care. Don't you get it? I want my life back. I want my choices back. And you are my choice. I want you."

Silence settled between them with her declaration. She stared up at him, breathing hard, terrified that he'd reject her. She didn't have answers. She didn't know how to fix all this. The only thing she knew was that she wanted Mitch, here and now and for the foreseeable future.

Afraid and a little desperate, she placed her hand on his chest. The rapid thump of his heart against her palm sent a shiver through her body. He was still shirtless, so nothing blocked her from soaking in his heat, savoring the smooth strength of his muscles, the crisp contrast of his chest hair. She swallowed to wet her dry throat and forced herself to hold his gaze.

"The others are watching." His voice was harsh and quiet, sounding strained.

"I don't care about that either."

"Kinky," he murmured.

The comment took her so completely by surprise in the otherwise serious moment, she laughed. She couldn't help it. He charmed her even in the worst circumstances, and she felt herself falling a little more.

To her relief, he reached up and cupped her cheek with one hand. She nuzzled into the touch as a sigh shuddered out of her. "Mitch, please…"

"You're asking for the impossible."

"Not impossible, just not easy."

He held her gaze for another long moment. Her own pulse was pumping hard, fear and hope tightening her chest. Her body was alive with nervous energy and that ever present need for him.

"Nila." With painful slowness, he lowered his head close to hers, bringing his mouth to her lips. "You don't understand what you're asking for, what you're committing to."

"Yes, I do."

"Whether you do or not, it's too late now."

His mouth found hers, hard and hungry. He tasted of need.

Nila sighed into the kiss, finally pressing against him fully, relief and an echoing hunger rushing through her as she wrapped her arms around his neck. Her every cell screamed,

This! Whatever the future held, this was what she wanted—this heat, this moment, this passion. And the rest of the world would just have to deal with it.

Aware of their audience, she hugged closer to Mitch, knowing a kiss was all they could indulge in, but she wanted all those other males to realize her choice had been made. She was with Mitch, in every way possible.

Angling her head, she opened to him as he deepened the contact. The taste of him sent her senses swirling, and some of the fear that had haunted her since their run from John's cabin eased, replaced by growing passion and an edge of desperation. She needed him, more than she'd ever needed a man before. To prove she was alive. To prove she still had a say in her future. To make her forget everything else.

His arms tightened around her waist, flattening her against his chest, and she groaned in satisfaction. She rubbed her breasts against him, gently, subtly, and savored the flexing of his fingers against her skin.

He broke the kiss first, pulling back reluctantly but firmly. "We need to stop. Or we really will give our audience a show."

She grinned. "It might not be such a terrible thing if they did see."

His eyebrows popped up. "You really are an exhibitionist."

Chuckling, she shook her head. "No, that's not my particular brand of kink. But they'll at least realize I'm not available."

"They might not."

"What do you mean?" Her humor faded.

"Remember, as far as tiger shifters are concerned, until you conceive, you're not mated. They might decide I'm your current choice, the winner of the proverbial Run. But that doesn't take you out of the running, so to speak."

"So much for the effectiveness of our show."

He brushed his lips across hers. "It affected me."

His wicked comment sent little flutters of excitement through her stomach, and she smiled again. "How do you do that? Make me smile when I'm busy being worried?"

"I don't know." He ran a finger over her cheek and across her lower lip. "But I'm glad I can because I love your smile."

Her pulse thumped faster. Funny how such a little compliment could turn her to total mush.

"So what is your particular kink?"

His change of subject made her blink. "Sorry?"

"You said exhibitionism wasn't your brand of kink. What is?"

"Oh, we should definitely save that conversation for a later date. Otherwise, we really will give our audience a show."

"I'll hold you to that."

He leaned in and kissed her again, gently, but tension tightened his muscles under her touch. Before they could get carried away, a loud throat clearing broke the moment. Nila glanced back up the dock, trying to pull her thoughts back to their current predicament. Sanjay stood several yards away, giving them space but not privacy.

"Gregory sent me to ask if you would come back up to the house. He would like to talk with you both."

"Something serious?" Mitch asked without loosening his hold on her.

"No. It's just rare to have a female and the grandson of an elder here at the same time. He's curious and wants to get to know you both better."

"He does, does he?" Mitch said. "Tell me, Sanjay, is your sense of smell okay?"

"Why do you ask?" Sanjay straightened his shoulders, looking almost offended.

Nila wondered at Mitch's question, too. What did Sanjay's sense of smell have to do with anything?

"Just curious. Is Gregory the organizer of this house?"

"He brought us together, yes."

Mitch nodded. "Tell him we'll be up in a few minutes."

Sanjay hesitated, as if he intended to wait for them. Finally, he said, "Don't keep him waiting long. Please." The please sounded forced.

"What's going on?" she asked when she heard the door above them close behind Sanjay.

"They should all know Gregory isn't right, smell it like I do. Hell, you're human and you can tell he's wrong. But they're following him, making him a kind of leader."

"You're making that sound like a very bad thing."

"It might be. For now though, let's not antagonize him. The longer we keep the peace, the better chance we have of getting away from here without a fight. We need to give whoever my grandmother called time to reach us."

She was loath to go back up to that den of tigers.

When she didn't move, he cupped her cheek and made her look at him, turning her away from the house. "I'll be right with you. Don't worry. You'll be safe."

She forced a smile. "I know I'm safe with you."

But would he be safe with the others? Would his reputation be enough to keep them from trying to hurt him?

She sure as hell hoped so.

Chapter Twenty-Three

They slowly walked to the house, delaying their return for as long as possible before finally stepping back inside the spotlessly clean, artfully decorated, and immensely uncomfortable main room. Gregory was sitting in a chair next to the fireplace. He stood when they entered and smiled. Showing teeth.

Nila held back a shudder, but inside she cringed away from Gregory. She wasn't sure what it was about him, but she didn't want to get too close. She looked toward the couch to see if their guns were still there and was surprised to see the weapons where she and Mitch had left them. But going for the gun would let the group know exactly how nervous she was—even if they didn't already. Mitch was right, it was better if they didn't antagonize Gregory.

He gestured to a couple of additional seats by the fire. Unable to ignore his offer, she sat in one and pasted on an expression she hoped passed for a smile. To her relief, Mitch actually sat on the arm of her chair rather than taking a separate seat.

She took a moment to study Gregory as he sat. He was very handsome, almost as good-looking as Mitch in an objective way. He was thickly muscled and tall with light brown hair, dark eyes, and strong features. At a glance, she might not have thought anything was wrong with him. He was also incredibly polite to them both, offering drinks and food, and reiterating his promise of sanctuary from Petrov.

But he sat like a king on a throne, commanding the other men hovering around the main room, and she just couldn't get past that glittering something in his eyes.

"We've only heard a little about you so far, Nila. You're a veterinarian?"

"I am. My specialty is big cats."

He smiled. "Appropriate. Did your father approve that choice?"

"Actually, he and my grandmother tried getting me to specialize in small animals, pets, something that would keep me closer to home."

"Of course." He nodded. "They tried keeping you from your tiger heritage."

"Not exactly." She didn't feel the need to explain her father's professed reasons for keeping her ignorant of her mother, but she also didn't want this strange man judging her family's motives. He had no right and not near enough information to attempt to condemn her dad for what he'd done.

She didn't want to start a fight, though, so she changed the subject. "What made you choose this location for your home?

The lake is beautiful but this place is very remote. Did you spend time here before? Are you from Maryland?"

Gregory's gaze shifted slightly. Did he realize she was looking for answers? Maybe he just assumed she didn't want to talk about her family.

"I was originally from Baltimore."

"That's how you know Max and Irina, then?"

"Yes."

"Did you know they have a friend who owns a cabin nearby? That was actually where we were staying." She hoped her questions sounded innocent and curious, but there was no telling what he thought from his expression.

"Really? I had no idea."

He was lying. Blandly and without really trying to hide it. He glanced at Mitch when he spoke, holding his gaze. Neither man flinched or turned for long moments. The tension in the air had the other men edging closer. Nila's fear spiked.

"Must be a popular area," she said, attempting to diffuse the situation, "if you're looking for a little isolation. And it really is beautiful here. Just gorgeous. Mitch, maybe we should look at cabins here, too." Her rambling brought the attention of both men back to her.

Mitch smiled just slightly, and she wondered if his approval was for the way she'd lightened the moment or for her reference to them as a couple. He'd told her the others wouldn't consider her "mated" until she got pregnant. But it couldn't hurt to emphasize that Mitch was her choice for all this mate business.

Gregory's expression was less approving, though not outright hostile. He looked curious. "Nila, did Mikhail tell you about the Mate Run?"

"He did."

"So you understand how we…do things. How mates are chosen?"

"I understand the elders have put a sort of competition into place to help protect the few remaining females."

"That's one way to look at it." He glanced at Mitch then met her gaze again. "I participated in the Mate Runs for Irina."

That got her attention. Though why she was surprised, she wasn't sure. Of course Gregory had run after Irina. He lived on this coast and she had been one of the few females available. She glanced at the other men. "Did all of you…run?"

"Not all," Gregory answered. "But most. Obviously to little effect."

"Hard to argue with love," she commented, holding Gregory's gaze with an effort.

He raised his brows. "Love? Love isn't the final deciding factor. Conception is. That's the only way we'll ever get a mate. We have to get a female pregnant."

Something in the way he spoke made her want to hide in the chair. He made getting a woman pregnant sound like a threat, a committing of violence. She shifted a little, closer to Mitch.

"Do you approve of the Run?" Gregory asked her.

"I don't really know enough to make a judgment," she hedged.

"And what about you, Mikhail? Do you approve of the Run? You've run before, though not for Irina as I recall."

"I ran during her very first estrous," Mitch said.

Shock reverberated through Nila. She tried hiding the reaction. Again, she wasn't sure why this came as such a surprise. Mitch had admitted to running. Why would he not run after Irina?

Gregory watched her closely as he spoke. "I missed that first Run. But I was part of every one after that. For two years, Max was the only male who ever caught her."

"They fell in love on the first Run." Mitch's voice was quiet and his tone held an edge of something a lot sharper than his words warranted. "Lucky for them he managed to finally get her pregnant."

"Lucky," Gregory echoed, a faint growl to his words.

"Why didn't you continue to run?" one of the other males asked Mitch.

The question diverted another staring session between Mitch and Gregory.

"Max is my best friend," Mitch said. "He loved Irina."

"But there are so few females, didn't you want to at least try?" Richard asked.

Mitch stared at Richard a moment before saying, "Things worked out in the end." With a very purposeful glance at Nila, he placed a hand on her shoulder.

The atmosphere in the room tensed, and Nila swore she heard a soft growl from somewhere off to the left. She didn't dare turn to look, afraid of what she might see. Her pulse pounded hard. Could they tell, could they sense her growing fear...smell it? If Mitch smelled Gregory's unbalance, she was sure everyone in the room could sense her discomfort.

"Don't you intend to run, Nila?" Gregory asked.

She frowned. "I'm not like you. I can't do that."

"You realize what you represent, though? You know what you mean to the tigers? To the males here? You have to at least give us an opportunity to plead our case. It's only fair."

"Not sure what fair has to do with any of this," she said.

"Oh, I couldn't agree more," Gregory said. "The Mate Run isn't fair. Irina being allowed to let only one male catch her wasn't fair at all. That will have to change in the future."

"You mean you want the Run to end? Or are you saying you don't think the woman should have a choice in who she mates with?" Nila bit out the words, anger mixing with her fear.

Gregory's eyes narrowed. "With so few females, no one female should be allowed to limit herself to one male. At least until she conceives. Whether she runs or not."

The threat had Nila bristling and next to her Mitch stiffened. "But all your females do run, don't they?" Nila said, making a clear distinction between herself and a tiger female.

"They do. It's the law."

Again there was threat to Gregory's words.

"Maybe the law should change. Maybe the Run isn't the best answer anymore," Nila ventured, though feeling a lot less secure in her arguments now. She believed the tiger females should have a choice in mates, and she understood the logic behind the Run and how it had protected the females for a long time now. She wasn't sure it had outgrown its usefulness, but then she didn't know nearly enough about their situation to be sure.

What she did know was that she wasn't a tiger shifter, so she had no intention of running with a bunch of male tigers chasing her. She intended to choose her own partner. No matter what Gregory thought was fair.

"Actually, I think it has," he said. "I don't think the Run works for us anymore."

The fact that Gregory agreed with her statement made her rethink the position. "What would you propose, then?" she asked.

"I have a few ideas." He shifted his gaze to Mitch. "What do you think? Is the Mate Run the best option for us still?"

Mitch shrugged. "I don't know. If the males of our species could control their baser instincts, we wouldn't have needed it to begin with."

Nila swallowed a surprised gasp at Mitch's not so subtle jab at Gregory.

"But you don't approve of it, do you?" Gregory asked, ignoring the slight.

"Why do you assume that?"

Gregory glanced between Nila and Mitch. "You appear to want to bypass it now."

"Nila can't run."

Gregory didn't immediately respond. Nila swore all the men in the room took another step closer. She tensed, ready to launch off the seat and run for it if necessary. Which was ironic given the fact that they were talking about how she couldn't "run".

"Well, as I said, there are other ways to decide the strongest male," Gregory finally answered.

"Yes, there are." Mitch's voice was flat, direct.

Nila's gaze shifted between the two men. She knew Gregory had just challenged Mitch, and Mitch had accepted, but they wouldn't fight one of those death challenges that had been outlawed.

Would they?

Oh, she and Mitch had to get out of this house and soon. She didn't want to stay the night. She didn't want to stay till dinner.

To her amazement and relief, Gregory broke the unrelenting tension by smiling and standing. "Well, I don't know about you two, but I'm hungry. I had a late lunch readied. Please, join us."

He turned his back to Mitch, a snub, Nila was sure, and headed toward the hall leading off the main room. Reluctantly, she rose after Mitch and they followed the other men trailing Gregory. A few men tried flanking Mitch, but he paused and jerked his head in a gesture for all the men to proceed him down the hall. For a moment, she thought Richard and another male whose name she couldn't remember would refuse. But at a glance from Dr. Ryan Yin, the other two reluctantly moved on. Ryan held back, still walking in front of Mitch but close enough to talk to them.

"You'll have to forgive their attentions," he said to Nila. "They are all…well, we're all in a very awkward position as you might imagine. Your existence has given us renewed hope.

Unfortunately, since you're the only one of your kind, so far, you're taking the brunt of our eagerness."

"It's fine. Just so long as no one gets the wrong idea," she said, as firmly as her shaken nerves allowed. "I'm not a tiger shifter, and we don't even know yet if I can have children with a tiger, so there's no point in getting too excited about my existence."

Ryan studied her a moment. "You're right. But we are excited. A lot of the community will be happy to welcome you into the fold. My sister, Sarah, is a genetics researcher at Chernikov Labs. She's been on the front lines of the hunt for people like you. She'll be thrilled to meet you." His half smile faded as he said, "Not all tigers think like Petrov." He met her gaze over his shoulder. "Remember that."

He jogged forward to join the other males as they turned into an open doorway. Nila watched him disappear. Ryan didn't give her the creeps the way so many of the other males did. In fact, she thought she might like him if she'd met him somewhere besides this hideously perfect cabin. Glancing at Mitch, she noticed him also staring after the doctor.

"What are you thinking?" she whispered.

"Later," he muttered back.

Despite her curiosity, she held her tongue. Mitch insisted on walking just in front of her into the room, blocking her with his body. The move sent another warm rush of gratitude through her. She was afraid that falling sensation she'd been worried about just sped up. How was a woman supposed to resist falling in love with a man so willing to put himself between her and a room overflowing with threat and danger?

Swallowing, she kept close to Mitch's side as they were directed to two chairs near the head of the table, unfortunately close to Gregory.

She was not looking forward to this meal.

CHAPTER TWENTY-FOUR

Nila's nerves stayed on constant alert throughout the afternoon and evening. She was exhausted by the time they'd finished dinner, but there was no chance she was going to get much sleep. Not in this place.

As night fell, she made excuses to get out of the cabin, pleading a desire to watch the sun go down behind the mountains. Mitch stuck close to her, a constant, solid, reassuring presence. Many of the other males followed them outside but then disappeared into the woods, a move which both pleased Nila and left her suspicious.

Unfortunately, she and Mitch weren't left entirely alone as they had been earlier in the day, so they couldn't discuss anything. But Ryan was one of the men who stayed behind, and Nila found she could have a relatively pleasant conversation with him without feeling on constant alert.

Mitch made a point of touching her constantly, a message to the lingering men that she was taken. To her surprise, they all seemed to respect the body language and kept their distance.

Ryan even smiled at them when Mitch very pointedly dropped his arm around her shoulders.

As darkness filled in around the cabin, Nila tried relaxing against the railing of the upper deck. She refused a very politely offered beer and remained quiet, listening to the men talk. The conversation was all very casual—sports, weather, food. If she hadn't known better, she'd think this was just a group of friend out camping; nothing strange or dangerous about it.

The fact that Gregory had gone out into the woods probably helped. Now that she was watching, Nila noticed the subtle tension that infused the group whenever he was around. Ryan in particular seemed to grow watchful and wary. If she wasn't so worried for her own safety, she'd want to question those reactions, ask him why they were all here following a man they had to know was dangerous.

She didn't dare voice her concerns to anyone but Mitch, though.

When full dark brought out the quiet hoot and chirp of night animals, Nila realized no one had discussed the sleeping situation. Not like she was going to sleep, but what did they intend to do with her and Mitch overnight?

She got her answer a half hour later when the other males returned. Gregory came directly to Mitch and said, "There's no sign of Petrov in the area. But he's sent others to watch us. They're keeping a distance, for the moment."

Mitch nodded. "Suspected as much."

Where the hell were the Trackers? Nila wondered yet again. Why was Petrov still wandering around out there intent on killing her?

"Don't worry, you'll be safe here," Gregory said to her. "We'll set out a guard tonight, to patrol and make sure Petrov doesn't attempt anything."

"Thank you," she said.

The tactic was sound, she knew. But a part of her wondered if the guard was as much to keep her and Mitch in the cabin as it was to keep Petrov's people away.

Gregory smiled, a nice, friendly smile that would have been charming if not for his creepiness factor. "I'm sure the day has exhausted you. Sanjay will show you both to your rooms."

"I'll be staying with Nila," Mitch said.

Gregory's dark gaze flickered toward Mitch, but he continued smiling as he said, "Then, Sanjay, be sure to give them a room big enough for two."

To Nila's surprise, no one objected, none of those quiet growls filled the air, and the tension didn't suddenly spike. Had the others finally realized and accepted that she was not available? Or were they all just biding their time?

Either way, she wasn't going to push the matter. She'd had no intention of staying in a separate room from Mitch. At least this way, they wouldn't have to sneak around.

Nila yawned as Sanjay led them up one of the spiral staircases to the second floor. She cast Mitch a half smile. "Long day."

He nodded but his attention shifted quickly back to studying their surroundings. The room Sanjay showed them to was a large one with two twin beds. The pair of beds made her furrow her brow. The room was decorated in greens and tans. The large windows along one wall looked out over the lake. When

Nila moved closer, she noted the very long drop to the sloping ground below and the lack of any trees near enough to reach from the room.

"If you need anything during the night, please call. Someone is always awake and will be happy to help you."

He didn't close the door when he left so Mitch did. "No lock," he said without surprise.

"Would a lock help?"

"No." He faced her and nodded at the two beds. "They're not exactly subtle are they?"

"And that comment about someone always being awake? They obviously want us to know we're being watched."

"Even if there weren't guards inside the house, the guards patrolling the area would be hard to get around."

"So we're…what…prisoners here? Under the guise of being protected?"

He crossed to one of the beds and sat down, holding a hand out for her to join him. "I think we already knew that."

"Even if your friend shows up first thing in the morning, will we be able to get out of here without a fight?"

"It depends on who my grandmother sends."

Nila took his hand and let him pull her down onto his lap. "I'm not going to sleep tonight," she said. "I keep thinking someone will sneak in here and try to kill you in our sleep."

He tilted his head back to study her, brushing her hair behind her ear. "You're worried about what they'll do to me? What about you?"

"They don't want me dead, so I'm not the one in immediate danger."

"They do want you, though. And I'm afraid some of them wouldn't object to force."

"Gregory?"

Mitch nodded as he let his hand caress down her arm.

"During that weird conversation by the fire, you two had some underlying thing going on. What was that about? He said something about other ways beside the Run to choose a mate. He wasn't talking about those death matches that happened before the Run, was he?"

"Before the population crisis, challenge fights were highly ritualized and most males didn't die."

"That doesn't exactly answer my question." Nila tried not to panic. "Gregory challenged you to a fight, didn't he? Would he fight to the death?"

"I don't know. Yes, he was challenging me. For you."

"And you accepted?" She smacked him on the arm. "You idiot. Why the hell did you do that?"

"Ow," he said with a half grin, rubbing his bicep. "Don't worry. The challenge was for future reference. He was basically telling me that at some point we will fight, and I told him I did not intend on backing down."

"He's crazy. Why on earth would you fight with an obviously crazy person?"

"To keep him from hurting you," Mitch said, his voice quiet and sincere.

Nila's righteous anger withered and her insides turned to mush. She cupped his cheek in one hand. "I do not want you dying for me," she whispered. "I like you as you are. Very much alive."

"Same," he said.

He tunneled his fingers into her hair and pulled her close, kissing her, his mouth soft, his touch gentle. She settled her hands on his shoulders, feeling the tension in his bunched muscles. But none of that strain showed in his kiss, only languid warmth and seduction. With a sigh, she pulled back and touched his lips with her finger.

"I wish we could do more of this, but I keep imagining Sanjay listening at the door." She couldn't sense him there with that newly developed ability to know where the shifters were, but she'd had trouble with that since entering the house. There were just too damned many of them and all she felt was her own tension and anxiety.

Mitch grinned. "You're not too far off. Remember we've got excellent hearing. Most of the tigers in the house will be able to at least hear the tone of our conversation if not our words."

"Oh, good. So they all know I'm weirded out being here."

"If they didn't know that already, they're blind with no sense of smell." He kissed the tip of her nose. "We're talking quietly enough that most will only hear our tones. The tiger they've stationed down the hall will know what we're saying."

She glanced at the door. "Before we got here, I realized I was feeling the other shifters—Petrov's people."

"Really? Is that new?"

"It must be. Or if I was able to do it before, I didn't know what I was doing since I didn't know tiger shifters existed. Can you sense me?" She'd never thought to ask. He couldn't sense humans, but she wasn't completely human.

"Not the way I can other tigers."

"Huh. Interesting."

"Potentially useful."

"I don't know how useful. Since getting here, I haven't been able to pinpoint individual shifters anymore. I think my fear is interfering. Or maybe it's just the number of them." She leaned in and murmured against his ear, "You're sure there's someone as close as down the hall?"

He nodded.

"Can they hear me when I talk to you like this?"

He murmured back in her ear, "No. But having you whisper in my ear is a little too sexy for our present circumstances."

His comment surprised a chuckle out of her. "So now what?" she said, pulling back to look into his face.

He frowned slightly as he wrapped his arms around her waist and his gaze drifted to the wall behind her. Then he leaned close and against her ear said, "I smelled rain coming when we were outside."

"You can smell that, too?" she whispered back.

He nodded. "We have a choice. We can stay here and wait for my grandmother's backup to arrive. Or we can take our chances and use the rain to cover our tracks."

"How do we get out of the house?"

He shifted so he could meet her gaze and mouthed, "Jump."

Nila widened her eyes. "You're serious?"

He moved his mouth back to her ear. "I can make the jump easy enough. It's not that far for me. Then I'll catch you."

She was shaking her head even before he finished speaking. "You can't. I know I don't look that big, but you cannot catch a full grown woman falling from a second story window while you're standing on slopping ground in the middle of a rain storm."

His breath brushed warmly against her ear when he chuckled. "You'd be surprised at what I'm strong enough to do," he said.

The promise in his words made her thighs clench. No time for sex, she reminded herself. "Are you sure? We won't get far if I break you in the fall."

"I'm sure. But you need to be prepared. It'll be dark and hopefully the rain will be strong. Running won't be easy. How are your legs after this morning?"

"Mostly recovered—food and rest helped, and I'm in good shape, for a human." She took time to consider their options. Staying in this house was not safe. She knew that in her bones. Gregory had some of the young males out there patrolling, and Petrov's tigers were still around somewhere. On her own, she'd never be able to outrun a tiger if one caught their trail. Plus whatever help Elizaveta sent would no longer be able to find them.

The question was could they risk missing the opportunity presented by the rain? Or was it ultimately better to tough it out here one night and leave tomorrow?

Then again, what if help didn't arrive tomorrow? What if Gregory, or Petrov for that matter, was able to intercept whoever was coming and send them away…or worse?

"What about the guns?" she mouthed.

They were both still downstairs. After dinner, Nila had tried to collect hers only to have Richard insist she wouldn't need it and set it to one side in the main room. She'd forgotten to grab it on the way upstairs, which was a stupid thing to have done, but it was too late to fix the mistake now. She just wasn't used to thinking about needing a gun, and she resented the fact she needed one with real ammunition in it now. A tranquilizer rifle was one thing. Using a weapon to cause harm sucked. It went against everything she'd spent her life doing. Yet she'd be stupid if she refused to use the only weapon she had in this fight.

Mitch glanced back at the door. "Going for the rifles now would tip our hands. If we were going to use them, we should have brought them up with us."

"I can't believe I forgot. I still have a pocket full of ammunition."

"I could make some excuse and go get them."

"No, you're right, they'd get suspicious. If we do run, we'll need as much of a head start as possible."

He nodded. "Are you decided, then?"

"We have time for me to think a little more?"

"Yes. Running will be difficult. Don't fool yourself."

"But staying could be worse."

He shrugged. "Possibly."

"What do you think we should do?"

"I want to get out of this house as soon as possible. I want you safe."

"Yeah, me too. On both counts. As well as keeping you safe. How much longer will these men hold off on attempting to get you out of the way?"

"Not much longer." He made a face and squinted at the wall behind her again. "I need to tell you something, but it's going to upset you."

"Oh, good." She shook her head. "I doubt you can tell me anything worse than what I've already heard."

"You're in estrous."

She blinked. Then she blinked again. She scowled at him, as if narrowing her eyes and frowning would somehow make his words make sense. A full minute passed before she shook her head. "No. I'm on birth control, an IUD, and I'm not cycling right now. Even in my ordinary human way."

"Well, more of your mother is showing because your scent is like nirvana at the moment. And if I'm affected, all those males downstairs are being affected, too."

"It's not biologically possible. It's just not."

"Did you think tiger shifters were possible a few weeks ago?"

"Well, no, but…"

"You're unique, Nila. As far as we know, you are the only one of your kind. You can hear, see, and smell better than a human. You can sometimes sense tiger shifters. Why wouldn't other elements of your biology also be different?"

"This is bad. What do I do? How long has this been going on?"

"I caught a hint of the scent earlier today, over lunch. It was faint, but it's gotten stronger all evening."

"Then why were the other males so much more relaxed around me this evening? I thought estrous would start a mating drive or something. It's a trigger in most animals."

"I think they relaxed because knowing you were in estrous confirms you'll probably be able to conceive with a tiger. And technically, I've won the proverbial Run this time around. They're conditioned to wait until your next cycle."

"They're socially programmed to do that, but will they? They don't seem to want to observe the current rules."

He grimaced and held her closer as they whispered. "This is another reason I want you out of this place as soon as possible. Gregory might not bow to my claim on you."

She narrowed her eyes and leaned back to stare at him. "You're not telling me something? What?"

Pulling her close again, he said, "They'll be able to scent you from farther away while you're in estrous. The rain will cover that. Water dilutes and muddles the scent. But when it stops, if we're not far enough away, they'll still be able to track us."

"Great," she mumbled. "You're sure this is tiger shifter estrous and not just my normal human cycle?"

"The scent of human women doesn't affect us the way female tiger estrous does. The difference is very clear."

"But you said I'm unique."

"You are. Your smell is uniquely powerful and delicious. You're in estrous, like a tiger shifter female."

"Shit. So we stay? If they can track me even easier now…"

His cheek brushed against hers. "Dangerous. They may decide I've won for this night, but the way Gregory thinks, he may demand you pick someone else for tomorrow night."

"I am not—," she started, loudly, before cutting herself off. With an effort she lowered her voice to a barely audible whisper and spoke through clenched teeth. "I am not fucking any of those men just because some crazy tiger thinks I should."

Mitch kissed her cheek. "Good, because I had no intention of letting you fuck anyone else but me."

She unclenched her teeth. "Good. So?"

"Estrous normally lasts about three days. If we put enough distance between this house and us tonight, and keep moving tomorrow, we should make it hard for them to find us. We'll keep you away from everyone until your estrous ends. It'll mean roughing it. I didn't want to force that on you, but…"

"We don't have a lot of choices." She sighed. "This is going to suck, isn't it?"

"Yes."

"We need to run, don't we?"

He let loose a long breath and squeezed her tightly to him. "I think we do."

"What about the help Elizaveta is sending?"

"With you in estrous, I'm afraid to wait."

She hugged him, in full agreement. Then a thought struck her and she pulled back. "Wait, does this mean my birth control won't work? It's designed for human women with menstrual cycles."

"I have no idea." He swallowed visibly, and his gaze shifted to her mouth. "Would it be so bad if you did get pregnant?" he asked so quietly she barely heard him.

She widened her eyes. "With an IUD in? Yes, yes it would." She swallowed down the knee-jerk edge of panic at the thought of being pregnant and considered her next words more carefully. "I'm not prepared to get pregnant yet, Mitch. I'm not ready. And while all this running is happening, it would be a very bad idea. I doubt it'll stop Petrov from wanting me dead. In fact, it might make things worse."

He nodded. "You're right."

Cupping his face in her hands, she met his gaze. "It's nothing personal. You know that, right? But we barely know each other. And while I want to be with you and get to know you better, jumping into parenthood isn't the answer."

He leaned forward and kissed her. "I know. We males are a little overeager to procreate because procreation is such a rare thing now. I have no intention of rushing you or forcing you into anything at all."

She briefly kissed him back, taking him at his word. The whole idea was too scary to contemplate right now anyway. They still had to survive, and she had to figure out how to live with her new identity. She had to convince all these tigers she intended to choose Mitch, despite everything he said would stand in their way. Then they had to figure out if they could make a go of a relationship. If they couldn't, she had no intention of choosing another tiger for a possible husband. She just couldn't bring herself to even consider that option. But if it turned out she and Mitch could be together and love each other, she wanted the chance.

Sometime after that, a long time after that, they could discuss children.

Nila hugged Mitch and stared at the bedroom door. Before any of that, though, they had to get out of this house.

CHAPTER TWENTY-FIVE

WILL they expect us to have sex? Do they think we'll actually fuck while they're listening?"

Her question surprised Mitch into pulling back to look at her.

"I mean, that's what you said happens when a male catches a female during a Run, right?" she said. "They have sex a lot during her estrous."

"True. And they probably do expect that." He didn't want to admit how difficult it was for him to keep his lust under control. Her scent was overwhelming his more civilized senses, but this was no time to lose himself to his baser instincts. He'd never had to exercise this degree of control over his body before and the internal struggle was only tempered by the fact that her life was in danger. If they'd been somewhere safe, he'd have her stripped naked and buried himself inside her before she could gasp.

Since even the thought of be inside her pushed him a little closer to the edge, he pulled his mind back to the danger. The more he concentrated on protecting her, the easier it was to ignore the way her pheromones were playing havoc with his body. The knowledge that the other males in the house were probably experiencing a similar reaction was like a cold shower to his libido, not completely drowning it but definitely keeping it in check.

"I'm not sure I can have sex while they're listening," she whispered as if embarrassed by the admission.

He smiled. "I have no intention of putting on a show for them. Don't worry." Despite his bodies very eager urges to do just that.

She rolled her eyes. "The thing is, I'm kind of wishing we had some privacy about now. Is that the estrous talking? I mean, to be honest, I've wanted you pretty badly since we first met, so that's nothing new."

His hands clenched against her waist and his mood shot up. Her admission flattered his ego more than he'd ever admit out loud.

"This is really no time to be thinking about sex, yet I don't seem to be able to stop noticing…well, how nice you feel."

Her words went right to his cock. Closing his eyes, he tried taking a few steadying breaths, but that only pulled her scent more deeply into his lungs, washing him with her essence.

"We need to talk about something else," he said through clenched teeth, "unless you do want to put on a show for our listeners."

"No. No, I don't. Maybe I should sit on the other bed."

"Probably a good idea." But he didn't let her go and she made no move to stand.

"What do we do now?" she whispered.

"Wait for the rain. Then we get out of here."

He kept her cradled on his lap, despite his discomfort, because the thought of letting her go was worse. Cuddling her close, he turned his addled brain to their escape. He hated to force her into rotten weather and a pitch dark woods, but as the day progressed, he'd grown more and more convinced they needed to leave as soon as possible.

Gregory probably realized his intentions since Mitch was sure the guard around the house wasn't strictly in place to keep Petrov's people away. With the rising of Nila's estrous, their desperate situation had gotten infinitely worse. He kept expecting the others to knock down the door and demand access to her. Or demand she run—which they all knew she couldn't do.

Those thoughts kept his desires in check for the next several hours as they waited for the approaching storm to hit.

He was sure Gregory would realize they might try escaping in the rain. With luck, the young man would assume Mitch wouldn't want to put Nila through the dangerous and difficult escape. Still, Mitch would have to pick their exit time carefully.

During the long, quiet wait, as he held Nila, he opened his senses to the location of the various males, timing their movements as best he could. Since his awareness of other tigers was better than most, he was able to keep track of the guard changes and the presence of the others inside the house.

When the first few drops plinked against the window panes, he knew exactly when they'd have a chance to escape.

Hugging Nila to get her attention, he murmured, "We leave in fifteen minutes, if the rain is strong enough. Otherwise, we'll need to wait an hour and hope it keeps coming down."

"Why an hour?"

"Guard changes will give us an opening."

"You know where everyone is, don't you?"

He nodded.

"Very handy, that sense of yours," she said and kissed his cheek. "You're gonna have to help me hone my newly discovered ability to do that when all this is over." She released a breath. "I'm ready when you are."

He heard the determination and the fear in her voice. With another tight hug, he patted her hip and they both rose. They'd turned off the lights in the room hours earlier in an attempt at giving the illusion they'd gone to sleep. Keeping their movements as silent as possible was easier for him than for Nila, but she surprised him by being very light on her feet. No floor boards creaked as they crossed to the window.

He stared outside, watching the rain fall harder, sheeting down within a matter of minutes. The torrent would be good for covering their tracks, but it would make moving through the woods a lot more difficult on Nila.

Nothing for it. They had to try.

He flicked the lock on the window and pulled the bottom pane up an inch. No sound. So far so good. He didn't dare lift it farther, though, until he was sure the patrol tigers were as far away from this side of the house as possible.

As soon as that moment came, he threw the window up. A very slight noise made him cringe. He paused, listening. No alert was sounded and none of the males were moving closer either in or out of the house.

Against Nila's ear, he said, "I'll jump down first. Don't wait too long to follow me. We don't have much time. Hang from the window and drop. Don't worry." He kissed her cheek. "I'll catch you."

She nodded.

He crawled legs first out of the window, hung from the ledge a moment and then dropped. Still without a shirt, the rain soaked him the instant he landed. His warmer than human body heat would help him, but in her tank top and loose canvas pants, Nila was going to freeze in this weather.

The ground underfoot was already slippery and muddy. He looked up at the window, pleased when he saw Nila throw her leg over the sill, a darker shape against a dark background. He got into position and when she dropped with a near silent screech, he caught her around the waist, her back to his front.

He felt her trembling and her sharp exhale. Against her ear, he said, "Told you I wouldn't let you fall."

She looked back and grinned, water dripping down her face. He put her feet on the ground, careful to hold her until he was sure she was stable. Then he took her hand and as fast as he dared, moved into the woods.

It was nearly pitch dark under the canopy, barely enough light for him to see, and the ground was slick and uneven. She stumbled several times, her free hand clamping onto his bicep to catch herself. The only good thing about the tree cover was that it blocked the torrent somewhat, making the rain more of a nuisance shower than a soaking blast.

Keeping his senses open to the location of the other tigers, he half jogged, half fast-walked in an uphill direction, moving them away from the lake and farther into the mountains. He had a vague idea which direction the nearest road was, and if they could reach that, they could find their way to the highway. But he didn't want to go that direction immediately in case Gregory sent cars out looking for them. With luck, they'd find a cave or some sort of cover to get Nila out of this weather. But first, they had to get far enough away.

So far, the tigers didn't seem to be aware of their escape. He hoped that lasted a little longer.

"How are you doing?" he asked over his shoulder. He wasn't worried that the others might hear them talk now. He could barely hear over the sound of the rain crashing against branches above.

She stumbled closer. "Can hardly see and I'm freezing already, but the running is warming me up. Keep going. I can manage."

He squeezed her hand and tried pushing them a little faster. He considered shifting so he could carry her on his back and move at full speed, but he needed time to shift—not a lot, but enough to delay them, and he wasn't sure they could afford even a short pause. He sure as hell didn't want to get caught mid-shift, unable to defend her instantly. If he carried her in human form in this weather, without his tiger shape to aid his balance and senses, all it would take was one misstep to cause them both serious injury. No, he had to get more distance between them and the house first. Then he could shift safely.

The tension of waiting for the other shoe to drop, for the others to realize they were gone, nipped at his heals and heightened his anxiety. Nila's scent still washed over and around him. She was leaving a trail, more surely than any footprint, but the rain would wash it away if they got enough lead time before being followed.

Instinct made him pause and opened his senses, taking note of the location of the others.

From the house, a dozen young males began their pursuit.

"Shit. Run!" He dragged Nila forward, racing through the underbrush, over fallen logs as fast as he could manage while still trying to keep her upright. She kept up better than he could have hoped, but she didn't have the physical ability to run like this for long. He wove through the trees, looking for a way out, a river to disguise their progress, something.

Even as he raced away from the house and the tigers coming from that direction, a new threat jabbed his senses. From another direction completely. More tigers. Closing in on them. Mitch paused again to get an idea of where the others were. Frustration punched him in the gut. "Fuck!"

"What? What's wrong now?"

"We're surrounded. There are more tigers in front of us, spaced out and blocking that escape route."

"So we go left or right? Can we double back?"

"Back is Gregory and they can cover a lot of ground with so many of them. Forward there are at least five other tigers."

"Not Gregory's group?"

He shook his head.

"Friendlies? The Trackers or maybe the help Elizaveta sent?"

"No. Petrov is in that group."

"You're sure?"

He was absolutely positive, but he couldn't explain how. The group of five wasn't close enough to pick up their scent signatures, yet Mitch knew deep in his bones those five tigers were enemies.

He tried to gage their chances. Squeezing Nila's hand, he took off in a new direction, hoping the rotten weather would work against their pursuers as much as it was hampering their own progress.

To his relief, Nila didn't waste breath asking questions or debating his decisions. She stumbled along with him, her grip on his hand firm despite the slicking of their skin in the rain.

He paused again to locate the individuals of each group, then took another sharp turn. The tigers were closing in from both directions. Closing the snare. He and Nila couldn't move fast enough to jump free of the trap.

He stopped, letting Nila suck in quick gulps of air as he located the others one more time. "They're all too close. We can't slip past them even in this weather. Your scent is too strong."

"What do we do?" she muttered around ragged breaths.

He stared into the rain, most of his concentration on the groups closing in. They had two choices. Gregory or Petrov. Only Petrov actually wanted Nila dead.

"Lesser of two evils," he hissed. Then louder so Nila could hear him over the storm. "Gregory doesn't want to kill you. And with his greater numbers, Petrov will likely back off once we're with Gregory's group."

"Frying pan or fire?" she asked and raised her brows.

He took in her soaked clothing and hair, her heavy breathing, the slight tremble passing from her hand to his, and bit back another curse. "Gregory is the frying pan."

Her shoulders slumped. "Damn."

"I'm sorry."

"No. We had to try. Do we head back toward Gregory or do we keep running and wait for someone to actually catch us?"

Both groups were close enough to sense each other now. He and Nila had nowhere left to run.

"Too late, they're practically on us." He kissed her hand, then cupped her cheek and kissed her fast and fiercely.

Without another word, he lead her back toward the house they'd just escaped from, weaving through the woods in an attempt to meet one of the least threatening of the young males. Ryan was close. Not the closest of Gregory's group, but near enough they could reach him before the others found them.

As they hurried toward the young males, Mitch realized Petrov's group had slowed, but they weren't backing off. Would they confront the young ones? A fight would be enough of a distraction, he and Nila might be able to get away in the mêlée.

Unfortunately, Mitch didn't seem to have that kind of luck. Even as they reached Ryan in his tiger form, Mitch sensed Petrov's tigers retreating.

So much for his great plan to get Nila to safety. Some protector he'd turned out to be. His only hope was that they could stay alive long enough to escape again, or for help to arrive. But as the young males circled them, bristling with aggression, chuffing and growling, his own future didn't look good.

Chapter Twenty-Six

Nila paced the room she'd been shoved into the instant they returned to the house. This was a room on the first floor, but the windows were barred and the door was firmly locked. She had no idea where Mitch had been taken. They'd been separated as soon as they cleared the front door. Her guards had gently nudged her into this room and thrown her a dry change of clothes—a flannel shirt and sweat pants presumably from one of the smaller males but still too large for her—then locked the door. All without a word.

She was so cold and scared at the time, she hadn't spoken either. Now, after hours with no word and no contact, she wanted answers. Where was Mitch? What was happening? Was Petrov still out there?

The faint light filtering in through the bars confirmed it was morning, though a dark, cloudy morning. The tension of waiting, of not knowing what was going on, made it feel like she'd been in this room for days rather than hours. She was on the verge of pounding on the door and demanding attention.

But she was afraid to face Gregory. She had no idea how to explain why they'd run away during a rainstorm without making it obvious they were as scared of these males as they were Petrov. She was terrified of what Gregory might do to Mitch now. Hell, she wasn't even sure if Mitch was still alive.

The thought tightened her already clenched stomach muscles, making her nausea rise. Folding her arms across her stomach to try relieving the churning, she forced the thought away. Mitch was alive. Somewhere in this house, he was alive. Probably pacing the floor just like she was, waiting for answers.

She tried reaching out to sense him, hoping to pick him out from all the other tigers, but with so many around, and her nerves so frazzled, she couldn't sense anything clearly. All she felt was an overwhelming aura of danger.

When she heard the lock click open, she spun to face the door.

Ryan walked into the room in human form, carrying a tray filled with food, and Nila felt a strange relief. She wasn't sure why, but the doctor didn't creep her out the way the others did. He seemed somehow less threatening.

"What's happening?" she asked. "Where's Mitch?"

"Safe for now. In another room in the cellar." Ryan didn't meet her gaze at first. He set the food on a table against one wall then rested his hand on the back of one of the two chairs flanking the table. Finally, he faced her. "Gregory is arranging a challenge. A fight. Mitch against… He'll fight Richard first. If he survives, he'll fight Jim. They're both our strongest combatants outside of Gregory."

"Isn't Gregory going to step up and face Mitch then? Is he afraid?"

Ryan's dark eyes flickered with an emotion she couldn't read. "Gregory would not be pleased with your assessment of his tactics. He intends to face Mitch himself. If Mitch survives the others. If he doesn't, Gregory will declare he was always an unfit opponent. None of the others will argue with him."

"And you? Where do you stand in all this blood sport bullshit?"

"I'll treat the wounds that are too serious to heal by themselves. Did you know we heal very quickly?"

She ignored his question. "Is Mitch expected to kill the other two?"

Ryan shook his head. "There are rules to challenge combat. Males don't generally fight to the death. Mitch will be able to follow the rules without repercussions."

"Meaning?"

"He'll only have to get his opponents to give up to be considered the winner."

He crossed to her, but stopped far enough away not to cause alarm or make her feel crowded. She wondered how many other males in the house were listening to their conversation. Without Mitch around to tell her where they all were, she was hopelessly out of her depth. Their scent, that musky smell she'd first caught at John's cabin when Petrov found her, that scent permeated the house, both subtle and pervasive, so she couldn't use it to help any more than she was able to use her ability to sense shifters.

When Ryan dropped his voice, she realized she'd been right in thinking others were probably listening. But since he wasn't trying to whisper in her ear, either what he was saying wasn't secret information or the others were far enough away they couldn't hear him at his current level.

"Gregory will announce that the challenge rules will be enforced. Such an announcement will make him appear very honorable to the others and that's how he keeps them following him. With promises and supposed honor. But make no mistake, Richard and Jim will both kill Mitch if they get a chance. At Gregory's orders. If Mitch somehow manages to survive that, Gregory will fight to the death."

Nila threw her hands in the air and turned away, trying to hold back the threatening tears. "When?" she forced out through a tight throat.

"I'm to take you to the arena after you eat."

"Fuck!" She let loose a further string of curses as she doubled over and braced her hands on her knees. "I can't believe this is happening."

She needed to do something. She had to help Mitch. But how? She had no weapon. They'd taken her useless-without-the-rifle-anyway ammunition. She couldn't call for help because they'd taken her cellphone. She wasn't strong enough to fight off twelve supernatural beings, and she had no idea if the man she loved would be able to survive the day.

The realization she was almost definitely in love with Mitch would probably have shocked her at any other moment. Just then, all she could think about was her growing panic and the urgent, hammering need to do something. Anything!

Ryan reached toward her, then pull his hand back before touching her. "You probably don't know this, but Mitch is very good in a fight."

She did know, but she wondered how much these tigers actually knew about him. "How do you know?"

"Has he told you about his family background? His status?"

She nodded but didn't go into detail. The less information she gave away, the better.

"Having to carry the burden of his father's punishment meant that Mitch ended up in a lot of fights when he was younger."

"So…"

He shrugged. "We all heard the stories of the fist fights and battles in tiger form that Mitch and his brothers got into. After the first few years of it, the Chernikov brothers rarely lost."

"Then Gregory is afraid to face Mitch."

That something passed through Ryan's eyes again. She still couldn't entirely read the emotion, and she was too panicked to try.

"Don't lose hope," Ryan said after a moment. "Mikhail is uniquely able to face this challenge."

She studied the doctor for a moment. She realized she had no idea how old he was. Mitch called this group "young males", but Ryan could be any age from twenty-five to forty-five based on his looks. Maybe that was why he was less intimidating? He felt more grounded, less…she wasn't sure. Flighty? Impulsive?

Overly aggressive? "Why don't you creep me out the way the others do?"

Ryan laughed, a charming, deep sound. "Because I'm a doctor?" he suggested. Then his smile fell away. "Just stay aware. Your scent is…" He swallowed and shrugged.

"I know. Mitch told me."

"It will affect the others. The combination of a female in estrous and the energy of the fights will raise their aggression. I'll stay close, but you need to be aware of the danger you're in, too."

"No one here wants to kill me."

"Not on purpose, no. But that's not the only damage a group of desperate and aggressive males can inflict."

"Great. Rape? Well, this just keeps getting better."

"Petrov would have been a worse option."

"You knew his was the other group in the woods?"

He nodded. "Why did you try escaping when he was still in the area?"

"The rain." She waved a hand vaguely at the window but didn't go into further detail. For some reason, she felt safer with Ryan than any of the other males, but he was still here with this group. She couldn't trust him.

"You should eat," he said. "I'll be down the hall. Your scent is distracting, so I don't think I should stay in the room with you."

"Oh, good. You, too?"

"All of us. Biology is hard to override."

"Fine. Get out."

He dropped his gaze and left, locking the door behind him.

Nila couldn't eat, though she did try forcing some of the food in. She knew she needed the energy for the ordeal to come. But she was too nauseated, knowing Mitch was about to face a death match. Throwing up all over the place wasn't going to help him.

What could she do? What could she do?

The question was still swirling through her mind with no immediate answer when Ryan returned. He looked at the plate.

"You should eat more," he commented.

"Can't. Let's go."

He hesitated, then shrugged and led her out of the room. They'd only gone a few yards when two more males came up behind her, boxing her in. She glanced back. She knew the faces but couldn't for the life of her remember their names. One, a bulky but short man with blond hair and brown eyes met her gaze and smiled. The expression chilled her. When he glanced down at her ass, she snarled then turned away.

Being surrounded and under threat caused her muscles to tighten further and adrenaline surged through her system. She scanned the hall, looking for options, weapons, but the area was clean and featureless. Not even a pen she could grab off a table.

Her guards led her through the main room to a door near the kitchen. She looked around for her rifle—which wouldn't do her any good since they'd taken the bullets—but it had disappeared, too. Ryan opened the door and revealed a set of brightly lit stairs leading down. The passageway was narrow but the wooden stairs were clean and dry. She balked at the top of the steps, her every instinct shying away from the confined space.

With a deep breath, she forced herself to take the first step before the guard behind her tried making her move. She did not want any of these men touching her. No point in giving them an excuse.

The stairs switched back once. At the bottom, they opened onto a large area the size of the main room above. This space, however, was not prettily decorated. In the center, a giant chalked circle filled the middle of the wooden floor, taking up the bulk of the room. Around the circle, stood the other tiger males.

Gregory was directly opposite the stairs and the first to catch her eye when Ryan moved out of the way. He smiled. She was starting to think of that expression as his cult leader smile. That smile made her want to turn and run.

She didn't run, but she did turn away without acknowledging his greeting. Scanning the others for Mitch, she was surprised not to see him. She realized as she looked at the various human faces, she didn't see Richard or Jim either, though she only had a vague idea what Jim looked like. With a frown, she looked back at Gregory.

He was still smiling. Sweeping his hand out to the side, he moved a step to his left and revealed a chair. "The seat of honor," he said, loud enough for the comment to echo.

She wanted to be brave, snarky, smart. But her muscles refused to move. Her instincts screamed at her to run away.

Her feet refused to take her farther into the room. The longer she stood in one place, however, the thinner Gregory's smile grew until it finally fell away. He nodded to the two males behind her and they each grabbed one of her arms. The exact thing she didn't want to happen.

Their touches started a fine trembling of terror in her stomach. She'd never felt so defenseless in her life. She wouldn't stand a chance if this group ganged up and raped her. Oh, she'd fight. She might even surprise them since she was strong for a human. But she wasn't a trained fighter and she wasn't a shifter. She'd lose.

The thought brought bile up her throat.

Swallowing back the need to throw up, she took the first step forward without being forced. That was the only power she had left. She refused to be dragged around. As soon as she started moving, another look from Gregory had the men dropping their grip.

Once freed, her nerve returned somewhat and she managed to get to the chair without actually panicking and bolting toward the stairs.

She didn't sit, though, and she refused to speak, despite the questions pushing at her clenched teeth. Where's Mitch? Why are you doing this? Who the hell do you think you are?

Gregory held her gaze for a long, silent moment. It was all she could do to remain still under his scrutiny. Finally, he took her arm and eased her with gentle but unrelenting pressure into the seat.

"Thank you for joining us," he said with a straight face.

Again, she wanted to come back with a smart, sharp comment, but her brain wasn't working fast enough for witticisms.

Gregory waited a beat for her to speak then turned back to the room as her two guards flanked the chair. "Bring out the combatants."

A door near the stairs that she hadn't seen before opened. Jim and Richard walked out first, both completely naked. Once they stood in the circle, everyone turned back to focus on the door. She held her breath, waiting. A beat later, Mitch stepped out.

CHAPTER TWENTY-SEVEN

Nila stared. Mitch was also naked, and like the others, he didn't seem conscious of his nudity. As he slowly walked toward the circle, she realized he was moving a little stiffly, not with his usual grace. Frowning, she looked over his body. He wasn't bleeding, but as she looked closely at his face, she could see a faint shadow around his left eye.

"You beat him already?" she hissed up at Gregory. "Cowards."

The room seemed to suck in a deep breath and all eyes turned from Mitch to her. She didn't care. She kept her gaze on Mitch. His mouth lifted slightly at one corner as he held her gaze. A growl from behind her made the hair on her nape prickle but she didn't turn or show the fear that trickled through her system, ignoring the fact that everyone in the room could probably smell it anyway.

Mitch glance up at Gregory, still with that faint smile lifting his lips.

Nila practically felt the others holding their breath. Gregory's presence behind her made her skin crawl, but she focused on

Mitch. When Gregory finally spoke, the break in the silence made Nila jump.

"Richard, take your place."

Jim moved out of the circle to stand in the middle of several of the other males. Richard passed around the edge of the circle until he was standing opposite Mitch and a few feet in front of Nila. She leaned to one side so she could keep an eye on Mitch.

Mitch finally turned away from Gregory and focused on her again. His smile lifted a little and he winked. Then he mouthed, "Don't worry." Aloud, he said, "Nila isn't used to watching us shift. May she close her eyes?"

"Of course," Gregory said, all politeness and chivalry. "Please, Nila, feel free to close your eyes as you need to."

She snorted but didn't otherwise reply.

"Combat rules will hold," Gregory said in formal tones. "Begin!"

Richard started shifting immediately. Nila tried ignoring the process, though he was only a few feet away, and held Mitch's gaze for a few seconds longer.

"Close your eyes," he murmured. "You can watch me shift later, when you're ready."

She swallowed and nodded. She wanted to be brave enough to watch this, but holding her sanity right now was a fine, delicate thing. She closed her eyes and counted slowly to a hundred. After watching Vlad shift, she knew the process took a couple of minutes, at least going from tiger to human. She wasn't sure how long the reverse process took but figured it would take close to the same amount of time. When she reached a hundred, she allowed herself to listen to her surroundings. A slight noise in front of her made her stomach clench and her eyes popped open.

A huge male Amur tiger paced back and forth in front of her, its body thick with muscle, its fur clean and rippling. Under the bright cellar lights, his stripped orange coat glimmered. He glanced at her during one of his passes, and she shivered. The intelligence in his yellow eyes was sharp and aware. She had the disorienting feeling of looking into a human's eyes while staring at the tiger's face. No one who looked at those eyes would confuse a tiger shifter for a real tiger.

Finally, she glanced across the ring to see Mitch, for the first time, in tiger form.

He was also an Amur, a little larger than Richard, his body a little bulkier, though not by much. He stood in a half crouch, not pacing, not moving, the full force of his gaze on his opponent. As a tiger, his eyes were still hazel green, a surprising contrast to the otherwise classic tiger features. He didn't glance at her, not once as she stared at him, but she could see that same sharp intelligence in Mitch that she'd seen in Richard.

And more. She saw Mitch. Looking into his eyes, she saw the man. Seeing him like this… He was magnificent.

Pulling in a steady breath, she waited for one of the tigers to start the fight and a part of her hoped they'd just posture and call it a day. She'd seen tigers fight before, in the wild and in captivity. It was an awesome thing to behold. Also terrifying. In this case, the fact that one of these tigers just happened to be the man she loved meant terror overwhelmed awe.

Both males growled and chuffed as they took each other's measure. Finally, as if they'd reached an agreement of some sort, both lunged at precisely the same moment. Nila bit back a scream as they met in the middle of the circle, claws swinging, rising up on their hind legs.

For a heartbeat, she lost track of which one was Mitch as the two males swirled together, a flow of muscles, claws, and teeth. But as they sprang apart to measure each other again, she immediately recognized Mitch. From that point on, she was able to keep track of him during the fight and she kept her gaze on him, following his every movement.

He was a clever combatant, she realized. He kept Richard off balance, drawing him close when he wanted him there and forcing him back a moment later. There seemed to be tactics in the way Mitch fought, not just pure animal instinct. As she watched, it occurred to her that any human watching this would recognize it was more than a normal tiger fight. There was too much planning, too many moves that weren't quite natural for a tiger.

With a deep roar, Richard lunged and Mitch swung out with his forepaw while neatly avoiding Richard's claws. Richard stumbled and was slow to turn. When he did, Nila saw the jagged red line along his shoulder. Limping slightly, Richard continued charging Mitch, but Mitch easily batted him away now, taunting the younger tiger with his lazy movements and casually inflicted hits.

Richard's wounds left streaks of red around the circle and filled the large area with the metallic tang of blood. Nila held her breath as Richard lunged at Mitch again, a lunge that left his underbelly completely vulnerable. Mitch slid under the assault and in a move too fast to follow, he flipped Richard onto his back. Almost gently, Mitch crouched over him and settled his mouth around his throat. Richard held still and stiff for several moments, growling quietly, then his body went lax.

Mitch rose and backed away, crouching at the opposite end of the circle as Richard got to his feet.

"They fought slowly so you could watch," Gregory said, leaning in close enough to speak in her ear. "Richard underestimated Mitch's skill at this speed. The next fight will be faster."

She didn't respond. She had no idea what Gregory was talking about as the fight had seemed to move pretty fast to her until Richard's wounds got the better of him.

As Richard, still in tiger form, slinked out of the circle, Jim in human form walked in. His body convulsed as he began changing. She turned away, keeping her gaze on Mitch's face, working hard not to see what was happening in her peripheral vision.

When Mitch stood, she took that as a sign she could look. Jim was a large white Bengal tiger, his blue eyes sharp with that same unnatural intelligence. His fur glowed in the lighting, giving him an ethereal quality. He was leaner than Mitch but equally tall at the shoulders.

She expected more of the growling, chuffing, hissing, pacing she'd seen in the previous match. Instead, in a move blurred by speed, Jim flew at Mitch. The two tigers rolled across the ground, leaving the circle and coming up hard against a wall. The sound of their bodies connecting with stone and wood made her cringe. They were on their feet and flying at each other a second later, again moving so fast all she saw was a white and an orange streak tangling together, moving apart then swirling together again.

Now she understood what Gregory meant. No real tiger moved this fast. Nila blinked and they were halfway across the room from where they'd been the second before. The fight moved back into the circle after that first charge but the men surrounding the circle had all taken several steps back, leaving the combat area larger.

One tiger howled, another hissed, then a roar shook the walls. Blood appeared, splashing across the circle, and Nila half rose from her chair. Gregory's hand came down gently but forcefully on her shoulder, pushing her back into her seat. He left his hand on her shoulder, which gave her a shiver of distaste, but when she tried dislodging his touch, he refused to move. She wanted to reach up and shove him away, but another howl and another streak of blood kept her too focused on the fight.

Was that red mixed with white fur or orange? Where they both wounded now?

Not being able to see the fight clearly made her want to scream. Despite the speed, the battle lasted longer than the previous one. Richard might have been a good fighter, at least according to Ryan, but obviously, Jim was much better. Or maybe moving slowly enough for her to watch had thrown the first tiger off his usual game.

She didn't care. All she knew was that Mitch was right in front of her, trying to stay alive, and she couldn't do a damned thing to help. Even yelling would only distract him. She ground her teeth together, keeping her shouts and cries of distress as much to herself as possible. She couldn't contain every gasp and once she tried launching out of her chair again. But her butt never left the seat thanks to Gregory's continued hold.

Minutes ticked by as white and orange streaks continued throwing themselves at each other. They separated and paused long enough for her to get a brief look at each. There was blood on Mitch, but she couldn't tell if it was his or Jim's. Jim's white coat was covered in blood along one side. They lunged together again so fast she couldn't see any actual wounds.

As the tigers came together, their growls and roars increased. They whirled across the floor in a tangled heap, and when they stopped, Jim was on top of Mitch, pinning him to the ground.

Nila choked on her scream as Jim dove his teeth toward Mitch's neck. Then more movement blurred the scene and a moment later, they were lying at her feet, this time with Mitch on top of Jim, Jim's neck already in Mitch's mouth. Jim hissed and thrashed beneath Mitch, attempting to dislodge Mitch with his hind legs and slashing at Mitch's sides with his forepaws. Mitch shifted, just a little, and Jim fell still beneath him. Blood trickled out of Mitch's mouth, staining the white fur of his opponent.

Gregory's hand flexed on her shoulder. Jim stared up at Gregory. She couldn't read the expression in those tiger eyes, but she knew he was waiting for something.

After a breathless moment, Mitch stepped back from Jim, once again moving to the opposite side of the circle and crouching down. He moved slowly though, and she stared in horror at all the blood covering him. He seemed to be bleeding from a wound on his right flank and one on his left shoulder. Claw marks crossed his snout. Again she tried rising, wanting to go to him, help him with the injuries, but Gregory kept her in place.

Jim rolled slowly to a standing position. He looked as bad as Mitch, his white fur covered in pink and red splotches. An ugly gash tore up his side and another laid open part of his chest. Blood dripped from the puncture wounds on his neck.

"Enough," Nila spit up at Gregory. "Mitch needs medical attention. So does Jim. Stop this nonsense now."

Gregory's fingers dug into her shoulder, making her wince.

"Dr. Yin will see to Jim's wounds."

"And Mitch?"

"He has to prepare for me."

She wanted to call him a coward again, to slap him or punch him in the nose and make him bleed, too. But his grip on her shoulder had made her entire arm go numb and she knew she'd only make matters worse if she said anything more. Instead, she tried catching Mitch's gaze, to see if he was okay. He didn't look at her. He focused on a spot at the center of the circle and stared as if in a trance.

Gregory finally released her and moved away. The two men who'd walked her into the room took up positions surrounding her again, standing close enough to restrain her but fortunately not touching her. Several moments passed in silence. She glanced around, trying to find Gregory. He didn't seem to be in the basement anymore. Then she saw a huge Amur tiger move out of the shadows and knew instantly who he was.

Mitch continued staring at the center of the circle, showing no signs of awareness that Gregory was even entering the combat area. Panic swirled through her stomach, making her nauseous again. Mitch was hurt, seriously hurt. He'd just fought off two strong opponents and he'd been beaten up the night before. He wouldn't stand a chance against Gregory now.

Gregory paced slowly around Mitch, moving inch by inch closer, keeping him in sight but not lunging. Mitch didn't look up or even stand from his crouch. Blood dripped onto the floor beneath him, creating a small puddle of red, the slow plink plink of blood into the puddle the only sound in the room.

While still several feet away, Gregory launched at Mitch, swiping his unwounded shoulder with outstretched claws. Mitch didn't even flinch from the injury as Gregory bound away. The younger male paced around the circle again, keeping his gaze on an unmoving Mitch. With a low growl, he flew at Mitch again, too fast for her to follow. Blurred movement and a flash of gleaming claws and Gregory was once again at the opposite side of the circle from Mitch.

Mitch still hadn't moved.

More blood appeared, along his side this time, a nasty looking gash that showed some of the muscle beneath his flayed skin.

What was he doing? Why wasn't he fighting back? Was he hurt that badly? She stood, unable to stay seated. Surprisingly, her two guards didn't try stopping her. But when she made a move to enter the circle, Gregory snapped his head around and growled at her. She took a startled leap back.

That's when Mitch attacked.

She never saw him move. One instant she was staring at Gregory, the next, two flashes of orange spun away across the floor. The angry roars and hisses echoed in the large chamber, but the two tigers moved faster even than the previous fight. She could barely follow even the blurred color of their fur.

A flash of red and orange, another shock of white from their underbellies, but even the shape of their tiger forms was lost in the speed. Around her, the men stepped closer to the circle, and it seemed to her as if everyone in the room held their breath.

She had to do something. She had to help Mitch. Blood trails marked the passage of the fight, turning the cellar floor red. He would never survive if he kept losing so much blood.

She looked around, desperate for a weapon, a way to distract the others, something, anything she could use.

When she edged back from the circle, her guards didn't move to stop her. She attempted a little more space and realized they were too focused on the fight to notice she'd moved behind them. Could they see what was happening?

Since she couldn't, and the sight of all that blood was turning her panic into near hysteria, she focused on finding a way to help Mitch. When she looked toward the door at the base of the stairs, she saw a flash of movement.

Damn it, what now?

Her first thought was of Petrov, and she wanted to scream at the universe for putting them into this mess. But Petrov might be at least enough of a distraction that she could get Mitch out of the house. She edged farther around behind her guard and when she was sure they didn't notice her, she worked her way slowly toward the stairs. She kept behind the other men, but near enough to the circle that she could move in and drag Mitch out the instant they had a clear opening.

How she thought she might drag a grown male Amur tiger up stairs and out of the house, she had no idea. But she had to try something, and details like that were trivial next to her desperation.

She checked on the doorway again. There was another slight movement. She bit her cheek to keep from calling attention to either herself or whoever was in that room. She was sure all the other males she'd seen at the house were watching the fight. This had to be either Petrov and his tigers, or another young male she hadn't met yesterday. But if it was a male who belonged here, why wasn't he coming out to watch the fight? It had to be Petrov.

She hesitated within sprinting distance of the stairs. She didn't want to get close enough to the doorway to make herself vulnerable. If Petrov wanted to get at her, he was going to have to come into this room full of males and go through them first. A definite distraction.

She hoped.

Her gaze flicked back and forth between the doorway and the fight. Tension kept her muscles tight and she forced herself to relax, keeping her balance on the balls of her feet so she could move instantly.

Almost before she realized what was happening, despite her attention, a blur of several large orange shapes charged from the doorway into the middle of the cellar. Male shouts, the sound of tiger roars, blurs of movement, flesh and fur.

Nila searched for Mitch in the chaos and found him crouching, face to face, with Gregory. An instant later, a large orange flash of fur barreled into Gregory, throwing him over and spinning them both across the room. Mitch launched up and ran toward her, but she could see he was limping and the amount of blood in his fur horrified her.

With a nudge of his head, he pushed her toward the stairs. She didn't need any further encouragement. She charged up the steps, taking them two at a time. Running through the main room to the front door, she was aware of Mitch loping beside her, but she didn't dare look at him. The sight of his injuries would slow her down.

They tore out of the house, heading into the wood without hesitating. Mitch nudged her thigh, angling her in a specific direction and she followed his lead. A moment later, two new tigers moved up next to them. Nila would have screamed if she had enough breath. Instead, she tried running faster, though already she was moving at the edge of her endurance. Terror clawed at her insides, pushing adrenaline into her blood and forcing her muscles to move.

But on two feet, an empty stomach, and a system overloaded with fear and panic, she couldn't manage the uneven ground smoothly. She lunged over branches and through the detritus, but her limbs grew heavy and one branch caught her. She hit the ground hard, her ankle twisting painfully, her left wrist jamming from the impact, and what was left of the air in her lungs whooshed out.

With a gasp, she sucked in oxygen and tried scrambling up, but it was too late. The two tigers giving chase surrounded them. Mitch stood just in front of her, facing the others. Nila tried breathing, panting as her chest burned and her body refused to move any further. She stared at the two strange tigers.

Chapter Twenty-Eight

One of the tigers looked beyond Nila and Mitch, toward the direction of the house, and let out a soft growl then looked back at Mitch. Nila watched in fascination and fear.

Mitch circled around behind her and with his head nudged her, as if trying to get her to stand. As he did, the other two tigers moved closer. She tried scrambling away, but her ankle protested and she cursed as pain shot through her. Mitch nuzzled her leg then looked up at the other two animals.

To her amazement, one of the tigers crept up next to her and crouched down parallel to her. Even more startling, Mitch nudged her toward it.

"Are you serious? What's happening?" She shook her head. "I know you can't answer and we don't have time for you to change, but…"

The second tiger crouched down too, and the first made a soft sound almost like a purr.

The help Elizaveta promised, she realized. Relief flooded through her but only for a moment.

"My ankle's twisted. I can't run anymore. But I might be able to walk. Are we being followed?"

Mitch growled and nodded his head.

"Close?"

He shook his head no.

She made an effort to get to her feet, but Mitch bumped her, urging her closer to the tiger crouching nearest her. "What do you want me to do?"

He pushed her again so that she was almost touching the strange animal. Then he made a head gesture, a sort of shooing motion.

Frowning, she glanced between him and the tiger behind her. "You want me on its back? Are you nuts?"

Mitch growled again and pushed her none too gently with his head. She nearly fell over.

Fine. She could take a hint. She scrambled onto the tiger's back, riding astride as if on a horse. This was never going to work. They might be strong and she might be small, but the tiger beneath her was never going to be able to run fast enough to escape the others with her as a burden.

When the animal stood, Nila leaned forward and wrapped her arms around its neck, holding on for dear life. No not like riding a horse at all. The animal was tall enough for her feet not to brush the ground, but she pulled them up higher and kept them pressed against the animal's flanks.

She still didn't think this would work. She continued thinking it wouldn't work right up until the tiger started running.

The world around her blurred as they sped through the trees. She realized with a shock that in all the previous running, away from Petrov and the young males, all the tiger shifters had been moving much slower than they were capable. The others had been toying with her.

A strange sort of terror for what might have been rolled through her stomach. She clenched the fur beneath her fingers and kept her head down, afraid a low branch at this speed would kill her.

Alternating sun and shadow made their run even more disorienting, almost surreal as the ground blurred beneath them. She lost all sense of direction and distance within minutes and she could no longer hear much above the sounds of the tiger's breath and the steady thump of paws on the ground. She risked a glance over her shoulder. Mitch was there, keeping pace surprisingly well given his injuries. The second strange tiger came in and out of her view, guarding their backs as they ran.

She tried looking ahead, to see where they were going, but the wind of their passage made that impossible. Tucking her head again, she concentrated on keeping her balance. Riding a tiger back wasn't all that easy. Especially when the animal jumped sideways and changed directions suddenly, making its loose skin shift under her so she almost slid off.

A third tiger came out of nowhere, charging up to them and then running beside them. Friend or foe, she wondered, tightening her grip. But before she could decide, the new tiger changed directions again and headed back the way she and the others had come. Her mount and escort didn't even pause. They ran at a steady uphill angle, weaving deeper into the woods.

Nila's muscles screamed from the effort of trying not to fall. When they finally slowed to a trot, then a walk, she nearly slid to the ground in a heap. Her mount stopped and let her crawl off. She tumbled onto the leaf strewn muddy ground and made no effort to get up. The three animals stood staring at her as if waiting for her to do something. She stared back with her eyebrows raised.

"If you need me to run on my own, you're gonna have to give me a minute." She wasn't entirely sure she could stand nonetheless run. Her muscles quivered from overuse and her limbs refused to move. A weird sensation of cement-like heaviness and an airy floating feeling ran through her body.

After a moment of staring, Mitch moved forward and nudged her arm with his head, then nodded toward something behind her. She glanced back. A large dark hole opened up in the side of the mountain-face.

"A cave?" she asked, facing Mitch again.

He nodded.

"You want me to go in?"

The tiger Nila had been riding moved to the entrance, glancing back once before disappearing inside. A moment later, to Nila's complete amazement, Irina stepped out of the cave.

She was fully dressed. Nila was sure there hadn't been enough time for her to have shifted so she knew the tiger that had gone inside wasn't Irina. Irina had even said she couldn't shift while pregnant. But the transition still took Nila a moment to process. Then she found her voice.

"What are you doing here? I thought no one wanted you involved in this? You shouldn't be here. You might get hurt."

Irina smiled a little as she crouched down in front of her. "Can you stand or are you hurt?"

"I can limp. I just need a minute for my muscles to stop shaking. Where's Max?"

"Covering your trail and confusing the scents. Your estrous scent is strong, but he should be able to confuse the others enough that we'll be safe for a while." Irina looked past her to Mitch. "Long enough for you to heal anyway."

Nila turned to Mitch and took in his injuries closely for the first time. She let her veterinarian's eye view the wounds, knowing that was the only way she'd be able to face seeing what had been done to him.

"You're going to need stitches," she said. To Irina, she asked, "Do you have a first aid kit or anything? Can we get him to a hospital?"

Irina shook her head. "No hospital. And he'll heal on his own pretty quickly."

"One of those wounds is nearly to the bone. Infection will set in. I can suture him up."

"No need." Irina laid a gentle hand on her arm. "See, the claw marks on his face are nearly gone? The wounds will all close up before infection can happen. He just needs to rest so he stops losing blood."

"You're sure?" All her medical training balked at leaving those deep gashes untended. They need to be cleaned and closed. But as she looked closer, she realized Irina was right, the cuts across his nose had nearly healed already. And that was while he was running. How much faster would he heal with some rest?

Mitch nudged her again, more insistently.

"He wants you inside," Irina said. "Out of sight. We should go. I have some food, if you think you can eat."

"I'm sure I'll want food in a bit, but I can't even think about it right now."

"Fair enough." Irina grinned. "You sound like me when I had morning sickness."

With a firm grip and surprising strength, Irina helped Nila stand. With Mitch on one side and Irina on the other, Nila shuffled to the dark cave entrance. "Any non-tiger creatures I should know about?"

She liked bats, but she didn't particularly want to try resting in guano. Irina chuckled.

"Nothing but us big cats," she said and flicked on a flashlight Nila hadn't noticed.

With the line of light, she gave Nila a quick view of the cave roof and front portion of the space. It wasn't very deep but went far enough back to keep them concealed. Irina flicked the flashlight off and Nila took a minute to let her eyes adjust to the dimness. Come nightfall, this place would be pitch dark, but enough daylight filtered in now to allow her to see where she was going. The tiger that had remained behind with them moved to the back of the cave, disappearing into the shadows.

A moment later, a woman walked out of the shadows. She was fully dressed in loose fitting jeans and a t-shirt, stood almost six foot tall, and carried the kind of lean muscle any professional athlete would envy. Her brown hair brushed her shoulders in a neat, simple bob.

She smiled as she crossed to Nila and held out her hand. "I'm Alexis Tarasova. Elizaveta sent me."

A soft growling rumble came from Mitch, a sound of greeting rather than aggression. Nila glanced down at him. This must be the Alexis he considered a sister.

She took Alexis' outstretched hand. "Thanks for your help. You didn't just go back there, did you?"

"That was my mate, Victor. He'll be out in a minute." She glanced down at Mitch. "We'll keep an eye on her."

Mitch nodded and padded toward the rear cave shadows.

"He's not going to try shifting, is he?" Nila asked.

"The change will help speed up the healing," Alexis said. "But he won't be able to shift back to human for another half hour or so. The blood loss has left him pretty weak. Victor will see he gets food and water and will make him rest until he can change."

"What about the others? Are we safe here for a half hour? Shouldn't we leave?"

"The young tigers were busy with Petrov's followers when we left. It'll take time for that chaos to break and still longer for them to attempt to track us. Meanwhile, Max is confusing the trail. We have time for Mitch to recover enough to get to the cars. We left them a few miles from here."

Nila glanced at Irina. "Are you okay hiking that far?" It was a silly question given she must have hiked to this spot to begin with. Still, everyone was so worried about her.

Irina rolled her eyes. "I'm perfectly fine."

"She's strong and the exercise is good for her," Alexis added.

Irina laughed. "Alexis is the only tiger I know who isn't trying to coddle me. It's great!"

"I've had a few cubs myself. I know how it goes."

"But…" Nila bit her bottom lip, not sure if she was allowed to know about the sex of Irina's baby.

"Irina's having a girl?" Alexis asked with her brows raised. "That's all the more reason for her to stay healthy and physically active while she can. It'll make labor easier."

"I'm all for an easier labor," Irina groaned. She tilted her head and studied Nila. "You look like you might fall down. Let's sit." She gestured to a few blankets spread on the hard ground and a single fold out camping chair. With a grimace, Irina said, "Max insisted on the chair. I can still get up and down off the ground, but try telling him that."

Nila smiled. "Did you all hike in in human form?"

Alexis said, "Max and Irina did, Max carrying some gear for us. Victor and I led the way in tiger form." She studied Nila as they settled onto the soft blankets. "You're taking all this tiger business pretty well, considering."

Nila snorted. "I haven't had much choice in the matter. I'll freak out and fall apart when we're somewhere safe."

Irina rested a hand on her shoulder. "You are safe now. Don't worry. We'll take care of you."

"What are you and Max doing here? Mitch didn't call Max on purpose."

Irina leaned back in her seat and frowned. "Well that's an interesting story. Vlad came to us, to tell us Petrov had tracked you to John's cabin."

"Vlad?"

"Max called Elizaveta," Alexis took up the story. "She told him that we'd been contacted, and we all agreed to come help."

"At my insistence," Irina said. "If Vlad came to Max, Petrov was close to you and you were going to need all the help you could get."

"Thank you," Nila said, as untimely tears stung in her eyes. "I didn't know how to help Mitch. Those others, they were going to kill him."

Alexis and Irina exchanged a long look, Irina frowning.

"Can you tell us what was going on at that house?" Alexis asked. "Elizaveta was sketchy in her details."

"To tell you the truth, I'm not entirely sure what was happening either. I was completely creeped out by the group of young men living there. Well, except one. But he was going along with the group so I'm not sure how I feel about him."

"How many were there? We didn't really have time to count," Alexis said.

"I lost track. At least twelve. I think. They were led by a man named Gregory."

Irina sucked in a sharp breath.

Nila focused on her. "He said he knew you and Max. That he'd participated in some of your Runs."

"He fought Max during my last Run, even though I'd conceived at that stage." Irina's frown deepened. "What did he say? Do you have any idea why he and the others have gathered here?"

"Not really. Only that Elizaveta was worried about it, and according to Mitch, the elders have known something was up for a few months."

"Max alerted them to Gregory," Irina confirmed. "But this gathering… And so close to John's place."

"I got the impression that wasn't a coincidence."

Alexis cursed under her breath. "Irina, he's still after you. You and Max need to keep clear of him. You shouldn't have come. As soon as he gets Max's scent, there's no telling what he'll do."

"He won't hurt me. Not right now. We're safe enough."

"But he might go after Max again."

"Again?" Nila asked.

"About two weeks after Max and I were married," Irina said, "Max saw Gregory stalking him. He never actually attacked Max." This last she said to Alexis. "Max beat him in their fight. He was hardly going to fight him again."

"I don't trust him," Alexis said.

"And you shouldn't. He's crazy," Nila said. "Mitch even said he smelled off. I don't know about the smell thing, but he definitely gave me major worries. I felt like I was in a scene from Psycho or something."

"See," Alexis said to Irina. "As soon as Max gets back, you two need to return to the cars. Victor and I can look after Nila and Mitch."

"No. Petrov is out there somewhere with his people, and there are at least twelve young tigers lead by a crazy man. We're out numbered as it is. We will stick together." Irina shrugged. "Besides, not a single one of them is likely to hurt me at the moment so what better security could you have."

"They might not hurt you directly, but they might go after Max," Alexis said.

"Max is tough. I'm not worried."

Irina might not be, but Nila sure as hell was. She wasn't going to feel safe until they'd put several states between them and Gregory's tigers. Not to mention Petrov. She felt what little energy she had left draining into the cold stone beneath the blanket. How could they survive this? They couldn't keep running indefinitely.

Out loud, she said, "Where the hell are the Trackers? Why is Petrov still free?"

Alexis and Irina exchanged another long glance.

"Good question," Alexis said. "I'd like to know the same thing. Elizaveta said they were zeroing in on Petrov, but…"

"But why did you all get here in time to help us and they didn't?" Nila finished for her. "Maybe the Trackers want me dead, too. Mitch said Petrov wouldn't be the only one."

A long silence descended, so quiet Nila actually heard a faint trickle of water from somewhere deeper in the cave.

Finally, Irina leaned forward and patted her shoulder. "You're safe now. We'll work the rest of it out."

Nila wished she could believe that.

Chapter Twenty-Nine

Nila managed to force down some food, and her muscles relaxed enough that she didn't think she'd throw it all right back up, which was a good thing. Max returned, in tiger form, just as she finished eating. He stepped up to Irina and rubbed his big head against her cheek, then moved into the shadows.

This time, no one immerged for long minutes. Nila kept checking the time with the two women, even as she attempted to recover enough energy to leave the cave. She almost fainted with relief when Mitch finally appeared, flanked by Max and the other man—Victor—all in human form. Mitch was even dressed, in jeans, a t-shirt, and tennis shoes, more than he'd had on when they ran from John's cabin.

Without paying any attention to the others, she rose and hurried to him, running her hands over his sides, looking for evidence of the injuries. "You're okay now? Are you still hurt? Have the cuts actually healed?"

He tugged her close with a hand on the back of her neck and kissed her soundly on the mouth in reply. Finally, finally, her body let loose the tension that had kept her muscles tight for days. She collapsed against him, wrapped her arms around his waist, and hugged him close.

Cupping her cheeks, he leaned far enough back to study her face. "You weren't hurt, were you? They didn't touch you after we were separated?"

"No, I'm fine. You?"

"All healed. I'll need some sleep and food soon, to fully recover, but I'm good for now." He looked at Alexis and Irina and shook his head. "Irina…" The censure in his tone was impossible to miss.

Irina shrugged, looking completely unrepentant.

To Alexis, he said, "Thank you for coming."

"For you, any time, sweetie."

The endearment reminded Nila that Mitch viewed this woman like a sister, a sister with several children. Nila looked closer at Alexis, for the first time trying to gage her age, but like all the tigers Nila had met, she found it impossible to guess.

Max interrupted her musings.

"We should go now. All that running around I did will only distract the others for so long."

Without question, Irina rose and with Alexis and Victor's helped, packed up the gear.

"Your ankle," Mitch said. "Can you walk all right?"

"I'll manage. Anything to get as far away from here as fast as possible."

"Victor and Alexis got us a few rooms in a small, off the trail motel not far from here. We'll be able to rest and make a new plan."

"I vote for Cancun. Or maybe New Zealand."

That earned her a smile. "They are heading into the summer in New Zealand."

"Perfect," she said with enthusiasm, which deflated a moment later. "Except I left my passport back at your cabin." She sighed, strangely disappointed. A trip with Mitch sounded like heaven right about now. But only if she could get her dad and grandmother out of the country, too.

Mitch rested his forehead against hers and murmured, "Petrov has contacts all around the world, unfortunately. He needs to be caught first. Then we'll take a trip."

"Deal," she whispered back and gave him a quick kiss.

They cautiously left the cave, studying the terrain as they moved. By unspoken arrangement, Nila and Irina were surrounded by the others, placed at the center of a protective circle. Since she was busy limping her way over the uneven ground, Nila couldn't really complain. The fact that Irina moved so smoothly despite being pregnant left Nila feeling, once again, way out of her depth. She was usually good in forests and jungles, for a human.

They reached the cars without any incident, which surprised her given the unending series of disasters over the last twenty-four hours. Minutes later, they were bumping over the back roads. Mitch stayed by her side in the back seat of Victor and Alexis' Jeep, his hand on her knee the entire time.

"Eventually, I need to get Bill's car back to him," she said quietly as they drove past a gas station and tourist shop that looked like they'd seen better days.

"I'll arrange it," he said, his tone neutral, but the hand on her leg flexed.

She stared at him as he concentrated on the view from the side window. "Why are you bothered by Bill?"

"I'm not."

Frowning, she decided this was a conversation they need to have in private. Alexis and Victor hadn't once spoken since they got into the car and somehow maintaining the silence seemed more comfortable.

They pulled into the parking lot of a small, single story motel a half hour later. The place also looked like it had seen better days, but it still had a sort of charm in the peaked wooden roofs and intermittent flower boxes which separated the sidewalk in front of the rooms from the gravel strewn parking lot.

The thought of a bed was almost overwhelming. Just last night, she'd been planning on roughing it in the mountains for a few days. A hot shower and clean sheets sounded like heaven just then.

Mitch let the others check them in, waiting in the car until Alexis came out of the small office with their room keys. They'd secured three rooms right next to each other and after some debate, put Nila and Mitch into the center room.

Nila stumbled into the cool darkness with a sense of overwhelming relief tempered by the knowledge that they were only safe for the moment. But safe for now was better than not safe at all. She turned to say as much to Mitch and found herself pulled up hard against him, his mouth covering hers in a kiss that drowned her.

She returned the passion, unable to do otherwise as the need she'd been keeping in check last night came roaring back at full force. Heat and an edge of desperation rose up to engulf her. "I was so scared," she said against his mouth. "I wanted to help but didn't know what to do."

He nibbled the soft spot beneath her ear before kissing his way down the column of her neck. "You weren't hurt. That's all that matters," he said before biting her shoulder none too gently.

She moaned at the feel, the slight pain a pleasure that sent heat and wetness between her legs. Her fingers slid into his hair so she could hold him close, keeping him with her. "No, that wasn't all that mattered, Mitch. You matter. I don't know what I would have done if you'd been killed."

"Survived. Escaped." He eased back and held her face between his hands, keeping her gaze. "No matter what, Nila, I want you to survive. To live. No matter what you make of that life, what you want to be, so long as you're safe somewhere."

"With you," she said, making sure he saw her conviction as surely as she saw his. "Somewhere, anywhere with you."

"Yes," he said, fiercely, possessively.

And his mouth was on hers again, his hunger a match for hers. His hands moved from her face to her borrowed flannel shirt and a sharp ripping sound made her pull back. He flung the now ruined shirt aside and, without pausing, stripped off the oversized sweatpants.

"They stink of other males," he said. "You're mine. From now on, you carry my scent. I'm the only man you'll ever smell like again. Do you understand me?"

"Yes, yes." She couldn't argue with something she wanted so badly, too. "And you're mine. No more Mate Runs, no more running."

"Yes." He lifted her off the ground and carried her to the bed.

She'd barely landed on the surprisingly comfortable mattress before he made short work of her panties and bra. Then he was naked too and she couldn't keep her hands from his skin, his body, every inch of him. She kissed his side, where he'd been injured, confirming he was well, then licked farther down across his hip bone. He smelled fantastic, better than she would have expected, and she realized he'd washed away the remains of blood and sweat at the cave, leaving only the deliciously male scent of him. She pulled in a deep breath, taking his scent into her.

When she took his cock into her mouth, he arched under her, his hands fisting into the sheets, his thighs clenching beneath her breasts. She loved him like this, seeing him as overwhelmed as she felt. She teased him, licked him to please herself, then she straddled him. Leaning forward to place her lips against his as she slowly lowered herself onto him, taking in each thick inch of him. When she moved, he met her, their hips rocking together in a steady, measured rhythm, drawing out the tension, letting her savor the slippery friction.

She hugged him close as they moved, afraid to let go. Here, now, he was solid and real. Alive and unhurt. And hers. All hers.

For as long as she was allowed to keep him.

The stray thought got swallowed up in sweat and passion as she refused to think about anything but the moment. Kissing his shoulders, his neck, she tasted and memorized, imprinting everything about him.

When her orgasm hit her, she screamed his name. He came a moment later, holding her hips tight against his as his head arched back against the pillow.

She collapsed against him as both their bodies relaxed, and he wrapped his arms around her, holding her tight, kissing her cheek and the top of her head.

She came awake suddenly, surprised to realize she'd fallen asleep. Sheepishly, she rose to look at him. She was still sprawled across his chest, and he still held her.

"I fell asleep," she said. "I've never done that before."

"Fallen asleep after sex?"

"Not instantly without even realizing it. While a man is still inside me."

He smiled, but there was a tension in the smile. "You're exhausted. I'm not surprised. I probably shouldn't have started this until after you'd slept. But I couldn't keep my hands off you a minute longer."

"You should definitely not have let me sleep first. I needed this, too." She frowned. "I wasn't asleep long, was I?"

"About ten minutes."

She nuzzled her face against his shoulder, still embarrassed. When he chuckled, she released some of that discomfort and met his gaze again. Something in his expression made her stop to study him more closely.

"What's wrong? Did I offend you, falling asleep like that?"

"No." He laughed and patted her ass affectionately.

"Then what's wrong?"

"Nothing."

"Don't. No lying allowed when we're naked in bed together."

"Lying is allowed when we're dressed?"

"No, not then either."

He smiled, but his gaze shifted to her mouth as he ran the pad of his finger across her bottom lip. "Don't get upset," he said.

"That's a terrible way to start! What am I supposed to not get upset about?"

"I really, truly, from the depths of my soul, hate the idea of you being with another man. Even in the past. Which I know is stupid since we didn't know each other. But..." His jaw tightened. "I swear every time you mention Bill's name, I feel like my head is going to explode."

She straightened a little. "You're jealous of my former lovers?"

He rolled his head to the side and stared at the bathroom door. "I know I don't have the right. But..."

"But..."

He shifted under her.

She put a hand to his cheek and turned his face so he had to look at her. She gazed at him, waiting for him to continue.

"You're mine now. That doesn't mean someone won't try taking you away from me. The other male tigers. Human men." His voice dropped. "I can't stand the idea of losing you."

Something in her chest lightened, leaving her feeling centered and settled in a way she'd never been before. Smiling, she leaned in and kissed him.

"I love you, too," she murmured. "Surprising, isn't it?"

His nod was full of emotion.

"So you know, I'm not going anywhere. You're stuck with me. We'll see whether you consider that a good thing in a few months."

"A very good thing," he said in all seriousness before cupping her face between his large palms and drawing her down for a long, slow kiss.

They napped until sunset, woke to bodies already eager for more sex, made love then showered, all in a sort of blissful calm Nila was afraid to ruin with talk of their next step. To her relief and disappointment, Mitch brought the subject up as they crawled back into bed from their shower.

"I'll see if Irina or Alexis have anything you can borrow to wear. I'm going to burn the clothes those cubs loaned you."

"Fine by me," she said. "Shame we can't stay naked here for the next few days. Or weeks."

He ran a finger across her collar bone, a sexy little lift at the corners of his mouth. "I will be very happy to keep you naked for weeks on end as soon as conveniently possible. You still smell like the best thing to ever exist."

She sighed when his hand closed over her breast and he gently toyed with her nipple. But the reality of her scent kept her from fully losing herself in his touch this time. "How far away will they be able to smell this estrous scent?"

"They'll only have to get within a few miles."

"Fuck. I feel like I'm wearing a flashing 'here I am' sign."

"Under normal circumstances, that's not a bad thing."

"For you maybe." She propped herself up on one elbow so she could face him more fully. "How am I going to do my job now? Does this mean I have to avoid going around any cats until the three days are up?"

"Probably. You'll have to make adjustments."

"Why the hell is this happening now?"

"You might have always had an estrous cycle, love. You were just never around any tigers to tell you so."

"I would have had trouble with my work if this had been going on all along. I even picked the IUD I have because it limits periods, which makes my job easier. No, this tiger estrous is new." She titled her head to one side. "Do you suppose it has to do with you? With us? It started the day after we had sex for the first time."

He shrugged. "Maybe. I have no idea. We'll have to ask the scientists when you're tested. But they might not know either. You're brand new to us. We have no idea what to expect."

"Well, they're not going to keep me locked up in a lab running experiments. Just so you know."

"Absolutely not."

"So now what?" She sighed and settled back against the pillow so she could snuggle closer to him.

"I'll get you some clothes. Then we'll talk with the others and try to find a new hiding place." He kissed her forehead before saying, "I'm worried about the Trackers."

"Why they're nowhere to be seen despite what Elizaveta's been told?"

He nodded.

"Alexis and Irina thought it was strange, too."

"If we can't rely on them to take out Petrov, something else might have to be done."

"Meaning?"

"Meaning we might have to take care of him ourselves."

"Kill him?"

"Not if we can avoid it. The elders want him brought before them for his crimes. It'll be important to the entire community how this situation is handled. If he's dead, there's no resolution, no chance for the elders to make an example of him."

"If, and that's a very big if, but if we can catch him and turn him over to the elders, and if they punish him severely enough, will that keep others who think like Petrov from trying to kill me?"

Will it make it easier for you to stay with me? But she kept that thought to herself. He might be in love with her—or at least think he was at the moment—but loving each other didn't solve their problems. She was prepared to face the uncertain future to be with Mitch, to make her own choices about her life, but she worried his resolve would waiver when faced with the realities of being with a woman who was always a target.

He didn't speak for a long, quiet moment. Then said, "Others will still follow Petrov's path. The elders' punishment will deter some. Not all." He swallowed audibly before he said, "You'd still be better off with a more powerful male."

"Don't start that again."

"I didn't say I'd let you go to another male. You're mine now."

He spoke so fiercely she had to smile. The tension that had started to build in her stomach eased. "I'm glad we agree on that point finally." She pursed her lips and let her gaze roam over his upper body, enjoying the view even as she worried. "I guess some deterrent is better than none. But that's if Petrov is brought in alive."

"The way he's pursuing you, and using humans, I doubt taking him alive will be easy."

"Do you think he got to the Trackers? Killed them? Bribed them?"

"We won't know until it's looked into. We have a bigger problem right now. We need a new safe house for you and a plan to stop Petrov. We can't rely on the Trackers anymore."

"What about Gregory and his cult?"

"I'll leave them to the elders."

"You don't think they'll follow, too? Try to find us?"

"I think they'll have to start planning for the fact that my grandmother's going to be pissed when she finds out they tried to kill me."

"Even without the elders' power behind her, that'll be enough to frighten them?"

"Yeah."

She chuckled. "I can't wait to meet this woman. She reminds me of my grandmother."

She snuggled into him, tucking her head beneath his chin. They fit well together. Now they just had to make that perfect fit stick.

CHAPTER THIRTY

Mitch hated leaving Nila alone, but he, Max and Alexis had some planning to do. Hiding Nila indefinitely wasn't an option. Even hiding her for another few weeks wasn't going to work anymore. Not with both Petrov and Gregory and his young tigers looking for them. Something had to be done now.

By almost unanimous decision—Irina being the dissenting voice—Victor was left to watch over Irina and Nila. The two women were ensconced in a single room together to make Victor's job easier. Irina insisted she would guard Nila and Nila insisted she could look out for Irina, but no one else wanted to take the chance.

Once Nila was dressed and settled with Irina, Mitch went to Alexis' room to discuss their options.

"You sure you want Petrov alive," Max said seriously. "She'll be safer if he's dead."

"But the elders want him alive." Mitch didn't finish his thought, but Alexis and Max were two of his oldest friends and they picked up the undercurrent.

"You want the elders' permission to mate with Nila," Alexis stated. "And you think they'll give it if you bring Petrov in alive."

"I don't need their permission. She's made her choice and it's me." He scowled a little at the defensiveness in his voice. His mood didn't lighten when Alexis raised her eyebrows. "I want her safe," he said, more quietly. "She'll need the support of the elders since I don't have the status she needs."

"Mitch, your friends will support you both even if the elders don't," Max stated. Alexis nodded her agreement.

"But for Nila's sake, having their backing—not just the support of my friends and Elizaveta's wrath—will be important for her to survive in our community."

Alexis let out a long sigh as her brow furrowed. "Mitch, you know not all the elders…well, you do know they don't all agree with what Elizaveta's been doing. There are a few who…" She met his gaze. "There are a few who wouldn't entirely object to Nila no longer existing."

Mitch sat back in his chair, feeling like he'd just taken a punch to the ribs. "Why hasn't my grandmother told me this? She said to stay away from the elders' compound until she said otherwise. She didn't say the elders were the ones we had to worry about."

"She probably didn't expect you to fall in love with Nila," Max said.

Alexis rolled her eyes. "Or maybe that's exactly what she expected. You never know with her. She's sneaky that way.

You heard the story of how she was already waiting in Vegas for Victor and me when we went there to get married?"

Max laughed.

"How would me falling in love with Nila help her cause?" Mitch said to keep them on point. He was still trying to process the idea that some of the elders wanted Nila dead.

Was that why the Trackers hadn't caught Petrov? He'd assumed Petrov was responsible for that, but what if someone even more powerful was actually protecting Petrov? Mitch should have guessed something like this when Elizaveta warned him to avoid the elders' compound in West Virginia.

Since Petrov killed his mate—or so they all assumed—the entire council wanted him brought before them for punishment. But maybe not before Petrov got to Nila.

Mitch's thoughts whirled in crazy circles. He dropped his head into his palms. What the hell were they going to do if one or more of the elders wanted her dead? If one went after her?

And he'd thought Petrov was a dangerous enemy.

"Mitch, if you and Nila mate, Elizaveta can probably put more weight behind protecting her. Nila would be family then."

"Elizaveta's not allowed to do anything for me and my brothers—"

"She can still assert her not insignificant power to protecting Nila. The punishment against you boys doesn't pass on to your mates or children. Elizaveta is good with loopholes, and she made sure that one was in place. She wasn't just thinking about her family line continuing when she insisted you boys be allowed to take part in the Mate Run."

Mitch sat back, startled. He'd assumed his status would pass on to his wife and children—which was one of the reasons he'd never tried hard to get a tiger mate. Did his brothers know if they married their wives and children would be protected by Elizaveta's full elder power?

"In fact," Alexis added, "I'd be willing to bet Elizaveta already has a plan in place to bring Nila safely into the community without having to worry about her mate's status."

"She might be on to something," Max said. "You know your grandmother. Her plans are always several layers deep and as convoluted as a Russian novel."

"Why the hell wouldn't she tell me, though?"

Alexis snorted. "Right. What was she going to say? 'Sweetie, I need you to protect this woman and also seduce her so she'll marry you. Spasiba'."

Her imitation of his grandmother, right down to the Russian "thank you", was so exact Mitch cracked a smile. But his humor didn't last long. "She took a huge risk, if that was part of her plan."

"I'm sure she had other options in place," Alexis said. "But I wouldn't put it past her to have this as one possible outcome. You are the most charming of the infamous Chernikov brothers."

Mitch laughed and rolled his eyes.

"So, how does that change what we do?" Max asked.

"It means I care less if we kill Petrov. And it means we can't trust any of the other elders, the Trackers, or most of the tiger community for that matter."

"Killing Petrov isn't going to endear you to some," Alexis warned.

"He killed his mate," Max growled. "There's not a single male in our population who will forgive that."

"Except no one's been able to prove it or the elders would have brought him in weeks ago," Mitch said. "He has other tiger males working with him. What of them? None of them seem to care that he killed Anaya?"

Max snarled. "A few may not understand the severity of his crime. But most will and most will be good with his death."

"We're forgetting the fact that a lot of the community will see Nila as hope, too," Alexis said. "As a possible way out of the biological mess we're in. Elizaveta's research isn't universally approved, but it hasn't been derided by everyone either. In fact, she's had a lot of supporters over the years."

Mitch shrugged. "It only takes a few like Petrov, though, and if some of them are elders…"

"I think you're underestimating the desperation of our males," Alexis said. "Gregory and his pack are a good example of just how desperate they're getting. We need an answer to the crisis soon. And Nila will help with that answer. Even if she can't produce tiger children, she came from a tiger female. If we can figure out how that worked, how the process can be duplicated, we can find a way to survive."

Mitch knew Alexis was right. He'd thought as much himself frequently over the last week. "What about Gregory? What do we do about him? We can't go after Petrov and the young tigers at the same time."

"Gregory is a coward. He'll back off and bide his time," Max said, his lip curled. "If he has the balls to face us again, I'll kill him."

"Not a bad idea," Alexis said, ever the pragmatic. "One less thing to worry about."

"You think he'll back off? You're sure we can leave him to the elders?" Mitch's faith in the elders had fallen apart in the last half hour. Outside of his family and close friends, he didn't know who to trust anymore.

All he knew was that he loved Nila. He wasn't even sure how that had happened in so short a period of time—how he'd gone from lust to possessive need to a place where his world wouldn't be right without her in it. But there it was. Her safety and happiness were the only things that mattered to him anymore. The elders be damned.

"Gregory's group is a challenge to the elders," Alexis said. "They won't let that go. They might not be unified against Petrov, but I can safely say it's to their benefit to take care of this possible uprising of young males."

"They're already on it," Max confirmed. "I don't know what they're doing exactly, but I know for certain they've been taking steps since I first told them about Gregory."

"What steps?"

"I'm not privy to their plans," Max said sardonically. "I just know there is a plan."

"Fine." Mitch sighed and leaned forward, his forearms resting on his thighs. "We'll leave Gregory's group alone so long as they leave us alone. We concentrate on Petrov. Draw him out. A trap?"

"You're not using Nila as bait?" Max asked.

"Of course not, asshole." Mitch threw a pillow at Max, who swatted it away and grinned. "We plan a diversion. Make him think Nila is somewhere she's not. And then we take him down."

"What did you have in mind?" Alexis asked.

Mitch outlined the plan that had been taking shape over the last few hours. With their help, he hoped to have Petrov out of the picture and Nila safe in the next forty-eight hours. Then he would fly her, her father, and her grandmother to someplace romantic and marry Nila before any of the other tigers got any ideas.

He finally understood the frustration Max had gone through during the two years he had to run after Irina. And his rushed marriage once they'd conceived. There was nothing like a little possessiveness to make a man move fast to ensure the woman he loved couldn't get away.

By the time Mitch returned to Max's room to get Nila, it was well into the early morning hours. Both women were asleep, so Mitch scooped Nila off the bed and carried her back to their room. Victor silently escorted them to the door, signed goodnight, and waited outside until the lock turn before continuing past to his own room.

As Mitch settled Nila onto their bed, he felt a wave of gratitude for his friends. They were the only people he could trust now. And he was going to need their support in the coming weeks.

Running his fingers down Nila's cheek, he was tempted to wake her, to tell her their plans. And to see if he could get her naked again. Having her in a spare set of Alexis' clothes was infinitely better than having the stink of other males on her. But he liked her naked best.

He had to remind himself, she wasn't actually a full blooded tiger in the middle of estrous. She wouldn't have the stamina or energy. And she'd been through hell the last few days. She needed sleep.

He curled around her, pulling her tight to him as he laid down beside her. She sighed and snuggled deeper into his arms. His chest ached with tenderness and a contentment that went to his very soul. Just holding her made him feel better, settled. Stronger.

In the morning, he promised himself, he'd wake her with his mouth and his hands and make sure she came before she realized the sun was up. For now, he was happy to sleep beside her and savor this feeling of contentment for as long as he was allowed.

Chapter Thirty-One

Nila wrapped a towel around her as she climbed out of the shower she'd shared with Mitch. "Tell me again how this is going to lure Petrov away from me and not get you killed in the process?"

"Nila…"

"Don't 'Nila' me, buddy. You're talking about going up against a homicidal madman with only Max and Alexis on your side." She held up a hand. "And don't even start on leaving Victor behind to protect me and Irina. I still think you'll need him more than we will."

"There's no way Max will leave Irina unprotected now."

"Then we come up with another plan that doesn't leave you isolated at Max's cabin completely outnumbered by Petrov's tigers."

"So far, Petrov has only had five with him. Max, Alexis and I are more than a match for them."

"Five against three doesn't sound like odds in your favor."

Mitch pulled her close. Her body still hummed from the lovely way he'd woken her up, yet she wanted him again, badly.

She was tempted to unwrap the towel around his waist and use his still-damp body as a distraction from the day ahead. This crazy need to take him again and again had to be the estrous. If this turned out to be how she felt around him all the time, they were going to have a hard time staying out of bed long enough to make a living.

If they had a future.

"Alexis is a former Tracker," Mitch said. "She trains Trackers. She is literally legendary for her fighting skills. And Max and I have been kicking tiger ass together since we were kids." His arms tightened in a hug. "You said yourself you can't stay in hiding forever."

She scowled at having her own words thrown back in her face. "Yeah, but my idea was to negotiate with Petrov, not try to ambush him."

"And you think you'd have better luck negotiating with a madman than I'll have trapping him?"

Huffing out a breath, she focused on his chin so she'd stop being tempted by his mouth while trying to concentrate. Unfortunately, for some really odd reason, even his chin turned her on. "Fine. Negotiation wasn't ever really an option. But this… At least let me go with you. What better bait than to actually have me there?"

He was shaking his head before she'd finished her sentence. "Already discussed and rejected. None of us want you anywhere near Petrov."

"You're sure the Trackers are no longer an option? I mean, it's their job right?"

"And so far, they haven't been very successful doing that job. I don't know what's happened, but we can't rely on anyone else anymore."

"I hate this. I really really hate this."

"The situation or the plan?"

"You know I hate the situation. The only good thing about all this was meeting you."

He smiled, that slow, seductive smile of his, and her heart did a funny little dance against her ribs.

"But," she said, keeping her hormones in check a few moments longer, "I was talking specifically about the plan. I don't like it. I don't like you risking your life for me." She frowned. "Any more than you already have, that is."

"I don't want you being in danger when there's something I can do about it," he countered. "And I can take care of Petrov." He brushed the back of his hand down her cheek, then tucked one finger under her chin and lifted her face so she had to meet his gaze. "I am very motivated to get him out of the picture. Trust me."

"You know I trust you, Mitch. But trusting your strength and trusting the universe not to throw a wrench in the whole mess are two different things."

He pressed his lips to hers. The contact was enough to start her pulse pounding all over again. Heat seeped through her belly and tingled along her skin, sparking need and hunger in her blood.

"You're doing this on purpose," she murmured against his mouth before kissing him again.

"Yes. But not to distract you." He set his forehead against hers. "I intended that to be a comforting gesture."

"Worked against you, though, didn't it?" She ground her hips against his full erection and chuckled at his groan. "That'll teach you."

He lifted his head and cupped her face, taking a deep breath. "We'll do everything we can to keep the odds in our favor. I promise. I fully intend on coming back to you."

"You better," she said, then kissed him, hoping to lose herself in his touch, to memorize his feel. Fear drove her already simmering passion into full blown desperation.

Both towels hit the floor at the same time and then his hands were on her naked skin again. She ground herself against him, sighing as his palms smoothed down her spine and cupped her ass, pulling her up tight against his cock. She wrapped a leg around his hip to get as close as she could.

Lifting her off her feet effortlessly, Mitch carried her to the bed. She was so hungry to have him inside her, she would have been happy with the bathroom counter. But once they were sprawled on the mattress, she found her need to memorize every inch of him, to touch and taste and savor, overrode everything else. She needed to show him how much she loved him with her hands and mouth. He answered with a slow seduction of his own.

They hunted out and explored each sensitive spot—her waist, his lower abdomen, the inside of her elbow, the palm of his hand. Unexpected places they'd been in too much of a hurry to spend time on before were given focused attention.

Slow and passionate, building the need beyond anything Nila had ever felt before, until her whole world was Mitch and the growing tension in her core.

He brushed his lips against the inside of her thigh, and her hips bucked as the tension moved into something more insistent.

He licked his way from her thighs back up her body, giving her clit only painfully brief attention before he trailed his tongue along her hip bone and up the center of her stomach. He paused at one breast, pulling hard at her nipple with his lips. She moaned and buried her fingers in his hair, tugging him up so she could kiss him.

He covered her, slid into her, and set her tension free with a few steady strokes. She came hard and for a long time as he continued an unrelenting rhythm that drew out her release. He followed while she was still wracked by the shocks and tremors of her orgasm. The feel of him shuddering in her arms made her heart swell with a deeper satisfaction.

When he finally relaxed, she hugged him close, burying her face against his neck and drawing in his scent. She didn't want to let him go. Her instincts warned her something was wrong, and she'd always trusted those instincts. Without them, she might have run from Mitch at the airport to find security people who would not have been able to help her.

Now, those same instincts were telling her that separating was a bad idea. They needed to stick together if they were going to have a chance at taking care of Petrov.

The problem was she didn't have a better plan. Mitch was right. Something had to be done. Luring Petrov to Max's cabin was a reasonable idea.

If they had more tigers on their side.

Maybe Mitch was right. Between Alexis' skills and his and Max's, maybe the other tigers didn't stand a chance. Maybe five to three wasn't as bad as it sounded. But if Petrov rallied more than five tigers to his side…

For the first time in her life, she hoped her instincts were wrong.

CHAPTER THIRTY-TWO

While Mitch and Max scouted the area around the motel, checking for any sign of Petrov, Nila returned her borrowed clothes to Alexis for a fresh set from Irina. Alexis put on the clothes Nila had been wearing.

"You're sure they'll be fooled by the scent?" Nila asked. Again. Her always strong sense of smell seemed to have heightened over the last week, but she still didn't have a tiger's sensitivity to all the nuances.

"Trust us," Alexis said as she came back from the bathroom, buttoning the top button on the jeans. "These reek of your estrous cycle. This will be what the men smell. If they had any female tigers with them, the trick wouldn't work as well. She'd sniff out the different female undertones as soon as she got close enough. But the males are so driven by the estrous scent, they're much more likely to overlook the other tones and textures from me until it's too late."

"And by the time they figure it out," Irina said, "you and I will be far enough away they won't be able to backtrack and pick up your scent again."

"I'm not worried about them finding me, at the moment, I'm worried about Alexis making herself a target for a madman."

Alexis smiled as she sat beside them on the bed. She looked completely relaxed and not at all worried. "I am extremely hard to kill, Nila."

Irina put a hand on Nila's leg to get her attention. "Mitch told you what Alexis used to do for a living? What she does now?"

"Yes. But… How long has it been since you were an active Tracker?" Nila asked.

"Over twenty years now," Alexis answered. "But I've been training the Trackers since, which means I've stayed in excellent shape. Don't worry."

"Can I ask…," Nila hesitated, wondering how personal a question this was. "Since there are so few females, I'm surprised the elders would allow you to do such a risky job. Are there many female Trackers?"

"None now. I was an exception. But I had Elizaveta on my side. The rest of the elders didn't stand a chance against our combined determination."

"Mitch has said the Trackers are like tiger police?"

"Similar. Sort of a combination police, bounty hunter, and enforcer. We make sure the laws are upheld, and when they aren't, we bring in the guilty to face the elders' justice."

"Did you know Mitch's dad?" Nila's curiosity got the better of her more polite impulses.

"I brought him in," she said quietly. "My first job after being confirmed as a Tracker. Elizaveta sent me because she knew he'd come with me without a fight. He always had a soft spot for women. And I was only nineteen at the time. He didn't see me as a threat, which made things easier."

"He went willingly?"

"Of course. He would never have hurt me. And I made sure no one hurt him."

"So you've known Mitch since he was a baby?"

"And I helped him and his brothers when other tigers picked on them, when I could. I contributed to their fighting skills." She smiled as if at a memory. "Speaking of which, if you're interested, it might not be a bad thing for you to learn a few self-defense techniques. I can train you—I do that for a lot of our females. Our world can be a little rough. You might feel more comfortable if you knew how to, say, break a tiger's knee. Or his face." Alexis' grin took on a feral edge.

Nila raised her brows. "Actually, that would make me feel better. I was so out of my depth at that cabin. I had no idea how to help Mitch. I mean, I should at least learn how to throw a punch without breaking my hand." She considered the strength and speed she'd witnessed during Mitch's fights. "Though, since I'm not nearly as strong as a shifter, would it do me any good?"

"Sure with the right training. Winning a fight isn't always about brute strength. Plus a lot of our males fight on instinct, without any formal training. I could teach you how to take them down."

"Thanks." She found herself wondering again about Alexis' age. "How long were you a Tracker?"

"A little more than twelve years."

Nila was absolutely fascinated. She leaned closer as she studied Alexis. If she'd been thirty-one when she went from being Tracker to teacher and that was over twenty years ago, Alexis was at least fifty-one years old. She didn't look a day over forty.

"How long do you live?" Nila asked. "I never thought to ask Mitch, but… I have to say, you look phenomenal for your age."

Alexis chuckled. "Thanks."

"Tigers can live on average about a hundred and twenty to a hundred and thirty years," Irina said. "Most of our elders have passed that mark, though. Elizaveta won't admit it, but Max said he heard she was at least a hundred and fifty. There are whispers she might be as old as a hundred and seventy-five."

"Wow." Nila could barely comprehend living that long. The things Elizaveta must have seen… Nila wasn't sure if she'd want to live that long or not. But if she could do so healthy, she could only imagine what the world would be like a hundred years from now.

Would she live longer than average for a human? She'd inherited so many other things from her mother. A long life span would be a nice addition.

Though to have a chance at taking advantage of that trait, she first had to survive her current predicament.

The thought brought her back to the present. She pushed the fascinating topic of tiger biology aside—she'd spent all last night talking with Irina about tiger reproduction anyway; that would have to do for the moment.

"Petrov and his men would have got your scent at the young tigers' cabin, right?" she asked Alexis.

"Probably. But I'm betting they'll assume I've been left to guard Irina."

"It's what most of our males would do, given I'm pregnant and having a girl," Irina said. "They'd leave a strong tiger to protect me if my mate couldn't."

"But we'll have Victor with us. Wouldn't they consider that?"

"Most males are so possessive of their mates," Alexis said, "they're more likely to assume Max would prefer leaving a strong female as guard. And that female would have her own mate as backup."

"So you're assuming Petrov will think both you and Victor are with Irina and Mitch and Max are with me?"

Alexis nodded.

"What if they don't? From what everyone tells me, Petrov isn't thinking normally for a tiger shifter. How can you anticipate what a crazy man might or might not assume?"

"We can't," Alexis said with a shrug.

"Then why do this at all?" Nila said. "Why don't we all just run away to some far flung place and gather a larger crowd to help?"

"We'll have a hard time finding more tigers we can trust, Nila." Alexis spoke quietly, gently, but there was an undercurrent in her tone.

"Because of me? What I am?"

She nodded.

"What happens after Petrov?"

Alexis exchanged a look with Irina that Nila couldn't interpret. Finally, Alexis said, "You'll go with Mitch to meet the elders. And there will be discussions."

Nila was already shaking her head before Alexis finished. "I'm not discussing anything. I'm telling. Mitch and I are a couple. If that doesn't work out for some reason, there's no way in hell I'm having anything to do with another male tiger. I'll donate my blood for your research, but that's it. I'm not going to be a pawn in this game."

Irina frowned and nibbled at her bottom lip. Alexis glanced at the wall behind Nila for a long, quiet moment.

"I know you've been through a lot in the last week or so," Alexis said, "and that all this is a shock. I know you'd rather leave it behind and ignore it, but you can't anymore."

"I have no intention of ignoring it. I just don't plan on playing into it."

Alexis looked at her again with a gentle smile. "You sound like me when I was younger, insisting I could do as I pleased and wouldn't be pressured by the community."

"So you understand."

"More than you realize. It won't be easy, though. You're talking about standing against a great deal of desperation and power. There will be a lot of pressure put on you to 'do your duty' and contribute to the tigers' survival."

"That's the thing. It's not my duty," Nila pointed out. "I'm not one of you. Not fully, anyway. There's a reason my mother left me with my father—to keep me out of your world. I am not going to change everything I am, my entire life, for a community I only just found out about. And after the reception I've gotten, with tigers trying to kill and rape me, I'm not inclined to embrace the community as my own."

Irina reached forward and gripped Nila's knee, giving it a reassuring squeeze. "Let's worry about this after we take care of the immediate problem of a crazy tiger out to get you. You might find you like our people more when you meet the non-crazy ones. Especially if you and Mitch…" She trailed off but raised her brows as if expecting Nila to finish the sentence.

Nila huffed out a breath. "Yes, yes, I'm insanely in love with the man." She made a face. "Which makes all my protests a moot point, because I've already played into Elizaveta's hands. If Mitch and I stay together, I will have done exactly as Elizaveta wanted and mated with a tiger male."

Nila put her forehead into her hand for a brief moment. When she looked back at the two women, she frowned at their suspiciously pleased smiles. "But I'm not running off and having children right away. Mitch and I might not even be able to. I've never tried for kids before. I don't even know if I could with a human man, nonetheless with a shifter. Don't get your hopes up."

Alexis raised her hands in surrender. "Fair enough. Victor waited a long time for me, and we still managed to work things out. I'm sure things will work out with you and Mitch."

The mention of Alexis' mate reminded Nila of something. "Does Victor ever speak? I'm not sure I've heard his voice since I met him."

"You wouldn't have. He was severely injured when he was a cub. He hasn't been able to speak since."

"How do you two communicate?" Nila asked.

"We use sign language. He's not deaf so I can just talk, too, if I'm feeling the need to ramble out loud." A sly smile lifted Alexis' lips. "But a lot of things don't require words."

Nila grinned, but before she could indulge her nosiness further, the door opened and the men joined them.

She caught Mitch's attention the instant he walked in.

He held her gaze, determination clear in every strong line of his face. "We're ready. It's time."

CHAPTER THIRTY-THREE

Nila glanced back at Irina, frowning. "You sure you're okay?"

They weren't even an hour out from the motel, and Irina looked pale. They still had at least three or four more hours of driving through the back woods to reach the hotel where they would rendezvous with the others after Petrov was caught. Nila wasn't entirely sure Irina would make that drive without a few stops.

"I'm fine," the pregnant woman said with a shake of her head. "Just a little nauseated. The movement of the car on these curvy roads isn't agreeing with Her Highness."

"We should stop, then, give you a break."

"Not yet. Let's get farther away from the motel first. Just in case."

The hotel they were heading for was in the opposite direction of Max's cabin, and required they leave the motel going a completely different route to the direction the others took. They were all counting on the very obvious trail Alexis had left with Nila's scent to disguise their movements.

Nila still didn't like this. She hated being separated from Mitch. For more than a week, she'd put her life in his hands, and despite everything, he'd done a fine job of keeping her alive. She'd grown used to having him around. Now, she felt exposed without him. Not entirely defenseless—Victor had a handgun under her seat as well as his own, both easy to reach in an emergency. But still… Mitch made her feel steady, and able to deal with this world she'd been thrown into, despite the fact that she was way out of her depth.

She hated that she might have to use a gun again. The last time had been bad enough. She was certain she'd have issues to deal with when this was all over, though what she'd tell a therapist that wouldn't get her arrested or locked away, she had no idea. She never did find out if she'd actually killed one of those men who'd chased her and Mitch from John's cabin. Just a couple of days ago? Had that been so recent? So damned much had happened since then, she'd never really had a chance to process the fact she'd had to shoot another living being.

And here she was with the very real possibility she might have to do so again.

Only if their plan went wrong, she reminded herself as she stared out the window at the passing trees. If everything went the way it was supposed to, she'd never even have to see Petrov or his people again.

She refused to think about the future after that, and the fact she was still officially stuck in this world she wanted nothing to do with. Nothing beyond Mitch, that was. As she let her gaze blur on the passing greenery, she wondered if she'd feel differently if her introduction to the tiger shifters hadn't been so fraught with danger. If no one had come to kill her and she'd been gently introduced to this species, would she be more comfortable stepping into their world?

Reluctantly, she had to admit she probably would. Under her fear and anger there was a lot of curiosity, both personal and scientific. If she'd been given the chance to meet with people not intent on killing her, she'd be full of questions and eager to help solve their problem with their female population. As a vet, preventing an entire species from going extinct was fundamental to her world view and lined up perfectly to what she'd spent her life doing. She had skills and knowledge to bring to the challenge the tiger shifters faced. She could help beyond the mere fact of her biology.

The question was could she get past this first introduction, to a place of mere curiosity and willingness to help? Or would she always be angry and afraid? Resentful of the position they'd put her in?

With a quiet, masked sigh, she accepted she couldn't answer those questions yet. Not while she was still on the run. Not while she still had to face the elders and insist she would have no other tiger but Mitch. The possibility that the interfering bastards might try to keep her and Mitch apart still hung between them. What would they do if his governing body forbade him to be with her?

For her part, she'd give his elders the finger and run away with him. But could he do that to his own grandmother?

She hoped so. Because she was so desperately in love with the man, imaging her life without him was grim. He'd said she'd be given a choice, and they wouldn't try forcing her hand. She held on to that with all her might, determined to make her choices for herself, no matter what.

If they didn't try interfering with her decision, she would get over her resentment. In time. Maybe she could find it in her to help their scientists in the effort to save the species. From the moment she took up her career, her goals revolved around helping big cat species survive and prosper—whether in zoos and sanctuaries or in the wild. When she looked at it from that perspective, how could she not do everything in her power to help these tigers?

If they let her help in her way. Not theirs.

That was the rub.

Nila turned when she heard Irina make a slight hissing noise as they drifted gently around a bend in the road. If anything, the woman looked paler. "Victor, I think we might have to pull over?"

"No," Irina said. "I really am fine. I promise not to throw up all over your car, Victor."

Victor looked at her in the rearview mirror and smiled. Nila realized it was the first time she'd seen him grin that big. He looked almost boyish with that expression on his face. She smiled despite herself.

Until his grin dropped, replaced instantly by a glare. Irina's eyes widened and her mouth rounded in an "o" of surprise.

"Son of a bitch," she cursed and looked out the back window.

Before Nila could follow her gaze, their Jeep was slammed from behind, throwing her hard against her seatbelt. Tires screeched, Irina cursed again, Nila screamed, and Victor worked frantically at the wheel. The Jeep lurched again as another hit came and the sound of crunching metal made Nila's stomach bottom out. She held onto the door handle, her other hand pressed against the dashboard, her muscles tensed and ready for the next impact.

On the third hit, Victor lost control. Nila couldn't even scream as they careened off the road and slammed head first into a massive tree.

Mitch tried to control the bounce of his leg in the back seat of Max's SUV, but the effort to keep still proved beyond him. He had never in his entire life had trouble holding still. Being able to freeze and remain unseen were so much a part of his internal make-up, his very being, the fact that he couldn't keep from fidgeting had him worried about his mental balance.

For the first time in his life, he was glimpsing the same emotions in himself that drove his father to kill after his mother's death. He finally understood, in the depths of his soul, how his father could go so completely crazed after losing his mate. Because Mitch knew if he lost Nila, he'd never recover.

"She's going to be fine, Mitch," Alexis said from the front seat beside Max. "We won't let her get hurt. Victor will protect her and Irina with his life."

Mitch didn't miss the tightening around her eyes when she said this last. They both knew she'd turn into an avenging angel if Victor was killed. She would respect his sacrifice for the women. But she would slaughter those responsible for forcing him to that action.

Mitch knew exactly how she felt.

The problem was, if Victor was killed, Nila and Irina would be in a lot of trouble. And Mitch wouldn't be there to protect her.

The farther they drove, the further apart he got from Nila, the more he regretted this plan. Not knowing, not having her beside him where he knew she was safe, was harder to deal with than he'd thought when they started this particular game. He pulled the phone out of his pocket and checked it, even though he knew she hadn't called. She'd taken a new cellphone Max had bought for them, so there was no way Petrov could track it. He held Max's phone, so if the others needed to reach them, he could answer immediately.

She hadn't called. As far as he could tell, everything was going to plan.

But he couldn't shake the feeling that something was wrong.

He finally forced his body to still, taking in several deep breaths to steady his rapidly beating heart. Then he stretched out his senses. What was wrong? What was…missing?

"No one's following us," he murmured, his eyes half-closed as he concentrated.

"We knew they'd stay far enough back that you couldn't pick them up," Alexis said, but she frowned as she looked past him out the back window to the highway traffic.

"But I did pick them up. When we were half an hour away from the hotel. Petrov was behind us. I felt him."

"He's probably just fallen back," Max said, keeping his concentration on the increasing traffic around them.

"No," Mitch said. He was sure now. "They're not back there anymore." He met Alexis' gaze as horror slipped into his bloodstream and he knew why he'd been getting more fidgety as they continued away from Nila. "They've figured us out. They know Nila's not in this car. They've found her."

Chapter Thirty-Four

Nila unsnapped her seatbelt as soon as they stopped so she could check on Victor. His side of the car took the brunt of the hit, and he wasn't moving. As she reached to check his pulse, she said, "Irina, you with me?"

Irina groaned in response.

"The baby?"

"We're both still here." Her voice was weak but lucid.

To Nila's relief, Victor had a pulse. She was about to lean back to check on Irina when the front two car doors were ripped away. She gasped, swallowing a scream as she faced the nasty end of a gun across a still unconscious Victor. Looking over her shoulder, to her door, she saw the man who'd tried kidnapping her from the airport smiling at her.

He motioned with his own gun. "Lean back now, Nila. Cooperate. Or we kill them both."

She eased away from Victor but couldn't force herself into her seat and so close to the sneering shifter. She didn't speak, waiting to see what the men would do.

The one beside Victor shifted his gun to settle it against the unconscious man's skull. He stared at Victor with his head tilted to one side. His intense concentration made Nila's stomach clench.

"Cellphones," her would be kidnapper said. "Toss them out."

Reluctantly, Nila pulled her phone from her thigh pocket. She was tempted to throw it at the kidnapper's head but was afraid he'd shoot her on accident. Or out of spite. Bidding her time, she did as he said and threw the phone past him, into the dirt.

Irina leaned forward, toward her purse. And the man's gun shifted her direction. "Easy, there, pretty. No sudden moves. Toss the entire purse out."

With a snarl, Irina did as told.

"I need to check her and Victor. To make sure they're not hurt," Nila said.

The man shrugged. "Why bother?"

"You said if I cooperate, you won't kill them. That's a pointless promise if they die from their injuries."

He chuckled. "Quickly, then, doctor. And only Irina. You have one minute."

Nila leaned between the bucket seats and tested Irina's abdomen. "Did you hit your head, does anything feel pulled?" Nila asked quietly as she ran her fingers along Irina's arms, then studied her face closely for signs of shock.

"I'm fine," Irina muttered, still glaring at the kidnapper on Nila's side of the car. "I can't believe you'd align yourself with a male who would kill his mate."

Nila didn't look at him, so she couldn't see his expression. His voice was neutral as he said, "She committed suicide. I can't blame her. If I'd birthed an abomination and my mate discovered the truth, I'd have killed myself, too."

Irina stared at him as Nila finished her exam. When Nila leaned back, Irina said, "Either you're a good liar, Stephen, or he's lied to you. Either way, you're pathetic."

Nila swallowed as she heard the man growl and watched him level the gun at Irina. "Please," Nila said to distract the man—Stephen—from Irina. His gun swung back toward her and he raised his brows. "You said you wouldn't hurt them. I'll do what you want, just leave them be."

Stephen snorted. "You'll do what I say anyway." He glanced at the other man then shrugged. "But Petrov wants the honors, so I can't shoot you yet. At least not dead. There are other places I can shoot you that will hurt like hell without killing you, though. So don't get any ideas."

Before she could respond, she heard Victor move and a gun click. Swinging around to face the other two tigers, she reached out for Victor. He was staring hard at the other man, who was staring back, the gun set firmly against Victor's temple. She tried squeezing Victor's arm, to get him to back down. But he ignored her efforts. She watched in tense horror as the tiger with the gun narrowed his eyes.

Stephen spoke into the heavy silence. "Do you really want Alexis coming after you? He dies from the car accident, she can't blame you. You shoot him, she'll rip you apart."

The man considered Victor for a long moment. He said in a quiet, gravely voice. "He's not hurt badly enough to die." He never moved the gun from Victor's head.

"Wound him if it'll make you feel better, then," Stephen said, unconcerned. "If he survives, she might not bother hunting you down."

Nila widened her eyes and her head spun. "You can't. We're too far off a main road. He'll bleed out before help arrives."

Stephen shrugged. Not the least concerned with the outcome. Nila leaned in closer to Victor, but Stephen jerked her back by an arm, sending her sprawling across the seat and bringing her hard up against his chest. Irina sat quietly, still glaring at Stephen rather than watching the other two men. Nila couldn't take her eyes off Victor and the gun at his head.

Several long seconds passed before the gunman moved his weapon away. Nila held her breath. She felt helpless as she watched, and though she pulled against Stephen's hold, she couldn't budge.

There was a gun just under her seat! She should have gone for that first, before checking injuries. Stupid, stupid. But her first instinct was to heal, not hurt. That instinct was going to get them all killed.

When the man staring at Victor finally looked up at Stephen, Nila realized how dead his eyes looked. Cold. Emotionless. She couldn't find any compassion, any anger, anything at all in his expression.

She was so sure he would kill Victor, she actually let loose a breath of relief when he walked away without spending a single bullet. Before she could savor her relief, though, Stephen jerked her backward, pulling her in a heap from the car.

As Stephen hauled her up to her feet, she looked back at Irina and Victor. They were both staring at her now, eyes identically narrowed. She couldn't read their expression, but she noticed Irina no longer had a seatbelt on. And Victor had unsnapped his, though the shoulder strap was still in place. She shook her head as Stephen set his gun against her temple.

"If you try anything, I'll kill Irina," he told Victor.

Victor's muscles relaxed immediately and his gaze jumped to Nila's. She nodded her approval. She wouldn't be able to live with herself if she knew Irina was hurt because of her.

Irina, on the other hand, was not so quietly accepting. She growled at Stephen. "You could try and kill me," she muttered. "But it'd be harder to do than you think."

Stephen chuckled. "I'd love to play with you, pretty, but I have somewhere to be." He pulled Nila backward, keeping his attention on the two tigers in the car. "If you move before we leave, everyone dies. Slowly. And painfully."

As he passed Nila's cellphone, he stomped on it, crushing it into the dirt. She searched the ground, looking for Irina's purse but didn't see it anywhere. Her hope that they'd be able to contact the others immediately using Irina's phone lasted only a moment before she saw the other kidnapper emptying the contents under the front wheel of a four wheel drive truck, kicking the phone close to a tire. The front bumper was bashed in, so she knew that was the car that had run them off the road.

She also realized there were two more men in the flatbed of the truck, holding large shotguns, both pointed at the damaged Jeep. They'd been outnumbered all along. Even if she'd gotten out one of the guns under the seat, she wouldn't have been able to do anything against all four of them.

Swallowing back her fear and keeping her feet under her with an effort, she stumbled toward the truck. Stephen released her to open the door, but he kept the gun at her forehead. He shoved her into the narrow back bench. She barely had a chance to right herself before the truck took off. She looked out the back window. Victor and Irina were both standing outside the Jeep now, staring after her.

One of the men in the back was still pointing his gun toward them. The sound of the shotgun going off seemed to happen at the same time as Victor went down, blood exploding from his leg. Nila screamed.

Horrified, she watched Irina kneel down next to him as the truck swung around a corner. "Why?" she demanded, facing Stephen in the front seat.

"There was a chance he could follow otherwise," he said with a shrug. "He'll heal. But his knee'll be tricky for a while."

"What if he bleeds to death? What about all that talk of Alexis' wrath?"

Again the man shrugged. "I don't care if she rips out that man's throat." He finally turned to look at her. "He's human. Good riddance."

Nila swallowed down her panic along with the bile in her throat. Tears filled her eyes, leaking down her cheeks slowly.

What the hell was she going to do now? She couldn't run, she had no weapons, and the only potential help she had might be on the point of death. Swiping away the tears on her cheeks, she tried focusing, concentrating on where they were going, and on the men in the cab with her.

There was nothing she could do right now. But she was still alive.

She just had to figure out how to stay that way.

Chapter Thirty-Five

The shiny, silver metal barn glared in the sharp sunshine. Nila squinted at it as if she could see inside but afraid to imagine what might be there. The truck pulled behind the structure so it was hidden from the road. There were no nearby houses or other barns visible beyond the surrounding woods. At least not from the direction they'd been driving. She couldn't be sure if there were neighbors closer on the other side, but she suspected not. Petrov wouldn't bring her to a place where screams would attract attention.

The silent man with dead eyes left the truck without looking at her. She felt the vehicle rock with the other two climbing down from the flatbed. Stephen was the last to exit. He stood just outside the truck door, looking around, his head raised. Then he looked back in.

"Come on," he grunted, motioning her out with his gun.

She looked for the other men as she climbed out. If she could surprise them, get to the woods before they shot her, she might be able to reach the main road and help before they had time to shift and chase her. Stephen must have sensed her intentions, though, because he grabbed her arm in a bruising grip before her feet touched the ground.

He set the gun to her forehead. "Petrov wants to kill you himself," he said against her ear. "But he's promised some of the tigers they can play with you first. So I'd rather not have to shoot you yet. Believe me when I say I will, though, if you try anything at all. I'm willing to face Petrov's displeasure."

He held her tight against his chest as he sniffed her neck. The gesture made Nila snarl in disgust, but jerking away would move her toward the gun so she held still.

"Estrous," he muttered. "You really are a mixed breed."

She held her tongue even as she continued scanning the area, looking for a way out, biding her time. The two human men from the back of the truck had moved inside the barn. The other tiger waited a few feet away, staring at them with his emotionless gaze.

Stephen flicked his tongue out, tasting her skin. Nila clenched her jaw to keep from reacting. Her muscles were tight so she forced herself to relax. She wouldn't be able to move well if she was too tense. She watched the dead-eyed tiger for reaction. Nothing. He just stared.

Stephen finally raised his head and pushed her forward. "Petrov is right to kill you," he said as they headed toward the small door inset in the larger barn doors.

"Why?"

The other tiger fell in beside them. He had his gun in his hand, but he held it down against his thigh, his finger along the side rather than over the trigger.

As they reached the open door, Stephen finally answered her. "You'll destroy our species." Then he shoved her into the dark interior.

Inside, the barn was much cooler than she'd expected. She'd been assuming all that metal in the sunshine would leave the place sweltering. Goose bumps rose on her arms as her eyes adjusted to the darkness. There were only a couple open windows, high up near the ceiling, so the space was twilight dim. When she could see enough to assess the area, she realized it was wide open and clean, the cement floor beneath her smooth and gray. The place looked brand new, but there was no indication what the barn would eventually be used for.

"Do you like it?" a deep and unfortunately familiar voice asked.

The sound echoed in the open space. She waited where she stood, just inside the door, flanked by Stephen and the dead-eyed tiger as Petrov walked toward her. He wasn't as tall as she'd expected, maybe six foot, and lean but in a coiled, well-muscled way. His blond hair was almost white, his eyes a piercing blue. Given Vlad's appearance, she'd expected Petrov to be darker. Anaya's traits must have been dominant. At least with the oldest son.

She wonder what Petrov's tiger would look like. Maybe a white Amur to match his white hair and eyes? Or did such things carry into their tiger forms?

"The barn," he clarified when she didn't respond to his question. "A fortunate find, don't you think?" He stopped in front of her, close enough to touch, and stared into her eyes. "Do you speak?" he asked with a slight smile.

He studied her face up close. She watched his blue eyes, his mouth, his expression, looking for hints to his state of mind. She saw anger there, tightly controlled, and the slight twitch of his lip into a faint snarl gave her a clear sign he felt disgust. But there was something else that passed over his expression as he stared, something she couldn't identify. Unfortunately, whatever it was didn't look gentle or forgiving.

"You look like her," he murmured.

He spoke so quietly, she wondered if he'd meant for her to hear that. "Everyone tells me I look like my father."

His expression froze. Nothing changed in the way he looked at her, but she saw he held the expression with difficulty. The creases around his eyes deepened slightly, the only indication of a reaction to her statement.

"You're small," he said, "and weak. So was your mother."

She had no response to that, so she just stared back, refusing to drop her gaze or rise to his bait. He wanted her dead and she was seriously outnumbered, but he seemed to want to play games with her rather than just putting a bullet in her brain. That meant she had time—to plan, to escape. She just had to avoid pissing him off further and forcing him to act.

But she had no intention of being cowed by her mother's mate either.

After a long moment, he finally nodded to Stephen. "The restraints."

Stephen grabbed her arm and hauled her toward the opposite side of the barn. She looked around for escape options and noticed the two human men were nowhere to be seen, but she didn't see another door. There was no sign of Vlad, or either of the tigers she'd shot.

She scanned the floor. There had to be a cellar entrance, someplace for the humans to have gone. Despite her search, though, she couldn't spot anything. The space was huge though and the ground near the walls was difficult to study as Stephen walked her in a straight line down the middle of the barn. There had to be another exit somewhere, something she might be able to use.

Her thoughts jumped to Mitch. Were some of Petrov's men following him and the others? Was he walking into a trap of his own? Or would Petrov leave him alone now that he had her? Not likely. He seemed too ruthless for that. But maybe Irina had managed to get help, to warn Mitch.

Halfway across the huge space, she finally looked up and noticed at the far end of the barn a set of leg manacles set into the cement and a matching set hanging from the metal wall. They gleamed silver in the dim light. The chains attached to the manacles had links the size of her fist. Those restraints were designed to hold someone a lot stronger than a mere human woman.

She balked, stopping her forward progress. If they chained her with those things, she was dead. There would be no escape. Stephen shoved her hard in the middle of the back, making her stumble a few steps forward and drop to her hands and knees.

"Up," he ordered, snatching a handful of her hair and jerking her head back.

She hissed at the pain and grabbed at the base of the clump he had to keep him from ripping her hair out. She rose awkwardly to her feet. With his hand still wrapped in her hair, he pushed her forward again. The closer she got to the chains, the harder her heart hammered.

"Why chain me?" she asked. "You've got me outnumbered and outgunned. Not to mention you're a lot stronger and faster than I am. Where the hell am I going to go?"

"You got away from me once before," Stephen said against her ear. "Not gonna happen again. And as I said, Petrov wants to play with you first."

She shuddered and ground her teeth together to hold in her fear. "He killed her," she murmured. "He killed Anaya. She didn't commit suicide."

Stephen didn't respond, just jerked her hair in a hard tug that almost sent her sprawling again. It mattered to him, how Anaya had died. She was sure of it. He wouldn't have told Irina that Anaya killed herself if he cared one way or the other. Petrov had lied to him. Knowing that might just get her out of this, though she wasn't sure how yet.

She needed to convince him Petrov had lied. But how? Especially when she didn't have any proof. One thing she was sure of, though. After staring into Petrov's eyes, at the violence and disgust there, Nila had no doubt he'd killed Anaya.

And he would kill her, too.

Her feet barely obeyed her commands to move the last few yards to the manacles. Panic made her breathe faster, and despite the pressure Stephen used to push her forward, animal fear had her trying to scramble away from the chains. Her terror lent her strength. She managed to throw Stephen off balance and get around behind him before he jerked hard on her hair again. This time, she did end up falling, landing hard enough on her ass to momentarily push the air from her lungs. Before she could suck in a breath, Stephen and the dead-eyed tiger had both of her arms.

They dragged her backward to the manacles. She fought, thrashing and kicking, even slipping free from Stephen's hold once, but he caught her up again. She couldn't shake them both off, not with their superior strength. She hated that her fear was driving her to this. She had to stay calm, she had to remain aware, but the thought of being helplessly chained triggered all her most basic animal instincts to flee.

Despite being half their size and nowhere near as strong, it still took both men to get her slammed up against the corrugated metal and the manacles snapped around her wrists and ankles. She fought and struggled until the last wrist restraint clicked into place. Even then she jerked at the bindings. She could barely move her legs and her arms where spread far enough apart, she had no leverage.

She only stopped struggling when Stephen took her face in his hands and set his nose against hers. The shock of his closeness made her jerk away, bouncing her head hard off the wall. That stupid move was enough to stun her into a momentary quiet.

When she'd calmed down, Stephen said, "Struggle more and you'll bleed to death slowly from the wounds you'll cause."

"I'm a dead woman anyway, right?"

"True. But you can choose to die quickly, when Petrov's ready. Or you can continue to fight the inevitable and make your death a lot more painful. Up to you."

"Bastard," she snarled, unable to help herself.

"I'm not the half-breed here."

"No. You're not good enough for that."

His hands tightened on her cheeks, and for a brief flash, she thought he might break her neck. To her surprise, the dead-eyed tiger grabbed his wrist and forced him back. The two men exchanged a long look. Then all of Stephen's muscles relaxed and he walked away without another word.

The dead-eyed tiger watched him until he left the barn by the same door they'd come through, then he looked at her.

"You do look like Anaya," he said in his low gravelly voice, but with absolutely no emotion in his tone.

She couldn't tell how he felt about her resemblance to her mother, if he felt anything at all.

"Stephen ran for Anaya. He caught her once. But Petrov succeeded in getting her pregnant after Stephen failed."

"Then how can he help the man who killed her? How can you?"

"You'll ruin us," he said.

Again his tone was so flat she had no idea if he cared about what he was saying. "I'm just one woman. I can't destroy your entire species."

"Yes, you can."

With that, he walked away. She jerked at her chains and called to him, but he ignored her. She wanted more answers.

She wanted to understand why these others were helping Petrov. Did the dead-eyed tiger think she was an abomination, too? What of the lie Petrov had told them about Anaya's death? Was that buying their loyalty?

So many questions. She jerked at the chains again, biting her lip when the manacles cut into her wrist and she felt blood drip down her forearms. She knew she had to calm down, to think and try figuring a way out of this. But as the dead-eyed tiger left the barn and she realized she was alone, chained to a wall by binding she couldn't budge, panic once again took hold, its fist tightening around her throat.

Her screams echoed off the distant walls.

CHAPTER THIRTY-SIX

Exhaustion finally forced Nila into silence. Her body ached from her attempts to escape the manacles and from being held in the awkward position. Blood dripped down her arms in grotesque stripes and her wrists burned from having the metal rings gouging into the injuries. Her ankles weren't as sore because she couldn't move enough to cause herself much more injury than bruising.

The longer she stood there, contemplating the huge, echoing space, the more numb her limbs grew. They would hurt like a bitch when she was released—if she was released. But numb was better than screaming pain.

As the overwhelming animal panic eased, she searched the area near her for some exit other than the barn doors. Her hope of finding a trap door or something to use for a weapon was short lived as the floors were scrubbed spotlessly clean, not a stray bit of straw, piece of wire, or plank of wood anywhere.

Waiting gave her too much time to think, to regret, to imagine the worst. She tried focusing on something good, something positive, and her thoughts turned to Mitch. Was he okay? Did he realize she'd been taken yet? Had they found Victor in time to save his life? Would Mitch try to find her?

Rescue might be her only hope, but she had no idea how they'd locate her. Could they follow her scent despite the smell of the truck? She was apparently still in estrous. Was that scent strong enough to leave a trail? They'd been counting on Petrov following the smell of her on Alexis' clothing. Did that mean Mitch would be able to track Nila to same way?

And would they kill her before he could find her?

She pushed that thought aside. Panicking had only hurt her. She had to concentrate, to study her surroundings, and be ready for anything. She opened her other senses, focusing on what she couldn't see. She had trouble smelling anything beyond the stink of her own fear and blood, but she could listen. And maybe with that newly discovered sense of the presence of tiger shifters, she could pick up how many were in the area.

Closing her eyes, she listened, searching for anything useful, and opened her awareness. In the distance, she could just hear the sound of a single car, but it never got closer so obviously wasn't coming her way. Birds were in the trees surrounding the barn. A breeze ruffled the leaves in quiet music. The barn itself was an echoing silence. Except for her own breathing, there wasn't even the scurry of rodents to distract her.

Beyond what she could hear, she did get that pinpoint sense of awareness that she'd learned indicated the presence of shifters. She felt three different points of danger, two together at the front of the barn, one off past the direction they'd parked the truck. So no more tiger shifters around than the ones she knew about—at least not near enough for her to sense. Since she was as scared now as she'd been at Gregory's cabin, she wondered if she'd been unable to sense individuals there because of the number rather than her fear, or if she just didn't know how to use this new sense well enough yet?

No way to answer those questions yet. It was enough to know, if she concentrated, right now she could sense the shifters in the area.

She frowned and finally opened her eyes, contemplating the barn's interior. Was it really new? Or was it this clean because Petrov had made it this way? If it wasn't new, what had it been before it was turned into her prison? Or had he built it for her? That didn't make sense. He hadn't known about her long enough for that. But he'd had almost a month to decide how he'd kill her. He could have found this place and cleaned it out. He had so much money, maybe he had had it built.

Since no one was around to answer any of her questions, she concentrated on the sounds surrounding her. If there was a cellar, it was sound proofed because she couldn't hear so much as a scratch of movement beneath the cement floor. A car whooshed by on the road, making her heart jump. It didn't even pause. Even if her throat wasn't sore from screaming earlier, she doubted passengers in the moving car would hear her anyway.

Every time she thought she sensed movement, she popped her eyes open. But the barn remained empty. When she concentrated on trying to sense them, she continued to feel the two shifters just outside the barn doors. They remained in the same location every time she opened her awareness—though when she wasn't trying, she couldn't sense them. The third tiger moved beyond her ability to feel not long after she started keeping track, so she was left wondering where he'd gone.

Hours passed as she listened and watched. And waited.

When the barn actually started getting darker, she realized it must be close to sunset. No one had come inside to check on her. Even though she knew there were still two shifters just outside the barn doors, she was terrified they'd just leave her dangling here to die a slow death. But since that meant she wasn't being raped and murdered, she had a hard time viewing that as the worst outcome.

She was parched, though, and her stomach rumbled with a combination of hunger and fear. She'd been standing in her forced spread eagle for so long now, her fingers were icy cold and chills raced over her exposed skin. The cool air was actually making her a little crazy. She liked heat and summer. Her personal Hell would be a frozen wasteland. The barn wasn't actually cold. Just cool. A temperature that might have been pleasant under different circumstances.

Her thoughts scattered when the barn door opened.

The dead-eyed tiger stalked in, carrying something in one hand. Surprisingly, she relaxed with relief that it was him and not Stephen. His utter lack of concern or interest in what was happening to her was somehow comforting. At least she knew where she stood with him. Sort of.

When he neared, he held up a water bottle. "You need to drink."

She studied the bottle as her dry mouth yearned for a sip. Caution had her asking, "Is it drugged?" She knew this man would tell her the truth. He had no reason to lie. He didn't care enough.

"No." He glanced at her wrists. "Should have been. But he wants you hurting."

"Why? I've never done anything to him."

"You exist."

"That's not my fault."

"Fault has nothing to do with this."

The way he said "this" made her wonder if there was something he found fault with in the situation, but he didn't elaborate.

He held the bottle to her lips and tipped it so she could drink.

When she'd gulped down a few large swallows, ignoring the excess that dribbled over her chin, she leaned her head back against the wall. "What's your name?"

For the first time, she saw a very slight change in his expression. His eyebrows rose just barely, but enough to assure her she'd surprised him.

"Joseph," he said, his voice even quieter than before.

"Joseph. What happened to you?"

"You should be worried about you."

"I am."

He turned and started back toward the exit.

"Thanks for the water," she called after him.

He didn't acknowledge her.

Then she was alone again. Her eyes narrowed to tired slits, she stared at the door, still with more questions than answers. Not the least of which was why had they bothered giving her water when they intended to kill her. And what the hell were they waiting for?

Chapter Thirty-Seven

It was full dark when Petrov, Stephen, and Joseph returned to the barn. As Nila watched them, she wondered where the human men were. For that matter, where was Vlad and his brothers? She had never sensed more than these three tigers all day—or at least three individual tigers; she couldn't tell who the tigers where just by sensing, not the way Mitch could. She kept expecting more shifters to show up to torment her. This waiting and not knowing was as tortuous as anything Petrov could do to her.

Petrov stopped a few feet away as the other two flanked her. He looked at her arms and shook his head. "Not very smart are you?"

She didn't rise to the bait.

He smiled. "You've led us a fine chase, Nila. I'm going to savor your death."

Petrov was sick, twisted. And like with Gregory, she couldn't understand why these other men would support him. Petrov didn't just want her dead to prevent her from bringing her human DNA into his lovely little tiger world. This wasn't just about preserving his species. He wanted revenge on her for something she had no part in or control over. Both Stephen and Joseph had to know that. Why did they go along? What had he offered them?

She remembered what Joseph had told her about Stephen, that he'd run for and even caught Anaya. "Did you savor your mate's death?" she asked Petrov, just to see how Stephen would react.

Petrov was in her face, nose to nose, so fast she never saw him move.

"She was a freak," he hissed. "An insult to everything we tigers are."

"Because she loved my father?"

"She never loved him. He was an accident, a passing fancy."

"You think she loved you? Why would she lie to you about me?"

His face turned red and a fine tremor shook his body while she watched. She was pushing too hard. He was going to lose control and snap her in half. But if there was a chance, even a slim shot at gaining help, she had to take it. She felt Stephen and Joseph both move in closer, but she didn't dare turn away from Petrov.

"How'd that feel?" she murmured. "Knowing you'd mated with a woman who didn't trust you?"

"She was a whore," he spit. "She deserved to die."

"You did kill her, didn't you?" she whispered, keeping her tone as even as possible, though terror and anger made her tremble.

He snatched her chin in a brutal grip. "The fact that you look like her will make it easier to kill you," he said. He set his mouth against her ear and said, "I'd kill her all over again if I could. She went too quickly. So you'll suffer for her betrayal. And I'll make sure nothing like you can ever happen again."

He pinched her chin so hard between his fingers, she thought he might actually crack her jaw, but then he released her with a sharp jerk and stepped back several paces.

"Take her down."

A blinding instant of relief at being freed from the chains was followed immediately by panicked fear. Joseph knelt in front of her and released her legs while Stephen freed one of her wrists. She wanted to look at Stephen to see if Petrov's admission had done any good, but she didn't dare look away from Petrov.

As soon as her one arm was free, her entire body sagged toward the floor and pain shot through her limbs. Her still manacled wrist screamed with pain as it took her full weight and her wounds were rammed against the metal. Fresh blood dripped down the inside of her forearm.

Stephen held her while Joseph released the final manacle. Once fully freed, she fell heavily against Stephen, unable to support her own weight. Her vision blurred as blood rushed to her limbs.

After several long moments, she got her feet beneath her and straightened away from Stephen. She had to keep her stance wide to keep from falling, but she managed. The fact that she managed to stand on her own, despite having gone without food since morning, barely any water all day, severely cut up wrists, and a full complement of fear chemicals racing through her blood, was a point of pride. She raised her chin a fraction and faced Petrov.

He looked over the blood on her arms and the abused skin of her wrists. "The smell of blood and estrous together…my tigers won't be able to resist." He practically purred the last statement.

Her stomach clench and her skin went cold, but she didn't respond.

"Let's go," he snarled.

Stephen and Joseph snatched her arms and dragged her toward the barn doors.

She couldn't resist asking, "We're leaving?" She'd thought for sure whatever he intended would take place in this huge, cool, bare space. Why bring her here otherwise?

"This was storage." He glanced over his shoulder. "Until night. But we prefer to play in the woods."

She scanned the floor. "What happened to the other two, the human men?" She didn't expect an answer, but the fact that she'd seen no sign of them since entering the barn left her with an awful suspicion.

Petrov gestured to the left, toward the barn wall. "Cold cellars are great for hiding the scent of dead flesh for a very long time. You'll join them. If there's enough left of you."

She bit the inside of her cheek to keep from saying anything more. She didn't want to know anything more. The fact that he'd killed the two men so casually, men who'd been working for him, only proved how deranged he was. Mitch had warned her Petrov would do this, but she hadn't expected him to kill off the humans so soon.

Thoughts of Mitch made her throat tighten. Was he even alive? She had no way of knowing and was afraid to even bring up his name to Petrov. If the man realized how much she loved Mitch, he'd use that emotion against her.

Petrov paused after opening the small barn door, his head up. He glanced around and seemed to scent the air before moving outside. His actions reminded her to open her awareness and feel for other tigers. Unfortunately, beyond the three with her, she couldn't sense anything. She knew more had to be out there somewhere, though, so she tried to keep her awareness open, though doing so took concentration.

She was pushed through the door without a pause. They marched her over the uneven soil past the truck and toward the woods. Full darkness and only a sliver moon made it difficult for her to see in the open area around the barn, despite her good night vision. Once they reached the woods, she'd be nearly blind. She knew if she was only human, with none of her mother's blood, she probably wouldn't be able to see as well as she could now. How well could the shifters see in the woods?

She squinted into the heavy darkness as they moved into the trees, attempting to make out something of her surroundings. She managed to see dark tree shapes against barely lighter space, but that was the best she could do. She had to rely on the two men still holding her arms to keep her from falling. As it was, they caught her several times when she tripped on downed branches or stepped into uneven depressions in the soil. She expected Stephen at least to curse her clumsiness, but both men simply hauled her back to her feet without comment each time she faltered.

Maneuvering through the rough undergrowth took all her concentration. After what felt like miles, they entered a clearing. Six men waited there, absolutely silent. No shuffling, no movement, no conversation. She didn't even realize they were there until they moved to surround her. She'd been so focused on staying upright, she'd forgotten to sense for other shifters.

Too late to bemoan the lapse now. She wasn't sure it would have done her any good anyway. Stephen and Joseph had never given her any room to escape. Even knowing what she was walking into wouldn't have prevented the inevitable.

A quick flash of light from a storm lamp brightened the area, casting the clearing in murky illumination. The men moved in closer, and her heart rate jumped. She opened her awareness and tried to gage if they were all tigers or not, but the number of them, all crowded so close defeated her. Like in Gregory's cabin, she just felt an encompassing aura of danger and couldn't pinpoint the location of any of the individuals. Was that the number of tigers around her now? Or were at least some of the men human?

They were all in human form—tigers or not. For some reason that worried her more than if they'd been in tiger form. While she didn't want her throat ripped out by a tiger, and she sure as hell didn't want them to tear bits out of her with predatorily sharp teeth, she didn't think they'd actually rape her in tiger form. In human form…

She swallowed and forced herself to remain still. Running from a predator was the worst thing she could do. They were sure to smell her fear already. No point in making things worse by triggering their chase instinct. But it took a great deal of control to keep still.

Joseph and Stephen held her at the center of the clearing as the others paced around her in a tight circle. Their silence drew her nerves out to breaking point. She tried to see their faces. Was Vlad one of them? His two brothers who'd been with Petrov at John's cabin? Would Vlad participate in raping and killing her, despite his earlier help? Despite being her half brother?

She realized she didn't recognize any of the men circling her. One looked a little like Petrov, so she thought that might be the brother she hadn't seen. But Vlad and the brother she'd shot weren't here. Questions rose, but she knew she wouldn't get answers and was afraid to give away a possible advantage. Vlad had claimed he didn't want her dead. If he was around, he might stop this.

But he'd helped her before behind his father's back. He didn't want Petrov to know. He'd hardly step forward now, surrounded by Petrov's allies, just to save her.

She was on her own.

And she had no idea how to get out of this alive.

Her heart hammered as the men circled closer, drawing out her tension and fear. She knew they were doing this on purpose, so she tried ignoring her growing panic, but it grabbed at her throat and tightened a band around her chest. Screams and curses clawed at her throat. Anything to break the silence, to disrupt the snap-wire tension drawing her tight.

When the men were close enough to touch Stephen and Joseph, they all stopped and faced her. The two directly in from of her looked her over, their gazes focusing on her breasts and legs. She was panting from fear, her chest rising and falling rapidly, and the movement brought a sadistic little smirk from one. Controlling her breathing was impossible, though, not when they remained quiet, unmoving and threatening all at once.

Her throat and mouth were so dry she wasn't sure she'd be able to scream now, even if she could force one out. She tried swallowing, but there was no moisture to wet her throat, and her efforts to relieve her lips only increased the one man's smile.

When Petrov cleared his throat, the sudden sound made her jump and an involuntary squeak escaped. The men chuckled. She snarled and cursed silently, but at least they were making some sound. Anything was better than the awful silence.

Then Petrov spoke, and she wished for the silence again.

"The first to have her," Petrov said, "will be the first to touch her."

The men surged forward in a wave of hungry violence.

Nila screamed as hard fingers and strong hands grabbed at her. Joseph and Stephen both dropped their hold, leaving her free. She didn't try running—she didn't have the room for it.

Instead, she fought, swinging her fists with as much force as she could muster, aiming for whatever bits of flesh she could hit, using all the strength she had left and the adrenaline of her fear to feed her fight. She clawed, punched, kicked, and bit anything that got close.

She wasn't strong enough to defeat them, but she had no intentions of allowing them to gang rape her. If she was going to die anyway, she intended to make them kill her before they had their fun.

Her size and their numbers actually worked in her favor. They weren't working as a single unit but were struggling against each other to get to her. She slipped around, dodging their longer reaches, slipping out of their holds. Her sweat and blood slicked her arms, making it difficult for any of the men to get a good grip on her. She cursed as she fought, swiveling to each new threat, clawing at clothes and flesh in kind. The men growled and cursed too, and when she connected particularly well, their howls made her shout in triumph.

Her satisfaction never lasted as their groping grew more violent. One managed to hold onto her arm long enough to toss her. She hit the ground hard, knocking her momentarily breathless. But the move had sent her beyond the circle of attackers. They all dove for her at once, getting in each other's way. She used their disorganized attack to scramble backward on her hands and feet.

She thought she heard laughter but didn't have the time to consider it. She already knew Petrov was enjoying this show.

His reaction fueled her anger, though, increasing her determination to hurt and maim and force them to kill her before they could rape her. Her limbs were heavy, her blows inaccurate and her body screamed, at the edge of its endurance, but adrenaline and being truly pissed off lent her power. She managed to gain her footing even as the six men tried pinning her down. She wiggled and thrashed, taking supreme satisfaction in every grunt of pain and curse of frustration from her attackers.

Then a roar filled the clearing, so loud, so full of rage, all other motion stopped. Nila's heart jumped, rushing to keep up with the new spike of adrenaline.

Death echoed in that roar.

Chapter Thirty-Eight

The six men attempting to molest Nila spun around, hunting the trees for the threat. She scrambled to put her back to a tree so they couldn't attack her from behind, then searched the clearing, too. Petrov, Stephen, and Joseph stood back to back facing different directions, staring intently into the darkness. A part of her noted that neither Stephen nor Joseph had joined the attack on her, but she was too busy worrying about survival to think about that too closely.

Another roar tore through the night. Goosebumps raced over her skin and her stomach muscles tightened. A moment passed in silent anticipation, then a single tiger flashed into the clearing, ripping out the throat of two men before Nila even got a clear look at the beast.

It only took one look to know who it was.

Mitch, in tiger form, spun to face the remaining four attackers. Two of them were backing off and beginning to shift. The other two attempted to circle him, making it harder for him to attack more than one at a time. She looked around for

Petrov, Joseph and Stephen. Stephen and Joseph had backed to the edge of the clearing, their backs also against a tree as they scanned the woods. To her surprise, neither of them attempted to shift to tigers. Petrov, on the other hand, had moved closer to Mitch and his body convulsed, muscle and sinew popping and stretching. She watched only long enough to know Petrov was changing into his tiger form before looking away from the grotesque vision.

Mitch crouched a few yards away, staring straight ahead rather than at any of the four combatants he'd engaged. Without hint or warning, he blurred and the man to his left screamed, a sound that was cut short by a gurgling noise. Before the man on his right could do more than lunge at him, Mitch spun and raked his claws down the man's face and chest, all the way to his groin. His sharp claws opened the man up, eviscerating him and filling the clearing with the stench of ruptured bowels.

Nila gagged at the acrid smell, though she felt no pity for the man. She held a hand to her nose to block some of the stench as she scanned the edges of the clearing again. Was Mitch alone?

The roar of another tiger answered Mitch's, this one belonging to one of the two attackers who'd managed to complete his shift. Rather than meet the tiger's attack, Mitch leapt away and mercilessly ripped a hole in the man still in the middle of his change. The sounds and sights of that death were so horrible, Nila's brain refused to recognized the details. They'd probably haunt her in dreams later, but for now, she couldn't process the sight and stay sane.

The sounds were impossible to escape, though, and the combination of blood and ripped guts made bile rise in her throat. She swallowed hard, forcing down the need to throw up. She turned toward Petrov. He was almost finished with his change.

She opened her mouth to shout a warning at Mitch when the clearing suddenly filled with five new tigers. Two cornered Stephen and Joseph, two charged Petrov, now in tiger form and roaring his anger, and one joined Mitch. The attacker facing Mitch and his new partner crouched low, looking as if he intended to leap at Mitch. Then suddenly, he bolted, so fast Nila's mind took several moments to realize he'd run away. Mitch's ally took off after him and Mitch swung around to face Petrov.

Petrov growled and chuffed at the three tigers circling him. His white fur was a bright beacon in the dark clearing. Nila took a deep breath. She assumed Petrov would give up now that he was outnumbered. Especially after Mitch, all by himself, had decimated Petrov's allies in a matter of minutes.

Her mother's mate didn't seem to take the same view, however. He launched at Mitch, ignoring the other two tigers. They blurred into motion too fast for her to follow, their fight rolling through the clearing in barely discernable patches of white and orange, light and dark. The storm lamp cast jumping shadows around the trees, a time-lapsed like display of violence.

She couldn't believe this was happening again. She couldn't believe she had to stand by and watch helplessly as Mitch fought a life or death battle to save her. Again! Would this be their future, with Mitch always having to defend her against monsters like her mother's mate?

She didn't dare follow those thoughts down their logical path. Not here, not now. But her throat closed up and tears threatened as she tried to see the fight swirling in front of her.

A furious roar rattled the trees, the ground actually shuttered under the battle. Nila gasped as a spray of blood shot out from the fighting pair, so much blood it looked like a river.

Silence descended on the clearing so suddenly her ears rang. She had to hunt for the two battling tigers because her senses were several moments behind their actual movements. When she spotted them, relief nearly brought her to her knees. Mitch was crouched several feet away from Petrov, his eyes open, his lip curling in a blood tinged snarl. Though it was hard to tell in the weak yellow light, he seemed to be breathing steadily and she couldn't see any mortal wounds.

Petrov lay on the ground, his white coat dark with blood, his throat a gaping hole of blood, ravaged tissue, and bone. More blood seemed to pool under his stomach, though from her position, Nila couldn't see that injury. Petrov tried to rise, despite his wounds, and took a single step toward Mitch. One of his back legs hung uselessly behind him, and more blood rained from his abdomen and chest. He made a wet, huffing sound before collapsing. He didn't move again.

Slowly, Nila edged away from the tree, careful to keep her distance from Petrov's body. She couldn't tell if he was dead, but she wasn't taking chances. She'd seen how strong tiger shifters were. She'd witnessed Mitch healing from some truly horrendous wounds in only a half hour. She didn't think Petrov could survive being gutted and having his throat ripped out, but she'd avoid his body just in case. She glanced at the others and realized one of the tiger's who'd arrived with Mitch had shifted back to human form.

Alexis motioned her closer. "Are you okay? How badly hurt are you?"

"I'll heal. Nothing is broken. They didn't get a chance to rape me before you arrived."

Alexis pulled her in for a hug. Nila was so relieved and so emotionally strung out, she couldn't even care that the woman was naked. She returned her hug, fiercely grateful to see her again.

After a moment, Alexis set Nila at arm's length, keeping her hands on Nila's shoulders as she studied her face. "You look like hell."

Nila chuckled, unable to hold in the reaction. "I feel like hell. How's Victor? His leg?"

Alexis nodded to one of the tigers guarding Stephen and Joseph. "He's fine. Though, I'm probably going to have to step in between him and Joseph soon."

"There's history there." Nila wasn't asking, she'd seen the way the two men had looked at each other.

"Yes, there is," Alexis said.

Glancing back at Petrov, Nila said, "I should do something to help him. I've never sat by and let an animal die before." She faced a frowning Alexis again and said, "But I'm finding it hard to care if he dies."

"Don't. This is a just end to his crimes. Killing a human is punishable by death among our people, and technically, you're a human and he was trying to kill you."

When Nila didn't immediately agree, Alexis gave her shoulders a little shake.

"I'm not letting you anywhere near him anyway," the former Tracker said. "Even after he's dead. You can blame me for preventing you from helping him if that makes you feel better."

"I'm too old to lie to myself like that."

Nila nodded to the other tigers. Everyone was standing in place, watching Petrov bleed. Even Stephen and Joseph seemed uninterested in helping their leader. Joseph's dead eyes remained as emotionless as ever. Stephen, on the other hand, had a fierce expression as he watched Petrov.

"You don't want to help him?" she asked the man who'd tried taking her from the airport and who'd been content to let her die.

Stephen shrugged, but he didn't turn away from his fallen boss.

Joseph surprised her by answering the question. "He killed his mate. Can't condone that."

Again, the lack of emotion in the man's voice made it difficult to know if he felt that way or if he was voicing Stephen's motives.

"You knew he'd done that," Alexis said. "Why follow him?"

"He told us she committed suicide," Stephen said, finally coming into the conversation. Unlike Joseph's voice, though, there was emotion in Stephen's. Dark, and deadly, and full of suppressed rage.

The fact that he'd still intended on letting Petrov torture and kill her, however, didn't redeem Stephen in her eyes.

"What will you do with them?" she asked Alexis, nodding to the two men who'd never made an effort to join the fight.

Alexis gestured to the tiger guarding Stephen. "He's one of the illusive Trackers. He'll take them to the elders for judgment."

"What about Petrov's sons?" Nila was more than a little worried about the fact that neither of the two sons supporting Petrov's hunt for her where here.

"On the run," Mitch answered.

The sound of his voice made her jump and spin to face him. She hadn't noticed him moving off to shift back to human form. But the sight of him, whole and here and remarkably uninjured made her heart rate triple. She let out a sound somewhere between a sigh and a sob and threw herself into his arms. The feel of his strong, warm embrace broke the hold she'd kept on her churning emotions and tears poured down her cheeks.

"I'm so glad to see you," she muttered inanely. "And unbelievably glad you're not dead."

"Same," he said as he tunneled the fingers of one hand into her hair and kept his other arm firmly around her waist.

She could feel the rapid thumping of his heart against her breasts and hugged him closer, giving and taking comfort as she let her relief flood her overwrought system.

"I need a holiday," she whispered.

His chuckle made her muscles finally relax.

Even more quietly, she said, "I love you."

His arms tightened. "I love you, too."

When she could stand to loosen her hold, she eased back and glanced at Petrov. "Is he dead?"

The white tiger wasn't moving, blood was a thick pool beneath his body, and from her vantage, she didn't see the rise and fall of his chest anymore.

"If he's not, he's close," Mitch murmured.

"Will he stay like that, in tiger form?"

Mitch nodded.

"There are at least two bodies inside the cellar of the barn where they were holding me. Human men who were helping him." She tried not to think about Petrov's threat to throw her remains into that very same cellar.

"See," Alexis said. "The elders would have had to execute him. We've just saved them the trouble."

Mitch stared at the motionless tiger for a long moment, then squeezed Nila closer and said, "Let's go. The others will clean this up. I want you somewhere safe."

Alexis fell in beside them as they all walked quietly through the woods, back toward the barn and her cavalry's waiting cars.

Chapter Thirty-Nine

Alexis and Mitch threw on clothes once they reached the cars, and Alexis offered Nila something to change into as what she had on was torn, dirty, and blood-stained. Since none of the tigers bothered about nudity, she went ahead and changed beside the car, too. She couldn't face being alone just yet, but she couldn't stand staying in her current clothes when she had an alternative.

"A shower will be good," she said as she pulled a t-shirt over her head. The spare clothes were Alexis' so they hung on her like pajamas, but at least they were clean. She studied her wrists. "I need a first aid kit."

A soft growl drew her attention. Mitch stared at her arms, looking like he could kill again.

"Don't worry," she told him. "This will heal."

He drew her to him, gently, and studied her wrists in the uneven light from the SUV's interior. "Shouldn't scar," he said.

She could still feel tension thrumming through his hands and the muscles along his arms bunched.

"I should have torn him to pieces," he said.

"He's dead. The rest is just…drama."

Her response finally cracked his serious mood, drawing out a very slight smile. But when he looked up, his expression was solemn again. "I'm so sorry we didn't reach you sooner."

"You found me. That was more than I was expecting. How did you find me anyway?"

"We should get moving," Alexis said as she climbed into the driver's seat. "There's a first aid kit under the backseat. Do you need help bandaging your wrists?"

"I'll help her," Mitch said before Nila could answer.

He helped her into the backseat, pulled out the first aid kit, then following her into the car, snuggling close. His presence proved so comforting, she refused to move to one side of the seat and had to use the center seatbelt so she could stay as close to Mitch as possible. Alexis put the car in gear and Mitch went to work cleaning and bandaging Nila's wrists. As they pulled onto the road, two cars sitting on the roadside opposite the barn pulled out behind them.

When Nila straightened, Mitch hurriedly said, "They're with us."

"More friends?" She settled down.

"Reinforcements from the elders," Alexis said. "More Trackers—ones I know we can trust."

"But…?" She looked at Mitch for explanation.

"The original Tracker team had problems as you might have guessed. That's still being worked out. Elizaveta mobilized this team in the last thirty hours. They found us just as we found Victor and Irina."

"So you tracked me with their help," she guessed.

"We tried. But that barn is sitting right in the middle of what used to be a pig farm and abattoir. The stink in this area kept us from pinpointing where they were holding you. We've been hunting every house and barn within miles of this location."

Tension radiated from his touch up her arms. He finished bandaging one wrist and moved to the other.

"So you found this barn through elimination?" she asked.

"No. Vlad contacted us."

"He told you where I was?"

Mitch nodded, but his jaw muscles jumped.

"Where is he? His brothers?"

"Petrov sent his sons away so they couldn't be charged by the elders in any of this," Alexis said. "Apparently, he knew Elizaveta had sent out more help and his time to kill you was limited. He wanted his sons away and safe."

"Vlad, too?"

Mitch nodded. "Clever bastard that one. His father never knew he was helping us. Took the sonofabitch a long time to tell us where you were though."

"He probably couldn't any sooner," Alexis said quietly, glancing at them briefly in the rearview mirror.

Nila had a feeling this point had come up before. She squeezed Mitch's forearm with her free hand. "He did contact you, and you found me. Everything is all right now."

Mitch shook his head and kept his gaze on her wrist as he finished the last bandage. Then he put the kit away and settled back with his arm around her shoulders, holding her tight to his side.

They fell silent. The quiet thrum of the car's engine, the solid wall of muscle and heat next to Nila, the gentle but firm grip of Mitch's hand on her shoulder all worked to make the rest of the day and night seem almost unreal. If not for the cuts and bruises, the raw red wounds around her wrist, she might have been able to imagine the nightmare she'd just lived through had been a dream.

Loath to break the quiet but too curious not to speak, she finally asked, "Where are we going?"

"To West Virginia," Alexis answered.

"The elders' US compound," Mitch added. "Elizaveta will meet us there."

"She's in the States now?" As far as Nila knew, Elizaveta had still been in Russia when Nila and Mitch were stuck with the young tigers, just two days ago.

"Along with the full council of elders," Mitch said.

All Nila's peace fled and her stomach tightened. "I'll be meeting the elders? Already?"

He nodded, his jaw clenching again as his mouth compressed to a hard line.

She wasn't sure what to say to this news, or what it would mean. She'd hoped for at least a day or two to recover, to make sure her dad and grandma were okay. To shore up her resolve so when she did finally face them, she could make her position clear in a calm and logical way.

Now, she didn't feel at all calm and logical. She was in shock. The last thing she wanted to deal with was a group of old, powerful tigers who thought they could determine the course of her life.

Finally, she grunted and said, "Well, they'll just have to wait. I want a shower, a rest, and to make sure my father and grandmother are safe. I'll deal with the elders when I'm ready."

She swore she heard Alexis chuckle. Mitch's mouth softened into a half grin, and he dropped a brief kiss on her lips.

"The elders will wait," he agreed, then kissed her more fully.

She sighed into his mouth, taking comfort and strength from his touch. With Mitch's love, she'd face the bastards and let them know exactly how she felt about this mess. And they'd just have to deal with it.

Even as she returned Mitch's kiss, though, worry crept in. Would they always have to fight? To kill just to survive? If they stayed together, would Mitch be forced to save her again and again?

Could she live with that?

Chapter Forty

Mitch stalked the corridor of the compound, pausing by the door Nila had entered two hours earlier as if he might catch something of the conversation, then continued his circuit when he didn't. The room was sound proofed against tiger hearing. He knew that. But he still stopped each time he passed the door.

Two hours. They'd had her locked in that room for two hours. He was going insane. What where they saying? What was she telling them? Was she safe? He hadn't wanted to leave her alone with the elders knowing that some of them probably wanted her dead. None of them would actually kill her here, in the seat of their power in the US.

Mitch still hadn't wanted to leave her alone.

Only his grandmother's insistence kept him in the hall. Otherwise, he would have barged in on the meeting an hour ago.

What the hell was going on in there?

On the drive here, she'd told him and Alexis about Petrov's confession to murdering his mate. Apparently, he'd been telling all the males working with him that Anaya had committed suicide. Nila seemed to think that, to Stephen at least, this made a difference. With Petrov dead, along with all but one of the tigers who'd attacked Nila, would Stephen and Joseph actually tell the council of Petrov's confession?

The murder of the four humans who'd been working with Petrov didn't look good for Stephen and Joseph. They could claim it was all Petrov, that they never knew he'd murdered humans, and had been told his mate was a suicide. There was very little the council could do to them if they stuck to those stories. They might see a few months in confinement for kidnapping Nila, but that was it.

Mitch hated it. He didn't care that Joseph used to be Victor's best friend years go, or that Joseph hadn't been the same since his sister's murder ten years earlier. Mitch wanted everyone involved with Nila's kidnapping locked away for life—or executed.

Mitch paced past the door again, scowling at it before moving up the hall. All of this was outside of the issue of him being allowed to mate with Nila permanently. That was an even more uncertain problem.

Last night, he'd have bet money on Nila overruling anything the elders wanted. He was sure their love was enough for her. But over the course of the morning, as she prepared to meet with the elders, she'd pulled back from him, forcing distance between them. He was no longer so positive he was her choice above all others. After he'd failed to protect her from Petrov, she had to realize what being with him would mean to her future. He couldn't protect her the way another male could. She'd had to face that reality. Would that change her mind about staying with him?

He wouldn't blame her, but losing her would kill something in him, something he'd never get back.

Farther down the corridor, beyond the council room, a door opened and Nila's grandmother and father walked toward him.

"They're still in there?" Leo De Luca asked.

Mitch shook the man's hand. "No word yet."

"I should go in," Rossa said, frowning at the closed door. "My bambina might need me."

Leo laid a hand on his mother's shoulder. The big man dwarfed his mother, but Rossa carried herself with such authority, she didn't come across as the least bit small. She really was a lot like his own grandmother. Though her motives were more straightforward. Elizaveta's machinations were too convoluted for even her own grandsons to follow.

Mitch actually wondered if Nila wouldn't be better off with Rossa by her side, but Leo spoke up before his mother could interrupt the session.

"Nila is strong. She'll be just fine in there. When this is done, we'll take her home." He glanced at Mitch. "Assuming there are no objections?"

Mitch wasn't sure how to answer that. If it were up to him, he'd run Nila off to the nearest Justice of the Peace and marry her on the spot. He met Leo's piercing gaze and decided to be honest.

"I love her," he said bluntly. "If she'll have me, I want to marry her."

Rossa smiled, a beneficent expression that reminded Mitch sharply of pictures of Italian saints. Leo was not so easily won over.

"She's my only child, young man. I will not hand her over to someone who can't protect her."

"Leo," Rossa hushed him. "Mikhail saved her life. How can you disapprove?"

Leo continued frowning, though he didn't say anything more. Neither did Mitch. He expected resistance from Nila's father. Hell, he expected resistance from everyone. In the end, the only person whose opinion on the topic mattered at all to him was Nila's. Unfortunately, he didn't know what her opinion was anymore.

Rossa filled in the awkward silence with small talk about the humidity here in West Virginia and what lovely boys his brothers had been, keeping her and her son safe. Mitch smiled at her descriptions of his two older brothers. He hadn't even known Nick and Dom had been recruited to watch after Nila's family. Elizaveta told him the less everyone knew about what was happening, the better. He didn't entirely agree with his grandmother on that point, but given how things had turned out, he couldn't argue with her either.

"And Nikolai, so polite. Wasn't he, Leo? A very good cook, too. He introduced me to…what was that called? Something Russian, with noodles. It was very good. I imagine his diner is very successful."

Leo held his tongue, not commenting on either Nick's politeness or his cooking skills. Like Mitch, his attention kept turning to the meeting room door.

"Such a shame neither are married," Rossa continued. "I am surprised they haven't found good wives."

"Momma," Leo finally murmured. "You know why."

"I do not. Human women make very good wives and there are plenty of children who need adopting. Silly to waste one's life on something that doesn't happen or cannot be."

Mitch watched Leo flinch and wondered if his mother had directed that reprimand to him before. Nila said he'd never remarried after Anaya. Did Rossa consider that a waste? Mitch faced the door separating him from Nila again. Would he eventually be able to love someone else if she left him?

The answer would have surprised him a few weeks ago. Now… Now, he knew what it meant to find the love of his life. The only love.

He and Leo exchanged a look and the older man's hard expression softened just a bit, the creases at the corners of his eyes relaxing. Mitch realized if he ever had the guts to say these things out loud to Leo, the man would understand.

Silence fell again as Rossa stopped trying to distract them with conversation. They watched the door from directly across the hall, and Mitch counted the seconds.

Finally, one of the elder's assistants slipped out of the room, closing the door the instant he was in the corridor so nothing that was said drifted out to them. Mitch couldn't remember the man's name, even though he was sure they'd met before.

The assistant stood respectfully, with his hands clasped in front of him and his shoulders straight as he addressed them. "They will be another two hours, at least. They've called for dinner, and I've been told to make sure you are all fed. If you'll follow me, we can adjourn to the elders' private dining room."

"Wait," Leo and Mitch both said at the same time.

"I'm not going anywhere until I'm sure my daughter is okay," Leo finished.

"I can assure you—"

"No," Rossa interrupted. "You cannot assure us. We will speak to her. For a moment." There was no question, no compromise, and a lot of steel in her tone.

Mitch smiled as he watched the assistant squirm under Rossa's glare. Mitch saw why his grandmother and Nila's grandmother got along so well. They were definitely cut from the same cloth.

After opening and closing his mouth a couple of times, the assistant finally nodded. "Excuse me for a moment, please." He disappeared back into the council room.

A minute later, Nila walked out.

Mitch's breath caught. She looked beautiful. And exhausted. He wanted to pull her into his arms and carry her off to someplace safe where she could sleep more. Despite her father and grandmother watching, Mitch did take Nila's hand when she got close.

"Are you okay?" he murmured, squeezing her fingers.

She squeezed back but didn't look directly at him. "We just have a lot to talk about. But I'm okay. Don't worry. You all go get something to eat. I'll find you when we're finished."

"You're sure, love?" Leo said, cupping her cheek in one huge hand. "You don't have to deal with any of this if you don't want to."

"It's okay, dad. I promise. This is a conversation that has to be had." She leaned in and kissed him on the cheek, then smiled at her grandmother and squeezed Mitch's hand before returning to the council.

Mitch's chest ached as he watched the door close behind her. She hadn't once looked up at him.

"Come," Rossa said when the assistant rejoined them. "Let's eat. Mikhail, you are too skinny. You are a big man. You need more food. Come."

She forced him to go with her by putting her small hand into the crook of his arm. A hand that should have been delicate with age but possessed a strength Mitch couldn't actually resist. He went, but he left his heart and soul outside the meeting room—waiting for Nila.

Chapter Forty-One

By the time Mitch finished dinner, made a phone call to Max, and met with his brothers, the council meeting had adjourned. Mitch returned to the floor where his room was located, but stopped at Nila's door. He'd been given a room next to hers, but her grandmother was on the other side and her father was across the hall, so Mitch had had to stay in his own bed last night.

As he stood outside her door debating whether to risk her father's disapproval by going in, he heard something that made the decision for him.

He knocked and opened her door without waiting for a reply. She sat on the bed with her back to him. He went to her without hesitating, sitting next to her and putting his arms around her. "Baby, why are you crying?"

She wiped her eyes with the sides of her hands. "First time I've had a chance to," she said with a half laugh. "These have been building for days. Lot of tension to release."

He hugged her closer but she didn't relax against him. "Is there something else wrong?"

"Besides being on the run for my life for the last couple of weeks, shooting living beings, being held hostage, kidnapped, nearly raped and murdered, watching people be ripped apart, facing off against not one but two crazy shapeshifters, and oh yeah, having to watch you fight a life-or-death battle because of me. Twice. Besides all that, no of course nothing's wrong."

"Nila…" His chest ached. He was desperate to take away her pain, to fix things he couldn't fix. Because he couldn't do any of that, he felt beyond helpless and frustrated. "What did the elders say?"

She waved a hand in the air. "Too much. God, those old farts can talk."

Her comment surprised a chuckle out of him.

"I had to literally slap my hands down on the table in front of them at one stage to get their attention."

"I would have paid money to see that."

"Yeah, their expressions were priceless. I don't think even Elizaveta was expecting that from me, and she at least knows something about me from my grandmother."

"So, what happened?"

She wiped her fingers under her eyes, removing more tears. The fact that she still had moisture leaking down her cheeks broke his heart.

"Well," she said, "they didn't believe me at first that Petrov admitted to killing Anaya."

"Not surprising."

"But Joseph, of all people, came forward and verified my story. You're completely off the hook for killing Petrov."

"I wasn't worried about me."

"Yeah, well, I was. But by unanimous decision, his… execution was deemed appropriate punishment for his crime against his mate, not to mention that he'd murdered humans."

"What about his crimes against you?" He already knew that was a different story. But he wanted to know what they'd actually said to her.

"Ah, that's where we got into a lot more discussion. Joseph and Stephen are being held in your version of jail for six months for their part in my kidnapping. The council couldn't decide whether to treat their crime as if they'd attacked a human—" she made air quotes with her fingers around the word human— "or whether to deal with their crimes as if I were a tiger. In the end, they compromised."

"Six months hardly seems enough." He heard the growl in his voice but couldn't stop it. In reality, he'd been afraid the two men wouldn't be held accountable at all. As the elders did see fit to punish them, he wanted the punishment to fit the crime.

"I think the elders made a deal with the men when I wasn't around and that got the sentence lowered. They didn't come out and tell me, but I got the impression it had something to do with the first group of Trackers, and why they never caught up with Petrov."

Mitch nodded. That made sense even if he still hated the minimal punishment. "What of Petrov's sons?"

"You were right. Because they weren't there when you all showed up to rescue me, and Joseph and Stephen aren't throwing them under the bus, they're being let off the hook."

"At least two of them still want you dead."

"And unless they actually try killing me, there's nothing the elders can do. An exact quote from your grandmother."

"Does she expect you to be bait, to draw them out?" Mitch's temper rose and his grip on Nila's shoulders tightened. He forced himself to calm down. She was still sniffling after her cry. He didn't want to make matters worse by losing control. She hadn't really relaxed into his embrace yet and that distance was bothering him more than her report on the meeting.

"Elizaveta didn't come right out and say she wanted to use me as bait, but of course if they do try finishing what their father started, Elizaveta won't object to bringing them in."

"Except that you could end up dead."

"Yes, well…" She turned her head away from him and swallowed audibly. "Anyway, after the crimes and punishments part of the session ended, we went on to discuss my…status in the community."

Mitch realized he was holding his breath again. He let it out quietly. "And?"

"And that was a difficult conversation," she said. "Some of the elders… They don't like me, like what I represent. They tried to hide it but not very hard."

He nodded but realized she couldn't see him with her head turned away so said, "Alexis mentioned that might be the case."

"Well, she was right. At least three of the nine would prefer I didn't exist. Besides your grandmother, there was only one other elder who outwardly supported my entry into your community. The others took a more wait-and-see attitude."

"What did you say to all that?"

She faced him then and smiled a little. "I said they could shove their community up their collective asses. I didn't need it or them. They needed me. And if they didn't want me that suited me just fine."

He barked out a laugh. Unable to resist, he kissed her. She pulled back before he could do more than take a brief taste.

"But they weren't prepared to wash their hands of me the way I was with them. Every one of them—some very reluctantly—admitted that they need to at least know how I was possible. To do that, they need me alive and cooperative." She snorted at that. "So we compromised. I cooperate with their scientists—give blood, let them run the necessary tests to see if I can procreate with a tiger, let them do genetic panels on me— the works—and they provide me with the necessary backing to discourage those who think like Petrov from coming after me again."

"What does that involve?" His heart thumped hard in his chest, and he wasn't sure whether it was relief or fear beating at his system.

"Technically, I'll be part of the community. Harming me would mean being met with the same punishment as hurting any female tiger. The elders themselves will be named my 'family' for the purposes of status and protection. Their power—Elizaveta's specifically—will cover me."

"So you'll be safe? No one would dare hurt you." He hadn't expected the elders to give her the full force of their collective protection. He'd expected them to force her into a mating that would give her the necessary status. "This means you don't have to mate with a tiger to be safe."

"Nope. I can do as I please. Though I'm not entirely sure that'll stop Petrov's sons. But Elizaveta seemed to think it would be enough."

She sounded so bitter he wanted to hug her closer. Given what she'd just said and how she'd been reacting to him all day, he no longer knew if he had the right. "Did they…did they ask you to consider a tiger mate?"

She stood and crossed to the window, looking out at the manicured lawn behind the huge complex. Mitch felt his limbs growing heavy and the ache in his chest intensified. Dread stopped him from saying more, from going to her even though he wanted to touch her more than he wanted to breathe. He briefly closed his eyes, prepared for the heartbreak he knew was coming.

"They did," she said, not facing him. "Just like you thought they would. If it turns out I can produce tiger children, they encouraged me to consider a husband among the men in the community. They even had a list of potentials. Ones likely to carry compatible genetic traits to make breeding easier." She snarled the last. "They have all these charts, tracing the various lineages. Did you know they suspect a few of the tiger lines may have the right genetic configuration to interbreed with humans? But they're worried all the children produced by such unions would be human unless the humans also carried certain traits."

"A human like you?"

"More so me than any other human lineage they've uncovered."

"I'm not on that list, am I?" He didn't want to dance around the topic anymore. If she was leaving him, he wanted to hear it now, get it over with so he could let his world shatter in privacy.

"No, you weren't on the list. Most of them didn't even consider you a contender. Exactly as you warned me."

"How will you…? You can't run so what did they decide would be the best way for you to select a mate?"

She waved a hand in the air, beside her head. "They went on and on about the best way to be 'fair' in my mating, how the males could compete for me without actually having a Mate Run. They're considering the option Gregory supported. Do you believe that? Going back to formalized fights. Winner takes all." Her voice dropped to a whisper. "Stupid."

"You don't think that will work?"

"I think the very idea they thought I'd go along with that bullshit proves just how delusional they all are." She finally turned and faced him. "Even your grandmother thought some sort of competition or combat would be the best way to get me a mate."

"What did you say?"

"Again, that they could stuff their list up their collective asses. I would not be given to a man who won me in combat."

Because he could picture her telling them just that, he smiled a little. But his heart wasn't in it.

"They actually said to me there were worse things than arranged marriages. Do you believe that shit? What century is this? What country?"

"So you won't take a tiger mate, then? You don't need one anymore to keep you safe."

She scowled at him but stayed by the window. "You were nearly killed. More than once. Because of me."

"And you nearly died because I couldn't protect you."

"No. Because a crazy man came after me. No one can plan against crazy." She looked away and shook her head. "The problem is, even with the elders' backing, there are still crazy tigers out there." She met his gaze and her expression was fierce. "I do not want you to spend your life having to fight and kill for me. I love you, Mitch. I can't ask you to live that way. I'd rather be alone."

Her word sunk in slowly, taking time for his brain to process. He'd been preparing for her to leave him, to tell him his love wasn't enough, that hers wasn't enough. She didn't need him now. She didn't need a mate at all.

But…she loved him. She loved him enough she was trying to protect him.

He rose slowly from the bed, approaching her as one did a wild animal on the verge of bolting. "I'd rather be with you," he said when he was near enough to touch. He cupped her cheeks in his hands, relieved when she didn't pull away. "If we'd met differently, if your introduction to the tigers had happened without all the death threats, or if we were both just ordinary humans, I would still want to be with you. I would always, always happily fight, kill, and even die for you."

She started shaking her head, but he stilled her movements and set his mouth gently against hers. "No matter what the future holds, Nila De Luca, the one thing I'm sure of is that I want you by my side. I love you. And nothing you can say will scare me away. If you don't want me, if you can't see a future with me, tell me so and I'll let you go. I'll hate it, but I will."

Tears dripped down her cheeks and pooled on the top of his hands.

"But don't send me away because you're scared for me. I'm not afraid of a fight. The only thing that scares me is not being allowed to love you."

"Mitch," she sniffed and gripped his wrists. "Life with me will make you miserable."

"Life without you would be miserable. With you, nothing else matters."

"You'll resent me one day."

He stared her right in the eyes. "Never. Nila, loving someone means you're willing to fight and die for them. That you'll be there with them no matter what life throws at you. Bring it on. Together, we'll be strong enough to face any future."

"Even if it's a dangerous one? Even if, despite the elders' backing, crazy people keep coming after us?"

"Even if. No more running."

"I do love you, Mitch. Enough to fight and kill and die for you."

"Then we're agreed. And the elders can deal with it."

She finally smiled, an expression both soft and mischievous. "That's what I told them."

He frowned.

"I told you before, you're my choice. The only man for me. I told them the same thing."

"How did they react to that?"

"By more talking! Do those people ever shut up?"

He chuckled, then he laughed, then he let loose a whoop of joy. "I love you so damned much, Nila." Picking her up in his arms, he spun her in a circle before setting her feet on the ground and kissing her with every ounce of love he had.

Finally, finally, she returned his kiss, her fingers tangling in his hair as she melted into him.

He eased slowly back so he could watch her expression as he said, "Stay with me."

"Yes."

"Marry me."

She grinned. "Yes."

He kissed her again, hard and fierce. "I didn't think you'd agree to marry me so soon," he said when he could drag his mouth away from hers.

"I surprised myself, too." She made a face. "We should probably have a long-ish engagement."

"You pick the date. I'll be there." If it were up to him, he'd marry her tomorrow, but if Nila wanted time, he'd give her time. He'd give her anything.

"My grandmother will be thrilled," she said.

"And your father?"

"Will come around. Grandma Rossa's already working on him." She cupped Mitch's face as her expression turned serious again. "You may be giving up the chance to have kids. We don't know yet if I can have children with you."

"If you want children, we'll adopt. I want you and whatever will make you happy."

She hugged him close. "You make me happy."

"I intend to keep making you happy for the rest of our lives." Then he kissed her and carried her to bed to show her just how happy they would be.

About The Author

Kat Simons earned her Ph.D in animal behavior, working with animals as diverse as dolphins and deer. She brought her experience and knowledge of biology to her paranormal romance fiction, where she delights in taking nature and turning it on its ear. After traveling the world, she now lives in New York City with her family. Kat is a stay-at-home mom and a full time writer.

For more on Kat and her future books:

Website: http://www.katsimons.com
Newsletter: http://eepurl.com/OxQQL

TITLES BY KAT SIMONS

Tiger Shifters Series

ONCE UPON A TIGER
ALONG CAME A TIGER
HERE THERE BE TIGERS
HER TIGER TO TAKE
TO TEMPT A TIGER
DOWN WILL COME TIGER
TO CATCH A TIGER
WHAT A TIGER WANTS